Storm in the Sky

THE BOOK OF COMING FORTH BY DAY
Part Two

LIBBIE HAWKER

The Book of Coming Forth by Day:
Part 2: Storm in the Sky

Copyright 2015, 2016
Libbie Hawker

All rights reserved.

Running Rabbit Press
San Juan County, WA

Second Print Edition

Cover design and formatting by Running Rabbit Press.
Original cover illustration copyright Lane Brown.

290 ½

MORE BOOKS BY LIBBIE HAWKER

The Book of Coming Forth by Day:
House of Rejoicing
Eater of Hearts

Baptism for the Dead
Tidewater
Daughter of Sand and Stone
Mercer Girls
The Sekhmet Bed
The Crook and Flail
Sovereign of Stars
The Bull of Min

For Paul.

The names of the sacred cattle are:
House of *Kas*, Mistress of All;
Silent One who dwells in her place;
She of Chemmis, whom the god ennobled;
The Much Beloved, red of hair;
She who protects in life, the particolored;
She whose name has power in her craft;
Storm in the Sky, who holds the god aloft;
The Bull, the husband of the cows.

-*The Book of the Dead*, Spell 148.

Ankhesenamun

Year 1 of Horemheb,
Holy Are the Manifestations,
Chosen of Re

I WAS HARDLY MORE than a year old when the court moved from the West Bank to the site of my father's new city. My own memories of that time are fragmented, darting, like fish in a pond, rising into the light and flitting back at once into the cool, blue recesses of shadow, leaving traces of brightness and the fractured flash of movement, fleeting impressions upon the heart. It is not my own memories that I record for you now. Not yet. But the tales I have been told—the histories I have collected, tending with meticulous care—are as vivid to me as if I had lived them myself.

Although I was only a babe, still I can tell you, reader—you who will find these words after I am gone—that throughout the House of Rejoicing, as the Pharaoh's court packed their fine, beautiful things and made ready for the trek downriver to a hot, barren stretch of sand, an air of impending bleakness hung within the palace's bright and lovely walls. It was a sense of sealing-up, for good and all, as when one sees their beloved laid in the tomb. (Iset, Waser, merciful Mut, how well do I know the feeling!) I can tell you that the three King's Wives sought one another out, like sisters reaching for friendly hands in the dark, and then lashed at one another with hard words and bitter eyes, because none of them knew how to give comfort to the others, how to wall off her own grief and fear, and face the future without trembling. I can tell you that Nefertiti's smooth, lovely face was creased by a frown that never left it; that Sitamun often wept; that Kiya stared ahead in blank, dense silence, her eyes unfocused, like one who has had a veil of blindness lifted but finds that sight is hateful to her—that the world is a blunt and ugly thing—and longs to return to darkness.

I can tell you all these things, just as if the memories were my own. Perhaps they are, now. I own them. I am their sole keeper, the last one who will hold and heft and count them. Perhaps, as each member of my family has walked into the depths of the Duat, their memories have walked into my heart, and there I weigh and judge them, just like Anupu at his scales.

Our new-built city, which my father named Akhet-Aten, rose quickly from the sterile sand. Egyptian builders have always been fast, efficient. We must be. We haven't the leisure of peoples in other lands, where the birthing of a city is the work of generations—where even as its older districts crumble and die, the city is still occupied with its own formation, spreading and sprawling, making itself anew, endlessly growing. The river's flood only covers our fields for a handful of months each year, and once the waters recede, carpeting the Black Land in the rich, deep silt for which it is named, every capable man must return to the farms and orchards. Much must be accomplished in only a season's time, and so we accomplish much.

Those *rekhet* who built Akhet-Aten, who went back to their farms and took up their old lives once the city was complete—I have often wondered what they thought of the Pharaoh's city in the sand. I have wondered what they thought of the Pharaoh himself—Akhenaten, passionate and brooding, wrapped in the insulating comfort of his own isolation. Once, Horemheb told me that the *rekhet* care very little for Pharaohs and King's Wives, for nobles in their courts and priests in their temples. So long as the river rises, he said—so long as the fields are fertile and the sun emerges each dawn in triumph over the terrors of the Duat—then the *rekhet* are content.

Horemheb knew of what he spoke, I am certain. And ever since he said those words, I have longed for the simple life of a *rekhet*. I have longed to care not at all about kings and thrones. I have longed to know nothing.

When I look back on the years of my father's reign, what amazes me most is the smallness of our numbers—the *fewness* of we who dwelt at Akhet-Aten. Oh, I do not mean to give the impression that Akhet-Aten was a small place, a shabby village like those the herdsmen occupy on the dry edges of the valley, where our Black Land gives way to the sweeping dunes and stony bluffs of the Red Land. No, indeed: Akhet-Aten was a city in truth, peopled by nearly all of the chosen favorites who had made their homes on the West Bank in my grandfather's time, and joined by some newly selected court pets—artists and craftsmen, mostly, who possessed the skills to bring Akhenaten's vision of renewal—a world built to his specifications and shaped to his whims—to stark and immediate life.

Nearly the whole court uprooted itself at Akhenaten's command. A great many people. And yet so few, when one considers *all* the people of the Two Lands: the *rekhet* in their simple mudbrick huts, the farmers in the fields, the merchants on their trade routes, the fishermen casting nets upon the river. The gods made so many men, and scattered them all down the length of the Iteru. Yet the dark and terrible drama of Akhet-Aten was played out by such a small cast. Our stage, the back-curved sweep of red sand that arched toward the cliffs, was a minuscule thing, compared to everything the gods have made. This was the greatest mischief the gods ever enacted: to hinge the fate of the river's flood, and the lives of so many people, on this scant handful of players.

I ponder the mystery of it, and it's enough to set me wondering—enough to send dangerous, seductive thoughts tumbling through my fast-beating heart: *Were we, those chosen ones of the West Bank, really human at all? Were we, of Akhet-Aten, something more? Perhaps our very power made us more than mortal men. Perhaps it made us gods in truth, with creation in our words and magic in our hands.*

These must be the same thoughts that haunted my father, the very seeds of his insanity. If so, then the goddess Meskhenet was kind to me. She set the bricks of my fate as the midwife set the bricks of my birth. She carved this destiny into my *ka* like glyphs into stone. She arranged for me an abrupt end, before my father's madness can claim me. The gods weave their mischief, and warp us into the fabric of one great, divine amusement. But still, in their strange and distant way, they are merciful.

West Bank living set us all apart from the *rekhet*, and made every noble and all his household dependent on the favors of the king. What, then, were they to do when Akhenaten gave the order to leave the West Bank behind, and take up a new life to the north? The court went with him to Akhet-Aten, because the court could do nothing else, after a generation of seclusion and *otherness*. Of course, many of those men—and women, I dare say—must have seen this disaster on the horizon, distant and thin, like the first amber smudge of a sand storm. But what could anyone do to prevent it? Who could stop what the king had set in motion? One might as well stop the river from flowing north, or the stars from swinging in their courses. One cannot simply kill a Pharaoh. Who would choose to curse Egypt so egregiously, striking against the man the gods had appointed, in their mystery—in their mischief—to see to the vital regularity of the river's flood? And who among any of us would strike such a blow against our own eternal souls?

Even if some daring assassin of the shadowy, scheming

court had been brave or foolish enough to try, Mahu would have stopped him as easily as swatting a fly or crushing an ant beneath his heel. Mahu loved gold—what man doesn't?—and Akhenaten kept him well supplied with riches. In return, Mahu kept Akhenaten well supplied with soldiers, and saw to the king's safety himself, a wary dog, lurking and growling, and always just at Akhenaten's heel.

At first, in the early days of the new city, the king used his army to police the cults of the gods—Amun's cult first, but the rest quickly followed. Whatever offerings the gods received, Mahu's men quickly diverted to Akhet-Aten. This arrangement was distressing enough, but we had not yet seen the worst of what Mahu and his fellow hounds could do.

Waset, once the great capital of Egypt, the very seat of the world's power, was left to wither in the hands of Amun, a god who found himself and his priests suddenly impoverished. Soon more cities waned like pale, sickly moons, fading to little more than shadows of their glorious pasts.

And it was not only the strongholds of the Two Lands that suffered. Egypt's client nations, to the north and east, to the south and west, received no assistance from their overlord. When enemies attacked, as they always did, they found chinks in these nations' armors, and gaps beneath their shields. First these client-kings sent demands for aid from the Pharaoh. Then they sent pleas. All their words went unheeded, drifting like whispers on the wind. Soon the kings of other lands reached in desperation for the one person in all of Egypt who they still thought might listen: Tiy, the former King's Great Wife. But Tiy's power was gone, dried up like a shallow well, and she could no more motivate her son to save his own empire than she could coax him out of his ornate temples, where he lay all day in worship with the sun beating down on his skin. Before the final bricks were laid at Akhet-Aten, the vast empire built by Thutmose the First and Thutmose the Third, only a few generations before, wavered on the brink of toppling.

What did it matter to Akhenaten if those far-flung kingdoms fell? What did it matter if the boundaries of the great sprawl of Egypt contracted, if the empire squeezed in upon him like the fist of a fallen soldier, locked in the stiffness of death? The only borders that mattered to him were the borders of his city—the river and the curving cliffs that delineated the world of his focused power. There, he formed his own divinity, a slick accretion, as when lightning strikes sand and turns it to glass. He set himself apart, and made himself otherworldly. The Pharaoh and his city were generated by terrible danger, forged by white heat and strife.

Nefertiti

*Year 7 of Akhenaten
Beautiful Are the Manifestations,
Exalting the Name,
Beloved of the Sun*

THE PAPYRUS PLANTS STIRRED as Nefertiti moved through them, finger-wide stalks parting and swaying, rustling their great tassels of silky green fringe. The sound was like a whisper in the dark, a hiss so soft she could discern no word, no individual voice, yet carrying all the urgency of a tense breath or a murmured warning. The heads of the papyrus did not even reach to Nefertiti's shoulder. The two years since their planting—since Akhet-Aten's founding—had not given them sufficient time to secure their roots in the river's bank, to take confident hold of the sandy earth and send their leaves and stems up in bold defiance of the sun's glaring heat. They were hesitant and crouched. They were small and huddled—oppressed—and their voices sighed in the sluggish breeze like captives surrendering to their fate.

Nefertiti parted the final row of papyrus with her hands and stood gazing down at the river while the plumes bobbed and shivered around her. Just beyond the toes of her sandals, the sandy bank broke and fell away from the spill of papyrus leaves, plunging down to the water, to the deep, gray-green, clouded rush of the current. The Iteru moved swiftly here. That, Nefertiti knew, was the reason for Akhet-Aten's dry, red barrenness. The river passed this place by, withholding much of the fertile silt it deposited so generously in other parts of Egypt where the waters and the gods felt at leisure to slow, to stay a while, to linger in the land and grace it with their blessings. At Akhet-Aten, the river's bank wore a thin fringe of green, no wider than the lanes of the city. Nothing else would grow here, save for the gardens inside the walls of the palace and the nobles' estates, which had to be watered by hand—a laborious process that occupied each house's staff from sunrise to sunset. Akhet-Aten, with its narrow margin of growing things, its thin, fragile, undeveloped shield, seemed laid bare to the dangers of the world, exposed and vulnerable. Nefertiti felt the river's rush deep within her blood, and her skin prickled with a thrill of danger. She watched the mobile surface of the water cautiously. What creatures might be lurking there, solid but unseen, malevolent in their patience, waiting for the right moment to burst from the current with a roar of broken water and catch her up in their wide-open jaws? She pictured the great, curving tusks of river-horses, the jagged teeth of crocodiles, the red expanse of greedy maws and the thrashing of scaly limbs in the shallows. She suppressed a shudder, and the heat of the sun was dispelled for a moment by her chill of fear.

Voices lifted from the palace, the faint sound of children playing, a high flutter of laughter that lost itself at once among the drone of the city and the crags of the red cliffs nearby. Nefertiti turned away from the water, gazing back at Akhet-Aten. The walls of the palace stood high and bright above the roofs of villas. Inside those walls, in the comfort of green garden shade, amid a tangle of flowers coaxed into blooming by servants' constant watering, Nefertiti's daughters played. They were like the gardens themselves—new and tender, fragile and bright. They did not belong in this place, and yet, against all odds—seemingly against the will of every gods of Egypt—they were taking root in the sandy soil, and thriving.

It filled Nefertiti with hot pride, to know that each one of her girls was strong and resilient. And it wracked her with guilt, to know that she had brought them to this sere, barren, dangerous place—that like a gardener of the palace, she would work tirelessly, day after day, protecting and nurturing them, ensuring they flourished and bloomed even in this parched, unblessed land. She would fit them for the rigors of this life. She would adapt them to Akhet-Aten itself, blighted and blasted as it was, and sink their roots deep into the hot, red ground. What else could she do? She would not see them wither. To watch any one of them fade would shatter her heart and burn her *ka*.

Nefertiti narrowed her eyes at the sight of the palace, at the sun beating bright and insistent on its high, square walls and on the pylons of the temples that surrounded it. Palace and temples—the heart of the Pharaoh's new city—had grown quickly and settled at once into the land, insinuating themselves against the bare, red stone of the cliffs as if they had always stood in this place. In these two initial years of the city's germination, the palace had towered above the tents which the court had called home—the crude shelters where they'd crouched like the poorest of *rekhet*, despairing in the heat until their fine villas at last rose, brick by brick, from the sand.

Those courtiers who had lifted themselves up from lowly origins in farming families set out across the river— with the king's blessing, of course—to establish a new agricultural district. Where the western shore yielded somewhat to the Iteru, patches of silty land could be scratched out between the rocky hills that reached down almost to the water itself. These fields would supply Akhet-Aten with the majority of its needs. Nefertiti suspected that the families who had settled the western bank considered themselves lucky—removed from the direct influence of Akhenaten, freer to come and go than any other denizens of the City of the Sun. Yet they were still isolated from the remainder of the Two Lands, connected as they were to the king. All of them—the merchants in the city, the women of the palace, the farmers across the Iteru—were stranded on an island of Akhenaten's making. Each and every one who had followed the Pharaoh north was exposed in a fierce, barren wilderness, far from familiar comforts and watched by the unseen eyes of predators in the deep.

As she stood gazing back toward the palace where her children played, movement caught her eye—a man striding alone, making his way from the still-unformed edge of Akhet-Aten toward the narrow strip of green where Nefertiti loitered amid the papyrus fronds. She squinted at the figure as he moved past the small mudbrick huts where the few *rekhet* of Akhet-Aten dwelt—those simple builders who labored to finish the villas and estates of the nobles. The man crossed a wide grid, lines of white lime that demarcated the boundaries of a new estate to be built, one of the last that would rise in the City of the Sun. His sandals tracked the lime in a careless streak. It was no matter, Nefertiti knew. Wherever boundaries were claimed, the wind of this exposed, red bowl quickly erased them—or they were brushed away by court rivals who wished this patch of land or that for themselves. The *rekhet* would re-draw the boundary in the morning, patiently renewing whatever the land or men themselves had attempted to undo. The king's will would be done.

Nefertiti's breath caught, and she drew herself up when she recognized the man's firm, direct stride and the swing of his tense, wiry arms. She had seen her father, Ay, but little over the past two years. Any such blessing from the gods was rare in this time and in this place, but if they'd wished to be truly merciful, they would have left Ay on the West Bank, or dropped him from the side of a boat into a crocodile pool. Even if she had managed to mostly avoid him while Akhet-Aten grew up in its improbable glory, Nefertiti still felt his influence in the City of the

Sun, an ever-present irritation like the burning itch of a fly's sharp bite. She stood regally still amid the papyrus and waited for him to approach, ignoring the tingle of danger at her back where the current whispered within its veils of green and gray.

Ay trudged across the final white line of the unbuilt estate's boundary. The prints of his sandals tracked pale against the red sand. His eyes flicked over her face and shoulders—all of her that could be seen above the papyrus—with their usual air of displeased assessment. Nefertiti frowned at him in silence as he sketched a shallow bow.

"Is there something I can help you with?" she asked impatiently when he straightened.

Ay raised one black-painted brow, taking in the strip of green bank with frank amusement. "Am I interrupting some important business, King's Wife?"

Nefertiti resolved not to dignify his impertinence with a reply. She waited, arms crossed. The papyrus tassels stirred and murmured against her skin.

Ay gave the softest, briefest of sighs. "Let us not dance about the issue. The time has come for us both to be forthright, Nefertiti."

"When have I ever been evasive with you, Father?"

Ay's thin mouth tightened in a half-smile, but he did not rise to her bait. His thin shoulders gave a little twitch, almost a shrug, as if he felt the weight of Akhet-Aten bearing down upon his back, as if he wished to rid himself of the city's stark reality, but could not. "You know this has gone too far," he said.

Nefertiti tilted her head, half an unspoken question, half a warning to the old man to proceed with caution.

"The city," Ay clarified. "Our isolation. This move away from the West Bank, and Waset, and the god Amun himself."

Resolute, Nefertiti kept her silence. The papyrus fronds brushed her bare arms.

"Your husband," Ay went on, lifting his voice with determined force, "is clearly insane."

"Then why did you follow him here, to Akhet-Aten? A man as great as you, Overseer of All the King's Horses, could have re-established himself in Waset if he so chose."

"Madness is weakness," Ay said. "And where there is weakness in a man, there is opportunity for another—for any man who is clever enough to seize that opportunity and make it his own."

Nefertiti watched his face as he spoke, calmly assessing the stillness of his features, the thin skin stretched over the shallow angles of his skull, the observant, coolly confident eyes. *Where is your weakness, Father?* she wondered. *Where is my opportunity?* For he must have a weakness. All men did.

All women, too. Nefertiti knew her own faults, those places where her heart was weak and friable, where the boundaries of her strength could be tracked away like lime dust through the sand. Gods help her, she had come face to face with her own monstrous frailties more than once. She remembered the sound of Mutbenret sobbing, pleading to be spared—remembered the sight of her sister trudging numbly off toward the Pharaoh's bedchamber—and Nefertiti suppressed a shudder.

Surely there was a way to crack Ay's hard, glassy shell and move the stunted *ka* that dwelt within him. Surely there was some path into his heart—some hold Nefertiti might place upon him, some strength she might exert over him. Her own influence at court was greater than his. It *must* be. She could not bear for him to be stronger, better—not after all she had sacrificed, and all she had done to others in pursuit of her own might.

"Opportunity," she mused aloud. "And what opportunity do you see here, Father? What fresh glory is Ay planning for himself, I wonder?"

Ay's dark gaze slipped to one side, as if he suspected listeners among the papyrus, as if the weight of Akhet-Aten pressed more insistently upon him. It was a rare display of hesitancy—uncertainty—and Nefertiti savored it like a fine, sweet wine.

"I have been searching," Ay admitted slowly, "for a ... suitable replacement."

"Replacement?"

"For the king."

Nefertiti's brows leaped in unfeigned surprise. She stared at her father in frank disbelief.

"If only I can find the right man," Ay went on, "one whom the nobles and priests alike seem disposed to support. Then I'll back that man strongly, and do all I can to see him to the throne."

Nefertiti pursed her lips, considering Ay in silence. Her lack of a response seemed to unsettle him—as much as Ay was ever unsettled. He twitched his bony shoulders again and said, rather defensively, "You know I can muster support for a new king. I have that sort of influence among the court, and my ties to the temples are still strong enough, I believe—"

Nefertiti cut him off with a curt wave of one hand. "You are speaking of dethroning a Pharaoh."

Ay tipped his chin in smug acquiescence.

"Such an audacity has never been attempted before. Whatever will the gods think?"

"What does it matter? The *priests* will be most enthusiastic about a coup, and it is they who hold the power."

"It is the priests who hold the *wealth*," Nefertiti corrected.

"What little wealth they still have left—what Mahu and his dogs haven't claimed for the Aten. It is the *gods* who hold the power—over the river, the land, our very lives. And it is the gods who put my husband on the throne."

Ay huffed a single, dry laugh through his nostrils. "Have you grown pious, Nefertiti?"

"I have always been pious, Father. It is you who have always disregarded the will of the gods. You may have sired me, but do not assume I am as reckless as you when it comes to matters of divinity."

"Ah, yes," Ay said, "how could I have forgotten? I am speaking to the devout and righteous High Priestess of the Sun, Nefer-Neferu-Aten herself."

Nefertiti's face heated at the sound of the name—her *other* name, the one used only in the temples, where she donned the robes of a priestess and carried out the daily pageant of Aten-worship, welcoming the sun and appeasing the demands of the Pharaoh. *Nefer-Neferu-Aten, indeed.* High Priestess of the Sun, Mistress of the Ben-ben Stone—empty titles—attachments to a distant and unfeeling god. The titles were meaningless to all who heard them, save for Akhenaten. To the Pharaoh of Egypt, Nefertiti's identity as Nefer-Neferu-Aten was a potent magic, a conferment of real and dazzling power. And because the titles were real to the king, it did not matter who else honored or accepted them. Nefertiti drew herself up to her full height and felt the heat flee from her cheeks. *Here* was her might, her strength over Ay. She may be a true High Priestess to no one but the king, but who in all of Egypt had greater power than he?

"You would risk the blasphemy of dethroning a king?" she asked coolly. "You would so blithely court the gods' displeasure? Why not simply kill Akhenaten, then? You will damn your soul either way."

Ay drew back—a subtle movement, the faintest shrinking

away, so slight that only Nefertiti, whom Ay himself had trained in observation, could have noted it. But she did note it, and it strengthened her spine.

The old man did not answer her challenge. He only slid his eyes away from her own, and contemplated the fast-moving Iteru with one hand on his chin, his lips pressed pale and tight. *Even he is afraid of reaching that far*, Nefertiti realized. *There is still some humility left in him—or some fear—small though it may be.*

"Have some sense," Ay said gruffly. "Cooperate with me, Nefertiti. For your own good—your own *freedom*—as well as the good of the land."

He is asking for my blessing, she realized with a rising sense of triumph. *He is loath to move against my pleasure.* That was *maat*, if ever Nefertiti had seen it. She was a figure of real power now, a force in the City of the Sun nearly as potent at Akhenaten himself. And anyone who wished to change Egypt—to remake the world—must contend with Nefertiti's will, if not Akhenaten's.

Nefertiti drew a deep breath. The fresh, green scent of the papyrus plants filled her head. It was a rich and soothing scent, as comforting as the perfumes of the West Bank gardens that colored the memories of her childhood. The strip of green that fringed Akhet-Aten was narrow now, and struggled to grow. But with time, it would flourish. Given enough time, the whole bowl of this dry, red valley would sprout with green, and blossom beneath the sun.

"Are you seeking my help in your schemes, Father?" Nefertiti said lightly.

Ay's lips thinned still more. He narrowed his eyes, glaring at her from beneath the fringe of his wig, and said nothing.

Nefertiti snapped one of the papyrus fronds and brushed its soft tassel against her lips, watching Ay as he maintained his stoic silence. Finally she turned and cast the stem into the Iteru. The current caught it at once and swept it from the bank, carrying it away to disappear amid the wink and glitter of sunlight on water.

"You will do well to remember this," she told Ay at last. "Akhet-Aten is as much my city as it is the king's. I rule here, as surely as he does."

"You have no great affection for your husband. I'm not fool enough to believe you've fallen in love with him. Why do you seek to defend him now?"

Fallen in love with him? Nefertiti thought drily. *Quite the opposite.* But what did it matter, after all? She could rule beside Akhenaten without loving him. She could take the power her titles gave her—the power she derived from Akhenaten's regard for her—and do with that strength whatever she willed.

She brushed past Ay, lifting the hem of her gown as she made her way from the strip of greenery, up toward the wide, new lanes of Akhet-Aten—her city. Imperfect and strange as it was, the city was her own. And here, unlike on the West Bank or in the House of Rejoicing, Nefertiti was stronger than Ay.

For as long as Akhenaten still reigned, at least.

Sitamun

Year 7 of Akhenaten
Beautiful Are the Manifestations,
Exalting the Name,
Beloved of the Sun

NEBETAH UNROLLED A SCROLL across her lap. Her narrow, brown shoulders stooped as she bent her head over the cream-colored papyrus. Sitamun watched as the shade from a nearby stand of roses slid over her daughter's slender form, the dapples of darkness and light flickering and playing over her soft skin and the red linen of her tunic. The breeze that stirred the rose bushes lifted their sweet perfume, twining the scent through the locks of Sitamun's wig, caressing her cheek with the gentlest and most fragrant touch. Nebetah's voice lifted, too, as she read the words of her scroll aloud in a careful rhythm.

The effect of sweet perfume and simple, musical words, of warm sunlight and kindly shade, should have been soothing—beautiful. But the quiet peace of the afternoon only pulled painfully at Sitamun's heart. Since coming to Akhet-Aten, she had felt herself haunted, followed through the gardens and the halls of the bright, new palace by a shadow, creeping and dense, that seemed to moan at her from the corners of rooms. It called out to her with words she could not discern, but sorrow and regret were evident enough in its hollow, echoing voice.

She clung to the quiet, lonely spaces, the abandoned corners of the garden, the little-used rooms of the palace. There had been a time when the thought of her brother's city—its promise, glittering like a single jewel set in a golden ring—had filled Sitamun with hope and joyous anticipation. That night, long ago, when she had sat beside Akhenaten on the deck of his ship, talking quietly of the new world he wished to build, still hung like a fog in her heart. Then, she had hoped they might build the city of the Pharaoh's dreams together and live alone there, the only dwellers in a land of the king's creation—together at last, and happy in their love.

Akhet-Aten was not the sanctuary of fulfillment Sitamun had yearned for. Day by day, she felt its crowds—its largeness and bustle—pressing in upon her *ka*, taunting her with the denial of her dreams. She could not be *comfortable* here. It was a strange, unfeeling place, and all its bright paint and new-laid plaster could not breathe warmth into the coldness of its walls. Every new villa that grew up from the sand only seemed to widen the gulf between Sitamun and Akhenaten, pushing her farther away from the companionship she craved. She had dreamed that Akhet-Aten would become her salvation, a refuge for her restless, searching heart. Instead, it had secluded her, walled her up, surrounded her by a gulf of fast-moving waters that no one cared to cross, and she was more alone and bereft than she ever had been in the House of Rejoicing.

"Therefore let us praise the god." Nebetah's words were cadenced and precise as she worked through her lesson. The girl's childish voice measured each sound and syllable with care. "For the Aten blesses all he sees." She paused and looked up at Sitamun, dark eyes serious in her long but pretty face. She tugged uncertainly at her braided side-lock, a gesture of habit that was quite out of keeping with the girl's usual air of confidence and self-possession. "Did I read it well, Mother?"

"Very well." Sitamun smiled in spite of her dark thoughts. "You always read well. You have learned fast, for one so young."

"I am seven," Nebetah said with a cool loftiness, bordering on scorn. "I am not a child."

Sitamun stifled a tolerant chuckle. "No, indeed you are not. Do you have more to read?"

"Yes. There is more written here. It's a new chapter."

Sitamun loosed the sun-cloak from her shoulders and stretched her legs before her in the grass, gesturing for her daughter to continue. The sight of Nebetah, bent in studious concentration over her scroll—the sound of her light, beloved voice—did what the roses and the breeze could not do, and lifted the heaviness from Sitamun's heart.

The child was the only person in all of Akhet-Aten who had the power to drive back the haunting shadows. Even Kiya, who was always kind, and admirably determined to make the best of life in this isolated new city, seldom brought a genuine smile to Sitamun's lips. What gave the girl such a rare and singular power? Sitamun wondered. Was it merely the fact that she was Sitamun's own daughter? She studied the girl's delicate features—the thin, straight nose; the wide-set eyes that sparked with quiet intensity; the broad mouth with its full lips and habitually thoughtful expression; the confidence, well-formed already but furled tight, like a bud not quite ready to flower. It was Akhenaten she saw there, his impression stamped on her features as clearly as a seal ring in wax.

You are Akhenaten's child, she told Nebetah silently as the girl read on. Sitamun's eyes prickled with tears, and she blinked them away. *You were never Amunhotep's seed. How could you have been? I did not love my father like I love my brother. My body would never have nurtured Amunhotep's get, nor made a child of his siring so lovely and strong, so perfect.*

That, at least, was some small comfort. If Sitamun was to be driven ever farther from her beloved's side—if the very foundation of her heart was to be worn away, grain by grain, like the sandstone cliffs slowly eroding before the fierce desert winds—then at least she could rest secure in the knowledge that Nebetah was a child Sitamun had made in love, and not in fear or loathing. If Akhet-Aten had not turned out to be the refuge of *maat* she had longed for, then at least the gods permitted her one small measure of peace.

From beyond the garden wall, the laughter of several men rose up abruptly, intruding on the quiet rhythm of Nebetah's reading. Sitamun jerked her sun cloak up around her shoulders, leaning irritably away from the wall as if the laughter had stung her. The men's accents were refined—nobility. Akhet-Aten was awash in noble men and their ladies. When Sitamun had first looked upon the valley, that bright morning when Akhenaten had watched the sun rise over the cleft in the hills, she had thought it a wide, spacious place. But now, filled with courtiers and artisans as it was, valley and city alike felt cramped and stifling.

Why didn't you listen to me, Brother? Sitamun sent the bleak thought flitting up from her heart, a dark bird on the wing. She imagined Akhenaten out there beyond the garden wall, closeted with Nefertiti or prostrating himself in the hot sand of his sun temple, and wished fervently that he might hear the pleading of her *ka*, and might, for once, care. *We should have come to this place alone, Akhenaten—just the two of us. We should have dwelt together with your zeal, your passions... your madness. I could have taken that burden upon myself. I know it. I could have loved you completely. I know you— understand you—as the rest of Egypt cannot. You are my brother. We are one.*

After everything Sitamun had given him, everything she had done to exalt his name, still Akhenaten could not grant her the small favor of dwelling with her alone in his dream world. True, it was a world that was half-formed and strange, a world of heat and fire—but Sitamun could find the dream beautiful enough, if she could only be alone there with the brother of her body and her heart.

"Mother?" Nebetah glanced up from her scroll. The dapples of light and shadow swayed over her fine features—Akhenaten's face.

Sitamun cleared her throat and dabbed quickly at the corner of her eye, where a tear had just begun to form. She had sighed with the darkness of her musings, and it had distracted the girl from her reading. She made herself smile at Nebetah, and tossed the braids of her wig with a light, carefree hand. "Dust in the garden," she said. "That is all. It makes my eyes water and clouds my lungs. You are reading well; don't let my sniffling drive you from the task."

Nebetah narrowed her eyes in a moment of stern brooding, an expression so like her father's that a lump rose in Sitamun's throat, and she could not tell whether it was love or loss that choked her.

"I think my reading is done for the day," Nebetah said with business-like formality. She must have learned the tone from one of her tutors, Sitamun guessed, but the crisp decisiveness suited the girl. She rolled up her scroll with a few practiced twists of her thin, brown hands and tucked it neatly into her embroidered carrying bag.

"If you wish."

Sitamun's delayed response only made Nebetah pause again in thoughtful contemplation. The girl's stare was so direct and intrusive that Sitamun felt it like a hand upon her skin, uncomfortably close in the afternoon's warmth. But the girl said no more. She climbed to her feet, brushing stems of broken grass from the bare legs that seemed to grow longer and more coltish every day.

Nebetah offered her hands to Sitamun to help pull her up from the ground, and Sitamun made a great ruse of being unable to rise. Nebetah braced herself and hauled at her mother's arms until the girl's sober mien finally cracked, and the high, tinkling chimes of her laughter burst out like morning birdsong. The sound of it gladdened Sitamun's heart.

They walked side by side through the garden, past groves of newly planted saplings as slender and graceful as Nebetah, skirting the small, raised pond with its sparse growth of lotuses. Sitamun kept one eye on her daughter's hands, enchanted by their dainty beauty, their absent movements as the girl carried her bright-stitched bag with its scrolls and the trinkets she treasured. An unfamiliar sensation welled up in Sitamun's middle, furry and warm, pushing back the dark cloud of sorrows that followed close on her heel. It was satisfaction, Sitamun realized with no small surprise. She hadn't felt *content* since moving to Akhet-Aten, two years ago. Nebetah was the wellspring of that pure, simple joy—the knowledge that the girl thrived, growing stronger and more capable day after day.

I have done one thing well, then, Sitamun mused, *in bringing her into the world*. A single righteous act was a tiny thing, only a pebble to counter-weigh the precipitous tip of a scale. But for now, it was enough.

Beyond the pond with its thin, patchy carpet of lotus leaves, a cluster of servants tipped jars of water into a stone-lined bed, pouring silver streams around the feet of newly planted palms. Nebetah paused to watch the gardeners at their work. Her fingers picked carelessly at the birds embroidered on her bag's strap, and as Sitamun watched, still wrapped in her pleasant enchantment, the girl pulled a flame-orange thread free, twisted it between her fingers, and let it go on the slight breeze. Then the absent, in-turned expression left Nebetah's features. She drew in a breath that lifted her narrow shoulders. The wide, dark eyes grew dreamy, and her lips parted in a silent sigh of gleeful, childish longing.

Sitamun glanced beyond the gardeners and their skinny palms. Four or five women of the harem drifted between stands of roses, the bright colors of their draped and folded linens blurring into one another, the soft brown of their limbs shifting into the leaves of the flower beds. They laughed musically together as they bent over the roses, inhaling the sweet perfume.

Sitamun pursed her lips and eyed her daughter again.

"They're so lovely," Nebetah whispered.

"They are very nice to look at," Sitamun conceded with a sigh.

"Oh, Mother—will I be a lady of the harem when I'm grown?"

The suggestion struck Sitamun like a blow, so hard and fierce that her heart lurched to a halt, then pounded again with a sickening, redoubled beat. Her face heated, prickling in the sun. "No!" she said, more forcefully than she'd intended.

Nebetah stared up at her, mouth hanging open, eyes glazed with tragedy. "But why? I want to be pretty, too."

"You are already beautiful beyond measuring, Nebetah. You don't need to belong to the harem to be pretty."

Nebetah burst out with an uncharacteristic whine. "But I want to *see* it! You've never even let me go inside the harem palace. Why? I suppose it's really the loveliest place in all the world, with flowers and birds flying and music and golden things everywhere. And I don't even get to see it."

"You aren't missing anything," Sitamun said drily. "The inside of a harem palace isn't as fine as the inside of the king's palace, where you are fortunate enough to live."

"And that's another thing." Nebetah balled up her fists

and braced them on her hips, facing Sitamun resolutely. "Nefertiti's girls get to live in the harem palace. And Kiya's daughter, Kayet, too. It's not fair. I want to live with my friends, so I can play with them whenever I please."

"You know why they live in the harem."

Nebetah's confidence crumbled away. Her head drooped, and she abandoned her fierce stance to clutch the bag to her chest with both hands. "I know why. Because they are the king's daughters, and I am not."

How could anyone look at you and believe you are not Akhenaten's daughter? Sitamun thought, pity mingling with fear. *But I must thank the gods for small mercies.* She would allow the Pharaoh and his courtiers to believe whatever they would, and for as long as she could maintain the ruse. If the City of the Sun believed Nebetah to be a cast-off of the royal family, of dubious paternity and born before Sitamun's marriage to Akhenaten, then it suited Sitamun well enough. Only true King's Daughters grew up in the harem, where they could learn the ways of the court. Sitamun would rather keep her child close, cloaked in the shadows of Akhet-Aten's periphery. Clutching at Sitamun's hem, relegated to the palace's forgotten corners, Nebetah would be safe.

"That's correct," she said. "You are not a King's Daughter, so it is not fitting that you live among Nefertiti's children."

"Or Kayet?"

"Or Kayet. But cheer up; you can still play with them in the garden, and sit with them at lessons."

Nebetah whirled and stomped back down the path, the way they had come, so she would no longer be taunted by the vision of the harem beauties. "I still say it's not fair," she grumbled. "And when I'm grown, I *will* be a lady of the harem. I'll *make* the Pharaoh love me, even if I'm not as royal as Meritaten and Kayet. And then I'll have the finest room and the most necklaces and the best gowns of anybody in Akhet-Aten!"

Sitamun's hand flashed out, catching Nebetah by the upper arm before she could pause to think what she was doing, and why. Nebetah squealed in surprise and indignation, and scowled up at her mother.

"You will *not* enter the harem," Sitamun said. She fought to keep her voice low and calm, but a blade seemed to press against the inside of her throat, and she swallowed hard to quell the pain. "You can do better than that—you can dream of being more than just an ornament in the king's household. The life of a harem woman is not as fine a life as you imagine, Nebetah."

Nebetah jerked her arm away, but she didn't storm off down the path. She stood in silence, watching Sitamun with wary expectation.

"When the time is right, I'll see that you're married to a good man. A man who treats you well, and gives you everything you desire."

The girl narrowed those great, dark eyes. "I *desire* all the pretty things the harem ladies have."

Nebetah was such a canny child, so insightful and clear-thinking, that Sitamun often forgot that she was only seven years old, and prone to the same foolish flights of any common little girl. She straightened abruptly and glared down at her daughter, using the withering, hard-eyed stare that Tiy had so often used when Sitamun was a recalcitrant child.

"I will not see *my* daughter consigned to the life of a harem girl."

"You will if I want it," Nebetah insisted.

"I will do *anything* to keep you out of the Pharaoh's pet-house. Don't think I'm incapable of enacting my will upon the world, Nebetah. You might be surprised by what your mother can do when she has a mind."

Suddenly the girl grinned. "Would you kick a crocodile in the teeth?"

Sitamun's forbidding mask cracked in a playful smile. "With my very hardest-soled sandals."

"Would you rob a vulture's nest and steal all her eggs?"

"If it would keep you safe, I'd let all the vultures in Egypt peck me until I was bloody."

Nebetah's hand crept into Sitamun's own. "Would you pull off Nefertiti's wig and throw it in the pond?"

"Gladly."

"Would you ride a river-horse through the marketplace?"

Sitamun pulled the girl close and tickled her ribs with her free hand. "Backwards!"

Nebetah's squeals of laughter masked the sound of footsteps on the garden path, and so when a hard, cool, hand landed on Sitamun's shoulder, she gasped and jumped, spinning to face whoever had intruded upon her small, fragile realm of happiness. Face to face with Ay, his expression as flat and unmoved as ever, Sitamun swallowed hard. Nebetah, alarmed at the sudden evaporation of Sitamun's levity, slunk behind her mother and clutched the back of her dress with one small fist.

"I beg your pardon, my ladies," Ay said smoothly. "I did not mean to interrupt your game. I called out to you, but you were... distracted... and so I believe you did not hear."

"It is no matter," Sitamun said, recovering herself.

"Have you seen Nefertiti today? I have a message for her."

Sitamun glanced down at Ay's hand. His sharp-boned fingers were locked tight around a small scroll of papyrus, and just behind his hand, tucked into the sash of his kilt, Sitamun could make out a neatly coiled length of cord. The leather was worked into hard, tight knots at regular intervals. The sight of the cord sent a twist of nausea into her middle, and made her limbs feel quivery and weak.

Once, when she was a girl hardly older than Nebetah, she had found herself walking beside Ay at a festival procession. She remembered watching his hand in the glare of the sun, his fingers moving in a slow, deliberate rhythm as he worked the cord through his grip, pinching one knot, then another, and another. His knuckles, jumping as he toyed with the cord, looked as hard and defined as the knots themselves. Something had startled him, and the cord had fallen from his hand, dropping into the dust at his feet. Sitamun bent to retrieve it, and handed it back to him without a word.

Ay had thanked her with cool grace. "I always keep such devices about me," he'd told her, using the amused, indulgent voice adults always resorted to with curious children—though Sitamun had asked him no questions. "For tallying up," Ay had said. "For making an account."

"An account?" Sitamun hadn't grasped his meaning, though she had understood, without knowing quite how, that Ay intended his words to mean more than what they seemed. "An account of what?"

"Of everything," he had told her, smiling his cold, flat smile.

Sitamun felt Nebetah's fist tighten in the linen of her dress, and she stood up straighter, her spine tingling, a she-jackal bristling over her pup. "I haven't seen Nefertiti," she said brusquely.

"I have," said Nebetah quietly. "She was with her daughters on the other side of the garden, not an hour ago."

"Go, then," Sitamun told her. "Run and find them. Tell the King's Wife that Ay has a message for her."

Nebetah bolted down the path, her thin, brown legs

kicking up the hem of her tunic in her haste to flee from Ay's sudden presence. Sitamun watched her go, scampering through the light and shadow that crossed the flat pavers of the garden path. The girl glanced back once, then turned and ran all the harder, until she disappeared around a bend.

"A lively child," Ay said. "And bright. One can see her great intelligence, like sparks in her eyes."

Sitamun nodded, but made no reply. Her hand tightened reflexively, and she imagined she could feel the hard, regular knots of a leather cord clutched in her fist, digging into the flesh of her palm. She pictured each knot in turn passing through her fingers, one by one—each wrong that had been done to her, and every ill that she had done.

Ay smiled patiently, waiting for Nebetah to return. But Sitamun could hear the memory of his whisper, rattling like broken shards inside her heart. *For tallying up*, it said. *For making an account. Of everything—of everything.*

Although the sun beat down fiercely and droplets of sweat formed beneath the locks of her wig, the skin on Sitamun's arms raised into pebbles, and she shivered.

Kiya

*Year 8 of Akhenaten,
Beautiful Are the Manifestations,
Exalting the Name,
Beloved of the Sun*

KIYA BRACED HER HANDS against the low barrier of plaster and mudbrick that ringed the outer wall of her palace. From this vantage, high above the sandy earth, she could peer over the tops of young palms and myrrh trees, south toward the vast bulk of the Great Aten Temple. Its lime-washed walls burned white, even in the weak winter sun, and between the powerful, straight arms of its outer walls, the temple's roofless interior spaces sank like deep wells, blue-black with shadow.

Beyond the temple, the massive, pale form of the royal palace crouched beside the waterline, its back turned to Kiya's sight. The high, square rooftop of the Pharaoh's personal quarters peeked over the walls of palace and temple alike, as if Akhenaten watched Kiya across that distance, holding her in his cold, steady gaze, tracking her every movement, hearing her every thought.

From this new, private palace, sequestered against stony cliffs in the far-northern corner of the valley, this was all she could see of the City of the Sun, except for the smudge of hazy smoke and brick-brown that delineated the city's southernmost district.

Nann's light, familiar footsteps sounded at the head of the stair. Kiya did not turn to greet her servant as Nann emerged onto the wall's terrace, but nodded in thanks when she set a tray of cool wine and melon slices on the barrier between them. Kiya did not touch the refreshments, and after a moment of thoughtful silence—during which Kiya, still staring out at the city, could feel Nann's eyes assessing her posture, her face—the servant took a slice of melon herself, sprinkled it with salt, and ate it with a matter-of-fact air.

"Put something in your belly," Nann advised, her mouth full.

"My belly is sour."

"All the more reason to put something inside it."

Kiya turned away from the sun-washed view, rounding on Nann with an abrupt shake of her head. "Put something inside my belly, you say?" She wished to speak on, to make some sharper retort, but her words froze within her, and the best she could produce was a defeated sigh.

Nann sucked the last of the melon juice from her fingers, then tipped her head in sympathy. "Oh, Mistress. Did you fall pregnant again?"

Kiya returned to her study of Akhet-Aten. She smoothed her linen gown with absent hands, and said calmly, "I did."

"And you... you took the herbs, yes?"

"I took them. The pregnancy is no more. Just like the last one, and the one before that."

What a cruel trick of the gods, Kiya mused bitterly. *When I wanted a child most, years ago, they withheld my heart's desire. And now that I wish only to be away from the king, they send him constantly to plague my bed, and plant one child after another in my womb.*

But she was resolved to keep herself barren. Since that terrible day, nearly three years ago, when Akhenaten had abused her and torn her clothing—overcome by lust in this same valley, enflamed by his own frightening zeal—Kiya had sworn she would bear the Pharaoh no more children. She had no power to cast him from her side or even from her bed. She must bear with brave indifference his affections, his touch, his intrusions upon her body. But she could decide whether she would set foot again on the birthing bricks. She could choose whether another child of her flesh should enter this fearsome world of the Pharaoh's making, this land of heat and terrible brightness. She could refuse to trust her own precious seeds to the hostile sands of Akhet-Aten.

"I'm sorry, Mistress," Nann said with real regret. "I didn't think before I spoke. 'Put something in your belly,' indeed."

She struck her own cheek in rebuke, but Kiya caught her wrist before she could punish herself again.

"Don't," Kiya said. "You weren't to know." She smiled lightly. "It is hot already, isn't it? And the New Year celebrations have only just closed. Can winter be slipping away so fast? Give me that wine. Is it cool? Ah—that's good."

She sipped from the faience cup, beaming at the wine though she hardly tasted its sweetness. It *was* well-chilled, at least—and the refreshment cleared her thoughts.

"What do you think of my New Year's gift?" She gestured with her free hand over the grounds of her private palace— the lower colonnades of gaily painted pillars, cool with shadow; the small menagerie of tame gazelles and silky-coated goats in stone pens; the long central courtyard with its glittering pond, where ducks with clipped wings paddled and flapped among the lotuses.

Nann's green eyes shifted from left to right, taking in the terraced wall and the estate it enclosed with a flicker of suspicion. "It's pretty," she finally said, sounding distinctly unimpressed.

"It is very pretty." Kiya sighed again and drained the wine from her cup.

"It's more prison than palace."

"I know. I'm as shut-up as those poor gazelles down in the garden."

"At least here, we will see the Pharaoh but little."

"Only when he comes to my bed."

"But he soon goes away again," Nann said practically. "And that is a blessing, at least."

Kiya took a slice of melon. "I fear what this means," she admitted as she ate. "Akhenaten hasn't showered such extravagant gifts on his other wives."

"Nefertiti still has her temple," Nann said with a shrug, "and she is still the High Priestess of the Sun."

"But she lives in the royal palace alongside Sitamun—with the stewards and ambassadors. Have you heard any rumors that the king might be planning another palace such as this one, as a gift to Nefertiti?"

Frowning, Nann shook her head.

"Well, there you have it." Kiya poured another cupful of wine from the flagon. "He has singled me out, and no mistake. He plans to name me King's Great Wife. Only a fool would deny what even a blind man can see." She swallowed the wine in another long draft.

"Why choose you?" Nann mused. "You, over Nefertiti, who has been so carefully trained for the court, and who loves power so—"

"I don't know," Kiya said. "Unless it's *that* precisely: Nefertiti understands power—craves it. She wields it so skillfully, just like a soldier with his blade. Perhaps the king fears to share his throne with a woman as strong and capable as she. Perhaps, to him, I am nothing—foolish, soft-headed—and so I am safe."

Nann raised her denials, and Kiya smiled at her staunch loyalty. But she listened with only half her heart. Bleak thoughts tumbled through her mind as she tightened both hands around her wine cup. *Perhaps the king actually loves me. Maybe that is why he has chosen me—because I am the one he most desires, the one he cares for.* Kiya was sure that Akhenaten visited her bed more than he did the other wives'. And he often stayed long after his pleasure was exhausted, stroking her bare skin, whispering endearments in her ear, while she schooled herself to stillness, driving away the quivers of fear and disgust that vibrated deep in her body. *If he loves me—if he does intend to make me his Great Wife—then I cannot cast his children from my womb forever. Sooner or later, he will begin to suspect...*

"Look," Nann said suddenly. "Someone is coming from the Great Aten Temple."

Kiya set her cup back on the tray, grateful for the distraction from her dark thoughts. "Coming here?"

"I believe so, Mistress. There is little else on this side of the valley, save for your palace."

"It's a woman," Kiya said, leaning once more over the wall to watch the figure, clothed in a flowing, white robe, make its way down the dusty road from the temple's gate. Kiya squinted. "It's Nefertiti!"

"Are you sure?"

"Very. Who else moves with such grace? Go, Nann—take this tray down to the kitchen, and prepare something nicer for our guest. Tell my gate-guards to admit the High Priestess at once. I'll be waiting to receive her in the game room."

Kiya had barely settled onto one of the couches in the cool seclusion of her game room when Nefertiti arrived. A light coating of dust clung to the hem and sleeves of her robe, but it shimmered in the light that streamed through the game room's windows, and Nefertiti seemed adorned with flecks of gold. Kiya invited her to sit, and poured the wine Nann brought herself. Nefertiti took the cup with a nod that was gracious, but her eyes traveled around the room, taking in the fine appointments of the palace in sour silence.

"It is so good to see you," Kiya said. In her over-eagerness to cheer away Nefertiti's silence, her voice sounded too buoyant and forced.

"It's clear the Pharaoh thinks highly of you."

Kiya swallowed a lump in her throat and looked away. Was there any response she could make that wouldn't be foolish—or worse, dangerous? Nefertiti's influence over the king had only grown since the advent of Akhet-Aten. She used the advantage of her own import, her significance within the two Aten Temples, with deliberacte precision. Only the gods knew what whims the High Priestess of the Sun might enact, how she might reshape Akhenaten's world, if she took a fancy to do so. And although Kiya had no desire to become King's Great Wife and to share still more of her life with Akhenaten, the position might give her some shred of power. Power was what she lacked now, save that one precious ability to control her own fertility.

She changed the subject. "With the move to—" she gestured feebly at the walls around them, painted in colors so dazzling and scenes so alive that they seemed almost chaotic—"I haven't had the chance to congratulate you on your new daughter."

"Yes." Nefertiti's brows lifted, and she sipped from her wine cup.

"Your fourth daughter. What a blessing from the gods." Kiya felt the emptiness of her own belly, and feared the hypocrisy of her words would show on her face, flashing and dancing there as wildly as the colors of her painted walls.

"Nefer-Neferu-Aten Tasherit," Nefertiti said. "The name is a mouthful, I fear. We call her Tasherit, to simplify the matter." Her words would have been light and playful on another woman's lips. But Nefertiti gazed into a corner of the room as she spoke, her eyes unfocused, taking in nothing of the mural, a tangle of papyrus and reeds rendered in a dozen shades of green, with white geese bursting up in joyous flight from the foliage.

Kiya nibbled a date to disguise her trepidation. "Is there anything wrong with your baby, Nefertiti? You seem—"

Nefertiti waved one hand, dismissing Kiya's concerns. Her dark eyes snapped into sudden focus, and she fixed Kiya with a stare as stern and assessing as a falcon's. "Nothing wrong, except that she is a girl. Again. Another girl. And that is what brings me here today, Kiya."

She fell silent, but her gaze lost none of its intensity. Kiya shifted uncomfortably under that cold appraisement. Did Nefertiti know about the herbs, the lost pregnancies? Did her position as High Priestess confer upon her some divine knowledge?

Kiya's eyes flicked to Nann, who stood with her back to one wall, between the images of two long-legged wading birds. The servant woman's hands were clasped below her waist, and her eyes were on the floor. Her body held an air of unpleasant expectation.

Has Nann told my secret? No. She was certain of little in Akhet-Aten, or anywhere in Egypt. But the assurance of Nann's loyalty reached deep into Kiya's bones. If Nefertiti had learned of the lost pregnancies, she must have gained her knowledge in some sly, secret way—having Nann followed into the marketplace, perhaps.

Kiya swallowed her date with an effort. It felt like a jagged stone in her throat.

"I am taking a great risk in coming to you, Kiya," Nefertiti said quietly, soberly. She, too, glanced toward Nann. "Send your woman away."

Kiya hesitated, and Nann looked up. The servant held

her eye for a moment, and Kiya could practically hear her thoughts. *Be brave. Remember that you have the king's favor, or you would not be here, in this fine palace. What have you to fear?*

Then Nann slipped from the room without being told, shutting the door softly in her wake. But Kiya saw Nann's head and shoulders flit past one window, and she knew the woman was heading in the direction of the front gate—toward the guards the king had dedicated to watching over Kiya's safety, day and night.

When they were alone, Nefertiti drew a deep breath, and Kiya had the impression that the High Priestess of the Sun was steadying rattled nerves. "There's a certain task you must do, Kiya. An important work, vital to Egypt, and after seeing your fine new home—" Nefertiti's mouth gave only the smallest twist to betray her envy— "I am convinced that you are truly the only one who may achieve it."

"A task? What task?"

For a long moment, Nefertiti did not answer. She turned the faience wine-cup in her hands, examining its smooth surface and bright patterns with an untroubled face, as if she hadn't a single care to darken her heart. Then she set it on the table before her with a decisive gesture.

"You must take a lover."

Kiya was so astounded that she gasped, and then laughed, a high, shrill titter of hysterical disbelief. Then, when Nefertiti's severe frown remained in place, Kiya gasped again.

"Examine the situation we have before us," Nefertiti said coolly. "I have borne my fourth daughter. Your own child is a girl, as is Sitamun's, if we can assume that Akhenaten is Nebetah's father. Every child the Pharaoh has sired is female. After so many years and so many children, I believe he is only capable of planting the seeds of girls."

"You mean—"

"Akhenaten will never have a son—an heir. Not unless we find some other man to plant the seed."

"But... but why me?"

Kiya clutched the collar of her robe tight about her throat, as if the flimsy linen might protect her. For more than two years, she had lived in fear of Akhenaten's unpredictable temper, his violence and dark urges. If he could abuse Kiya merely for the sake of his own lust, he would surely not hesitate to kill her if she took a lover and the king found out. She recalled the roof of the Pharaoh's quarters, peering over the temple wall toward Kiya's palace, like a man slinking through the reeds to watch women bathing in the river. She imagined that Akhenaten could see her now, staring through solid brick and painted plaster, noting the way she trembled and swayed within the heart of her palace. She was not safe from his gaze anywhere, not even here.

"Let all remain as it is," Kiya blurted. Her tight-pulled collar bit into her neck. "What does it matter if he has only daughters?"

Nefertiti's reply was so low, Kiya could scarcely catch her words. "Because, you fool, the sooner we have a clear heir to the throne, the sooner we can restore Egypt. Move the capital back to Waset—or the West Bank, at least. Set the true gods back in their places, soothe the anger of the priests."

"But Akhenaten will... will still reign. He will still live, for the gods know how long."

Nefertiti said nothing. She only arched one kohl-black brow.

"Why not you?" Kiya pleaded. "You must do this task. I've had only one child, but you have had many! It's likelier to work with you; you'll fall pregnant sooner, and the danger of discovery will be less."

"I've thought of that already," Nefertiti admitted. "I would do it if I could, but Ay—my father.... He has hopes of securing my *cooperation* in certain plans. He keeps a close eye on me. He's constantly watching, waiting for me to make a mistake."

"And then he will have you deposed?" Kiya asked, wide-eyed. "Strip you of your position at the temples?"

Nefertiti gave a short, dry laugh. "No. He's waiting for a chance to blackmail me—to hold some bit of information over my head, so that I am once more firmly in his control. If I were to take a lover, Ay would be like a child with a New Year gift. He'd caper down the Royal Road with glee.

"So you see, Kiya, I have risked much, just in coming here—in speaking to you. I know you and I have never been especially close—at least, not for many years. But I am placing my future in your hands. Now you know how precarious my position is, how close I am to falling back under my father's sway. You could do it, if you chose—hand me back to him, strip away everything I've earned for myself, and make me a little girl cringing in fear of her father once more."

Slowly, Kiya released her grip on her collar. Her hands fell limp on her lap. "I see," she said. "I see how you trust me, Nefertiti. I will not harm you. I won't sell your secrets to your father."

Nefertiti's smile was tentative, almost shy. "I know you won't. You're a person in whom anyone can trust, Kiya. It may be the rarest quality in all of Akhet-Aten, but it's all the more admirable for that."

"I won't tell your father, but you must understand that I cannot do it. I can't take a lover. The risk, if the king found out, is too great."

The dark, falcon-fierce glower returned. "I thought perhaps you'd say so."

"You saw how Akhenaten treated me, that day... when we first came to this valley. I fear him, Nefertiti. I have feared him ever since."

Tears misted Kiya's vision, blurring the brightness of her murals into a senseless clamor of color and light. She hung her head, ashamed to weep before this woman, who had always carried herself with poise and confidence, through the darkest of trials, through Akhenaten's most frightening bouts of zeal.

"Besides," Kiya went on, sniffling, "I have no desire for a lover. I only want to be left alone, to keep to myself."

"Desire?" Nefertiti spat the word. "This has nothing to do with desire, Kiya. Don't play the fool."

"I just want to stay inside my palace," she pleaded. "To shut Akhet-Aten out, to pretend the Pharaoh doesn't exist." The tears broke from their dam and spilled down her cheeks, a hot flood that scoured away any pretensions she'd had toward poise and composure. "I can pretend he doesn't exist, you know, between his... *visits*. I can make believe that I'm back in Mitanni, that I never left. Oh, Nefertiti, I have been such a fool!" She pressed both hands to her face and sobbed, hunching over her lap, filling her palms with tears of shame and loss.

"A fool?" Nefertiti asked quietly. "What do you mean?"

"To think there was ever a time when I believed myself in love with that monster! To think there was a time when I delighted in his touch. To think I ever thought him safe, or trustworthy, or *sane*. Oh, the gods curse me, I am a simpleton."

With an effort, she stilled her sobs. Her eye-paints had run, and her fingers were streaked with the mess of her face. Nefertiti silently offered a kerchief, and Kiya took it with a trembling hand, then dabbed at her cheeks and eyelids.

"I was young," Kiya said, more calmly now, "and new to Egypt. But still, I behaved like a child, too innocent for my own good."

Nefertiti rose from her couch opposite the one where Kiya huddled in her misery. Kiya thought for a moment that the High Priestess would leave, but to her surprise, Nefertiti glided around the table and sank down beside her, pulling Kiya into a brief embrace.

"What choice did you have?" Nefertiti asked. "You did what you were bidden. You were as much at your father's disposal as I ever was."

Mollified, Kiya sniffed in agreement.

"But choice or no choice, this is where we find ourselves. The gods have brought us to this point, for reasons of their own. Egypt is in the hands of an unstable man. We might be able to save the land—and ourselves, Kiya—but we are running out of options. And we must be willing to take risks, if we are to succeed.

"No woman who takes a lover will be entirely safe. But secluded as you are, here in your little palace, you have a better chance of surviving the gamble than Sitamun or I."

"Sitamun—are you sure she can't handle the task?"

Nefertiti's pretty mouth tightened in a distasteful frown. "Sitamun? She would likely throw herself into a crocodile pool rather than lie with any man other than Akhenaten. The poor creature; there's no one in the world I pity more than her. And before too many more years have passed, she may have further troubles to weigh on her heart."

"What do you mean?"

"Sitamun does her best to keep Nebetah hidden away. She secludes the girl as much as she can, and forbids her from going near the harem. But despite Sitamun's efforts, Akhenaten has begun to notice that Nebetah exists."

Kiya gaped at Nefertiti, winding the kerchief around her

fingers.

"It won't be long before the Pharaoh sets his sights on that girl, mark my words. He..." Nefertiti's voice cracked, and for the briefest moment, she glanced away. Kiya noted the shame darkening her cheeks, the guilt staining and distorting her fine, flawless features. "He seems to enjoy very young flesh. You know he lay with Sitamun when she was just a girl, long before he married her. And... and my sister, Mutbenret, too. Soon Akhenaten will make of Nebetah what the old Pharaoh made of Sitamun. Once that happens, I fear none of our girls will be safe. Nebetah is only the eldest. The rest of our daughters will soon follow."

Kiya covered her mouth with one trembling hand. Her daughter Kayet, growing up in the waterside harem after the royal Egyptian tradition, suddenly seemed impossibly far away, and more fragile than an eggshell.

"The rest of our girls will follow," Nefertiti repeated with grim force, "unless we can move first—work together—come up with a male heir, and then... well..." She shrugged. "Let the will of the gods be done."

Kiya drew a shuddering breath. "What have I done, to bring my daughter into such a world? Oh, how I wish I'd never left Mitanni. Egypt is a terrible place. For all the brightness of the sun, it's darker here than the bottom of the deepest, coldest well."

Nefertiti pursed her lips in thought. "If you cannot see your way to taking a lover for Egypt's sake—and I don't blame you for that; you are not Egyptian, after all—then at least think of what you might gain if you run the risk and succeed. If you can bear the king his heir, Kiya, then one day you will be King's Mother. The title will give you nearly as much power as I have, as High Priestess of the Sun."

"I don't want power," Kiya said flatly.

"You might, if you realized what that power could mean. Bear a son and when he is grown, you can go anywhere you please. You can leave Egypt—go back to Mitanni. You can take Kayet with you, out of Egypt forever."

Kiya knotted the kerchief in her fist, struggling to hide the desperate desire that welled up in her middle. *Back to Mitanni. I might see it again.* She could walk the seaside cliffs once more, smell the cool breezes gusting down from the pine forests. Feebly, she beat at her surging hope. But she was too late, or too weak to quell it, or both. Nefertiti's dark eyes narrowed, and the tiniest smile of satisfaction spread across her lips.

"Think about what I've told you," Nefertiti said, rising and heading for the door. The note of triumph in her voice told Kiya, as plain as words, that Nefertiti already knew her visit to the palace had been fruitful.

AS EVENING APPROACHED and the fiercest of the day's heat ebbed, Kiya set out from her palace with Nann for company and a pair of guards trailing several paces behind. Too restless to remain in a litter, she walked down the long road toward the Great Aten Temple, her sandals scuffing up clouds of golden dust, her face cooled by the small canopy of plumes that Nann held overhead. Here, at the northern reach of the valley, the cliffs arched close to the water, and their hard, vertical faces seemed very near—intrusively present, towering over the city of Akhet-Aten like the king himself. The cliffs still held the memory of mid-day heat. Kiya could feel it radiating from the stone, beating against her side and the skin of her bared shoulder.

She eyed the high, square-topped walls of the Great Aten Temple as she made her way ever closer. They were tall and austere, their outer surface unadorned except by plain white plaster, as if the only beauty they needed was the reflected glory of the sun itself. That very sun was setting, far across the river, casting a warm hue over the temple's façade as it sank into a red horizon with a slow, deliberate ease that seemed rather gloating to Kiya.

"Where are we going?" Nann asked. "You haven't left your palace for nearly two weeks, since the king moved you in."

"I must pay a visit to Sitamun."

Kiya did not need to look her servant in the face to know that Nann was squinting at her, trying to read the meaning of her errand on her features, through the bobbing, shifting shade of the canopy. Kiya willed herself not to meet Nann's eye, afraid she would break down in tears again. She kept her gaze resolutely on the temple walls, and forced herself to hold her chin up high.

They passed the gate to the Great Aten Temple, which reached nearly down to the water's edge and the largest stone quay, which stretched out into the Iteru's swift current. No ship waited at the quay, and the temple's outer courtyard was silent, emptied of priests and the nobles who often spent their days there, hoping to be seen by the Pharaoh, angling to earn his favor. The devotees of the Aten would return, Kiya knew, when the sun rose once more, ready to welcome its spill of light over the cliffs, its cascade of life-giving warmth that poured over the temple's walls to heat the sandy floor within. Kiya gathered her skirt in her hands and quickened her pace, the faster to leave the gateway behind. She hated the Great Aten Temple, its stark light and stiff formality, the way the sun's power seemed to gather within its courtyards and sanctuaries, redoubling itself, heating the interior like a baker's oven.

It was only when she passed the temple's far wall that she slowed, and finally stumbled to a halt. She stood gazing out at the city of Akhet-Aten. It unfurled from the temple's southern wall like a carpet of white and gold, filling the bowl of the valley, a grid of wide streets running between fine estates. Here and there, noble women moved in tight clusters as they made their calls for conversation and wine, and on the nearest rooftops, she could see men, bare-chested, their white kilts glowing softly in the setting sun, their heads close together in private discussion. A patrol of three city soldiers, wearing kilts striped vertically in Mahu's red and blue, came out of a nearby alley and swaggered down the center of the street. The women who had gathered at a friend's doorway made haste to get inside before the soldiers came too near.

Kiya gestured for her personal guards to draw closer, then struck out toward the waterside palace, refusing to look at the city soldiers. *Mahu's dogs*, she thought with grim mistrust. She hadn't been able to think of Mahu without a shiver since the day Akhenaten had raided the Temple of Amun. Neither Mahu nor his men had struck any sort of blow against a citizen of Akhet-Aten—at least, not that Kiya had heard. But there was not a man or woman in the City of the Sun who didn't fear them. Their display of power at the Temple of Amun—their reckless disregard for all that was sacred—was enough to make the citizens of Akhet-Aten wary of the Pharaoh's soldiers.

Kiya glided past Mahu's men, refusing to acknowledge their bows or their murmurs of *King's Wife*. She told herself, *If I do become Great Wife, the first thing I shall do is drive Mahu and all his creatures from the city.* It made her feel somewhat braver, made her knees less inclined to tremble, even if she knew the plan was a futile one. No King's Great Wife could induce Akhenaten to forsake his bodyguard, nor banish the men who had seized Amun's treasury in the Pharaoh's name. Not even a Great Wife he loved—if indeed it was love that had motivated him to set Kiya apart from the others.

She found her way to the rear gate of the palace, but

before she could approach the guards who watched it, Nann stalled her with a hand on her elbow.

"Mistress, what will you do if you see the king?"

Kiya shrugged. "He never told me I must stay in my palace. It was a gift, not a prison." *Or so he intended me to think.* "I shall tell him the truth: that I've come to visit Sitamun. He knows that Sitamun and I have always been close. It's not so unusual, that I should wish to see my friend and fellow King's Wife."

She swept past the palace guards, nodding in response to their deep, respectful bows. She encountered no one but a few servants, toting water for the garden or fresh linens from the laundry, as she made her way through the long, straight corridors of the great palace. To steady her nerves, she counted the pillars she passed, brushing the brilliant paint adorning each one with a soft, glancing touch. Like the cliffs outside, the pillars of the great palace still retained the heat of the high sun, and it seeped through her fingertips, accumulating within her body until her hand and arm tingled with a sensation of distant warning.

Sitamun's private apartments were tucked in the southeast corner of the grounds, backed against the palace's outer wall and half-hidden by a grove of young palms and a bank of tangled roses, still glossy with last year's leaves. Kiya bade her guards wait beside the palms, then took Nann with her to tap at Sitamun's door-frame.

Nann raised her brows curiously as she leaned her feathered canopy beside Sitamun's door. "I'm to come with you, then?"

"Yes," Kiya said. "But you must swear secrecy. I fear this is a dangerous errand."

"Nefertiti?"

Kiya nodded.

"She's too ambitious by half," Nann hissed under her

breath. "You shouldn't involve yourself in her schemes. You have only to wait—you'll be King's Great Wife soon, and then you need never bow to Nefertiti's whims again."

"It's not like that," Kiya said. "And anyway, I fear I have little choice but to become involved with this particular scheme. All afternoon, I've considered what Nefertiti and I discussed, and I believe she's right. You'll understand, Nann, when you hear it. Only wait until we're alone with Sitamun."

A household servant admitted them. The woman, speaking in a low voice, directed them to a small chamber that looked out, through one narrow window, onto a tiny, raised pond encircled by papyrus plants set in bright-colored pots. Birds flitted amid the papyrus leaves and dodged over the water, hunting the evening's hatch of insects. But Sitamun, leaning against the window sill, looked beyond the peaceful scene with distant, sightless eyes. The servant announced Kiya and paused, waiting on orders to bring refreshments or to summon musicians. But Sitamun remained silent, staring fixedly out into the sunset garden. After a moment, the servant withdrew.

Kiya and Nann shared a wary glance, then Nann led the way to Sitamun's small couch, and together, they sank down on its edge.

"It's good to see you, Sitamun," Kiya said. The other King's Wife made no reply, and Kiya said cheerily, "I walked all the way here, you know. It will be a fine evening, and I wanted to enjoy it."

She bit her lip, watching Sitamun's back, her motionless study of the garden. These long, distracted silences had started with the court's move to Akhet-Aten, and had only grown more plentiful and protracted with time.

Nann nudged Kiya in the ribs. She tried another angle. "I've come to speak to you on an urgent errand. Sitamun, it's about your daughter. I believe she may be in danger."

Sitamun turned from the window with a jerk, blinking rapidly as her eyes focused on Kiya. "What did you say? Nebetah?"

Kiya held out an arm, beckoning her friend to sit close beside her. Sitamun approached the couch warily, and sat as far from Kiya as she could manage, watching her with a cautious frown.

"Nefertiti came to see me today. She gave me a warning, Sitamun. She believes Nebetah may be in danger of... of ending up in the harem."

Sitamun shook her head abruptly; the thin braids of her wig lashed the air. "Nonsense. My daughter will be no harem girl." The mist of distraction left Sitamun's face, and her eyes were as keen and determined as Kiya had ever known them to be.

"I hope that is so," Kiya said gently. "It's why I've come today: to warn you, so that you can protect Nebetah before it's too late. So that *we* can protect her, and all our daughters. We'll have to work as one, Sitamun. We'll have to join together, and trust one another—Nefertiti, you, and I."

Quietly, mindful that servants might even now be listening from adjoining chambers or lurking outside the garden window, Kiya told Sitamun of Nefertiti's plan. Nann's mouth fell open as Kiya proposed what Sitamun must do, but Kiya sat calm and straight on the edge of the couch, resolute in her decision.

"It's the only way," Kiya finished in a whisper. "Nefertiti must be correct: the Pharaoh will never sire a son. But once there is an obvious heir to the throne, perhaps the gods will grant us some relief, and provide a way for the throne to pass to the heir. Soon Nebetah will be old enough for the king to show her... *favor*. If we're to produce an heir before that day comes, we must begin soon, or none of our daughters will be safe."

Sitamun glowered past Kiya's shoulder as she spoke, as if her eyes might bore a hole through the plaster, paint, and mudbrick of the palace, or knock the whole structure down with a great burst of fury. But when Kiya fell silent, Sitamun's expression softened. A look of hopeless sorrow crossed her face—raised brows, wilting mouth—then vanished behind a mask of hard amusement. Sitamun huffed a small, bitter laugh.

"What a great lot of work," she said. "What trouble to go to."

"But the girls—"

"The girls will come to no harm," Sitamun said harshly. "Count on that. I will not allow it. Akhenaten will not touch my daughter. I won't allow him to make of her what he—and my father—made of me."

She clutched at the heavy necklace around her throat, a thick chain of overlapping, golden leaves. Kiya thought for a moment that she might tear the thing away, but she only tugged irritably, like a hunting hound worrying at its collar. Her hand fell away again, and she turned to Kiya with wide eyes. Their dark depths flamed with a sudden intensity that made Kiya draw back, pressing herself against the silken cushions as if shrinking from a hissing asp.

"You and Nefertiti," Sitamun said, "plotting, scheming. But it's all so complicated, isn't it? So risky."

"What other choice do we have?"

Sitamun smiled, a tight, eerie grin. Her face went pale around the lips, and her teeth flashed, catching the glow of the setting sun. "It would be simpler," she said softly, "to kill Akhenaten."

Kiya lurched to her feet and was halfway across the room before she'd even realized she had moved. Was she rushing to check for listeners in the hall, she wondered as she caught herself, slowed, and stopped—or fleeing for the door? Trembling, she made herself turn and face Sitamun coolly.

Sitamun laughed. "How Egyptian you've become! Afraid the river won't rise if the Pharaoh is killed?"

Nann, still seated on the couch beside Sitamun, stared at Kiya with pleading eyes. Kiya could see how she shivered, how her body vibrated faintly with the rapid beat of her heart. Nann held herself perfectly still, as if she hoped she might vanish from Sitamun's sight, or the King's Wife might forget that Nann had ever entered her chamber and witnessed this talk of treason.

"Sitamun," Kiya said carefully, "are you well? Such talk is so unlike you. Your words are dangerous. Surely you know that."

"How dangerous is this talk, truly?"

Sitamun rose smoothly and drifted once more to the window sill. She turned her back on Kiya and stood poised and aloof, watching fire die in the sky, watching the merciful cool of the night's shade creep over paths and flower beds. Kiya had never noticed before how very much Sitamun resembled her mother. The hard stillness, the confident, lonely strength—it was as if Tiy stood before her, as practiced and adept as a charioteer racing steeds beneath the open sky.

Kiya hastened back to Nann and took her hand in comfort. Nann's fingers were stiff and cold.

"Your words frighten me, Sitamun," Kiya said.

"I'm not frightened." Sitamun's voice was untrembling, as placid as a lotus in a pool. "I'm not afraid to do what I must. To kill a king—again."

The breath left Kiya's chest in an icy rush. Her heart seemed everywhere at once, pounding painfully in her throat, her stomach, the soles of her feet, behind her eyes.

Her soul turned itself inside out, all her thoughts fleeing from her like a flock of birds exploding from the reeds, flapping, clamoring, crying out in a chaotic fury. There was a sound in her ears like the ringing of a gong. Her mouth tasted of blood.

One thought returned to her—one thought alone, beating its frantic wings inside the cage of her chest. She whispered, "Amunhotep."

Sitamun turned her head, and her sharp, regal profile—Tiy's face—stood out in bold, warm colors against the square of gathering night. "Shall I tell you how it was done?" she said. "How *I* did it?"

Kiya shook her head. "But you... you were only a child," she whispered.

"And the king was a sickly, bloated, indolent thing. When we were alone together, I mixed his poppy drink, as he often had me do. I made it stronger than I ought—that was all." She smiled again, that tense, feral leer. "The poppy made him drowsy, but I did the thing before he could drift off to sleep. I wanted him to know it was I who would send him down into the Duat to face Anupu's scales—that it was I who would throw his heart into Ammit's mouth. I looked into his eyes, and then I pushed a pillow onto his face."

"I don't want to hear this," Kiya said. "You mustn't speak of it."

Sitamun ignored her. "He struggled, of course. But the poppy and his own illness had weakened him enough. And anyway, I was stronger than he. I always was, even as a child.

"When he was dead—I stayed beside him for some time, to be certain he was truly gone—I simply walked back to my chamber and left him for his servants to find. I never slept so well as I did that night, before or since. All my dreams were sweet."

A hard fist seemed to tighten around Kiya's throat. Another black bird had joined the first, fluttering inside her, insisting she ask the question that choked her, that tasted so very bitter on her tongue. "And Thutmose?"

Sitamun sighed. Her head sagged as if it were a puppet's whose string had been cut. For a long moment she said nothing, and remained with her slender shoulders turned to Kiya. The night's first stars had begun to shine outside; they limned Sitamun's delicate form with a faint, ethereal trace of silver.

At last Sitamun said, "Thutmose—that is my one regret. I loved him, Kiya. He was a good brother to me, kind and gentle. I loved him, but not as I loved Amunho..." she shook her head, then amended, "Akhenaten."

With a great rush of pain and fear, Kiya remembered Thutmose in the West Bank garden, his casual grace, his startling beauty. She remembered his fingers in her hair, stroking its golden-bronze softness, and saw again how his eyes had closed in ecstasy when he'd lifted a lock of her hair, brushing it with his lips and inhaling her perfume.

"Why?" she said plaintively. "Why Thutmose? Your own brother...!"

"I thought..." Sitamun hesitated. Her hands drifted up to cover her face. "I thought it would make Akhenaten love me again, if I cleared his way to the throne. Even then, I felt him pulling away from me, discarding me like a broken cup, or a tawdry bit of jewelry. I thought if I gave him what he truly desired, he would see how I loved him, and he would give me his whole heart once more.

"And to think, Tiy thought it was Akhenanten who'd done that awful deed. She sent Smenkhkare away for it."

"But..." Kiya faltered. "But Smenkhkare is dead. He drowned. We all stood beside his body at the funeral. You were there, Sitamun. You remember."

STORM IN THE SKY

Sitamun shook her head. "Some other boy's body—a *rekhet*, no doubt, the same age as my brother. The funeral and the body were all part of Tiy's plan. Smenkhkare still lives, as far as I know, and if Akhenaten is dead, the throne will pass to him. But first Akhenaten must die."

"Sitamun..." Kiya's eyes stung as if flooded with tears, but Sitamun remained mercilessly clear in her vision, unblurred—and Kiya's cheeks were dry. She wiped them anyway with cold fingers. "You cannot do this thing. You'll become a monster—a demon!"

Now at last Sitamun turned to face her, and her eyes were terrible to see—haunted, hollow, their centers as dark as the caverns of the Underworld.

"I know," Sitamun said simply. "We're all demons already, all mad—each of us in the royal family. Every one of us is vile, in one way or another. But some of us are viler than others."

"That's not true. It can't be. You cannot all be mad."

"It is true. This madness is an infection in our blood. Perhaps it's the stamp of divinity, the very thing that makes us near-gods. It's what ties us together—what makes us who we are. It's what damns us, too. It was our beginning, somewhere back in distant generations, and it will be our end."

"But Nebetah—"

"Her madness will come," Sitamun replied sadly. "No one of this bloodline will escape it. Not a single one."

Kiya moaned wordlessly, pressing the heels of her hands hard against her eyes.

"Thutmose was more difficult to kill than Father," Sitamun said. Her voice sounded very small and weak, a child's voice in the darkness.

Kiya shook her head and pressed still harder, until bursts of purple light erupted behind her eyelids. She shook her head, silently pleading with Sitamun to spare her this dark knowledge.

But Sitamun spoke on. "I know what you must think; a girl as small as I was—as I *am*—could not possibly have overpowered a man of Thutmose's strength. I got the idea from Ay, from a knotted leather cord he used to carry. He still does carry it, you know—carries it all about Akhet-Aten, and plays with it when he's distracted, as if the gods wish to taunt me with its presence whenever I cross Ay's path.

"When I decided that I must kill Thutmose, I thought of Ay and his knotted cord. I realized such a device would give me the leverage I needed to overcome my brother, and subdue him quickly—"

Kiya tore at the air with her nails, flailed her fists in Sitamun's direction. "Stop!" she cried. "I don't want to *hear* this, you creature, you beast!"

Nann caught Kiya by the wrist. "Mistress! Hush! The servants will hear!"

"I am a beast," Sitamun said quietly. "I have never regretted killing old, lecherous Amunhotep. But not a day has gone by when Thutmose's death hasn't dragged at my heart. I know, Kiya, when I face my judgment, that it will be Thutmose who stands at the scales to weigh my heart against the Feather of Truth—not Anupu. And I have no hope that my heart will be light. I can feel its weight already. It's a stone inside me, and it sinks deeper every day. Thutmose will be waiting there, ready to push me into Ammit's maw, ready to send me to the Eater of Hearts, just as I did to Father. And it will be no more than I deserve."

"Oh, Sitamun!" Kiya could think of nothing else to say. For it was true—a murderer, especially one who killed her own kin, had no hope of an afterlife. Sitamun's revelation seemed to fill the room with palpable impurity, thickening

STORM IN THE SKY

the air Kiya breathed, coating every surface with a skin of oily filth. She was Sitamun no longer, but something sullied and damned—a vision from a nightmare. And yet she was Sitamun still, the frail, frightened girl whom Kiya had comforted after the birth of her child; the small, pale hand Kiya had held; the one she had defended from Nefertiti and sheltered from the darkness of the world. Sitamun was her friend—one of the few she had in all of Egypt. The tears broke at last, flooding Kiya's sight and spilling down her cheeks in two hot streams that burned her skin with their salt.

"Don't weep." Sitamun came to her, and Kiya drew back against the cushions, but Sitamun ignored her flinching and sank down beside her. One thin arm reached around Kiya's shoulders. Thin, but it felt strong and warm—capable. "I'm not afraid, Kiya. I will do what I must do, for Nebetah's sake, and Kayet's, and for the sake of Nefertiti's girls. I'll do it for your sake—and for mine. Once we are rid of Akhenaten, you will all be free."

"But you—"

"I am damned anyway," Sitamun said. "For Thutmose. Let me do some good to counter the evil I have wrought."

"But you love the king!"

"No." Not the slightest hint of sorrow showed on her face—no knitting of her brows, no paling of her cheeks. She spoke with the dull, hard certainty of one who finds truth revealed at last—truth as enduring as carved stone. "I thought, since I was a child, that I loved Akhenaten. I thought he loved me, too. I thought we could dwell together here, alone with our madness in this valley, where the world would be safe from us. I thought we could be content here—together—just my brother and me. But you see what he's made of this place. It's a shrine to his own vanity, the whole place—a temple for his madness. He couldn't be content with me alone; he brought the whole of the court with him.

"How could I have loved a man like him, Kiya? His heart is incapable of loving. Was it the work of some demon, to trick me, to cloud my judgment for so many years? Or was it only the curse of my bloodline?"

Impulsively, Kiya clutched Sitamun's hand. "But you can't kill him. Not until there is an heir. We can't leave the throne unoccupied. Who will be king?"

Sitamun shrugged. "Egypt has faced that challenge before and survived. The conqueror, Thutmose the First—he came to the throne a common man, you know. The Great Wife chose him when her husband died without an heir. And his grand-daughter, Hatshepsut—she ruled from the Horus Throne. Why should a woman not hold Egypt when my brother is dead?"

"But who?"

"Tiy," Sitamun said at once. "She is more than capable. Or even Nefertiti. It doesn't matter, Kiya. An heir is not as necessary as you and Nefertiti think. But Akhenaten's death *is*."

"Murder isn't the answer," Kiya begged. "It cannot be! The gods abhor the killing of a king, and will curse those who slay their kin!"

Sitamun rounded on her, stilling Kiya's voice with the force of her stare. "I will do what I must to protect my daughter. Nebetah will never be his plaything—*never!* I swore that on the night she was born, and I will uphold that vow, even as I go down into the Duat. My *ka* is already damned for my sins; the gods have cursed me already. They may curse me a hundred times more and I'll never care, so long as Nebetah is safe from that madman."

"Oh, Sitamun—I wouldn't feel so frightened if only there were another man to rule, or even a woman. But I know the chaos that falls on a land when its throne is left unclaimed. It was so in Mitanni, and it will be so here. The war, the rape, the destruction! How can any of our daughters be safe if we upend the order of the world?"

Sitamun twined her fingers in her lap, and stared silently at her garden window. Her slight body was very still; even her chest barely stirred with the faint rhythm of her breath. For a long pause, she watched the starlight gleam in the garden, dusting the leaves of the palms with a shimmer of silver.

Then, with a timid, almost pleading smile, she turned to Kiya. "There is another man who might take throne. I have one brother still living."

Confounded, Kiya shook her head. "I... but all your brothers are dead, save for Akhenaten."

"No. Smenkhkare still lives. For his own protection, Tiy sent him away from the House of Rejoicing when Thutmose died. She felt sure Akhenaten would kill him."

"Smenkhkare?"

"Tiy planned to recall my little brother when the time was right—*if* the time was ever right, if the need to depose Akhenaten—or dispose of him—ever arose." Sitamun stood, and returned to her pensive vigil at the window. "I believe Tiy would have brought Smenkhkare back long ago, if she hadn't lost all her influence at court. She has kept Smenkhkare's existence secret all these years, and so have I. Tiy no longer has the power to recall him. But I do. And so do you, Kiya."

Nann leaned close to Kiya's ear. "A clear heir to the throne," she muttered. "It would alleviate your fears, Mistress. The transition from one Pharaoh to the next could be seamless and quick."

"You are talking of murder! The slaying of a king!"

"A thing not done in Egypt, perhaps," Nann admitted, "but not so unthinkable in Mitanni."

Sitamun smiled faintly at the gap-toothed servant. "Yes. Are you Egyptian in truth now, Lady Tadukhepa, or is your heart—your *ka*—still Hurrian?"

"I cannot agree to murder." Kiya insisted. "Not even the murder of... of that man. Why do we not simply recall Smenkhkare, and allow the court to depose Akhenaten once they see that a better alternative exists?"

"Because," Sitamun said smoothly, "the court is more Egyptian than you are. They will not depose a Pharaoh, no matter how they hate him. We are the only ones who may secure Smenkhkare on the throne—we who have no cause to fear the gods of the Two Lands. They were never your gods, and they have already damned me. And so let us act now—the two of us—before our daughters come to any harm."

Tiy can stop this, Kiya thought frantically. *Tiy can stay Sitamun's hand.* The former Great Wife was perhaps the only person in all of Egypt who could keep Sitamun from this mad, impulsive feat. And only Tiy might have the ability to extract Kiya from the plot, to absolve her of her unwitting participation and restore her to the safe seclusion of her palace. *I must find Tiy—tonight. But Sitamun mustn't suspect...*

Kiya took one deep breath to steady her nerves. On the cooling night air she could taste the sweetness of lotus flowers and the crisp dampness rising from the pond. The night seemed so innocent, so serene. She stood carefully, smoothing her skirt with slow, deliberate hands.

"For our daughters," Kiya said. "We must speak of this again, and determine how it ought to be done."

Sitamun nodded once, and half her mouth curled in a smile that might have been satisfied, or might have been amused.

"Shall we meet again tomorrow evening, at the same time?" Kiya said.

"If you like. Until then, Lady Tadukhepa of Mitanni." Sitamun turned her back, sinking at once into the same distant reverie in which Kiya had found her.

Kiya took Nann's hand and pulled her from the chamber. The night in the garden embraced her, brushing her skin with cool, soothing hands. But a fire of panicked desperation flamed in Kiya's middle, and her limbs felt hot and shaky. She marched quickly through the garden, towing Nann behind her.

"Mistress," Nann said, struggling to keep the pole of her shade canopy from tangling in the flower beds as they rushed by. "Slow down! There's no need to—"

"There is every need," Kiya hissed, glancing back toward Sitamun's little cluster of apartments. The window where Kiya had left her was obscured by the dark, blue-shadowed shapes of the garden, which seemed now to be animals crouching in the darkness, lions ready to spring, leopards with their claws extended. "We are going to Tiy's estate. Now—as quickly as we can get there."

"Mistress, I—"

"Hush, Nann! There is no time. If we're to stop Sitamun from this foolishness, then we must act quickly."

Nann's frown was as deep as the shadows of the night. "*Should* we stop Sitamun, Mistress?"

"Of course!"

Nann slung the pole of her shade canopy over her shoulder. "Should we, indeed?" Scowling, she marched ahead of Kiya, leading the way down the path, making for the western wall of the palace and the quays beyond. But Nann's footsteps did not slow. If anything, she moved through the darkness faster than Kiya had, and Kiya was obliged to lift the hem of her skirt high, stepping quickly to keep the pale, bobbing plumes of Nann's canopy in sight.

Tiy

*Year 8 of Akhenaten,
Beautiful Are the Manifestations,
Exalting the Name,
Beloved of the Sun*

NIGHT HAD FALLEN like a heavy blue cape across the land, shrouding the valley beyond the river in folds of shadow. Tiy, alone on the small, riverfront terrace of her modest estate, watched the torches and lamps of Akhet-Aten flicker, pale-gold, against the black flank of the distant cliffs. From her isolated home on the western shore, set amid meager farms and new orchards, Akhet-Aten seemed a small, insignificant thing, and smaller still beneath the cloak of darkness. But appearances, she knew, could be deceiving.

Even with the Iteru between them, Tiy could feel the presence of her son. Akhenaten, who day by day retreated ever further into his temples, yet managed to grow in potency with each new sunrise. He had tightened his grip around the city, using Mahu as his fist, forbidding citizens to leave Akhet-Aten on any sort of business except that which he approved himself. There had been reports of men—and women, too—trying their luck against Akhet-Aten's borders. But the cliffs that surrounded the city on three sides concealed Mahu's soldiers in every cleft and cave, and the docks of the Iteru were patrolled day and night by squadrons of the king's men. Akhenaten was determined to make his city a world apart—a place immersed in the worship of his god, a place concerned with no other business than gratifying the Pharaoh and the Aten.

Tiy squinted into the darkness, certain she had just seen a shape moving across the current, gliding fast and low over the water's surface. *A crocodile?* she wondered, taking a few wary steps back from the terrace's edge. The thin fringe of reeds just beyond her small stone platform rattled in a soft breeze. Perhaps it was a river-horse. The great, ill-tempered *deby* preferred the marshes and grassy swards of Lower Egypt, far to the north, and seldom ventured this far south. But they had been spotted in Upper Egypt now and then. They, too, could be dangerous.

This is a night of unsettling shadows, of demons and ghosts, Tiy thought with a shiver. Perhaps it was better to remain inside, where her servants kept lamps burning gaily and where the painted walls of her small villa could blot Akhet-Aten from her sight.

She peered once more into the heart of the river, at the place where she'd imagined that low, swift form to be. It was difficult to make out any shape upon the river, for the glimmer of starlight and the flicker of Akhet-Aten's lamps toyed with her vision, distorting distance and suggesting movement and form where none could truly be. But the darkness rippled again, and now Tiy was certain she'd heard the quiet splash of oars in the water.

A boat? Who would cross the river at this hour, and without a lamp to guide them? She turned and hurried toward her garden path and the golden, glowing squares of her windows. But a soft voice caught and held her. The cry was stifled, barely more than a whisper, but its urgency was plain enough to hear.

"Tiy! Lady Tiy!"

She wheeled and returned to the fringe of reeds, watching the water. As she blinked against Akhet-Aten's distant glow, the shape of a small rowing-boat resolved out of the gloom. It glided toward Tiy's narrow quay and bumped against her own moored boat with a hollow thump.

Tiy watched in wonder as two women clambered from the boat and hurried down the quay. Starlight robbed the color from their linens, but she could tell by the ornately draped and flowing robe of one, and the short, plain tunic-dress of the other, that it was one of the King's Wives who had ventured across the river, attended by a servant. *Nefertiti?* But Nefertiti would never move with such graceless speed, with her skirt hitched up carelessly in tight-clenched fists.

Kiya burst through the veil of reeds, onto the little stone terrace. Even in the starlight, the flush of her cheeks was evident, and her eyes were wide with some terrible excitement. The Hurrian servant with a missing tooth hovered close behind.

"What is it?" Tiy said at once. "What has happened? How did you come to be here, at night?"

"My guards rowed me over." Kiya glanced toward the boat, where her guards apparently waited, then took Tiy's elbow and guided her up the path. But she stopped well short of Tiy's house and stared about her into the darkness of the small garden. "Are we safe here?" Kiya twitched anxiously. "Is it private?"

Vexed by the mystery, Tiy jerked her arm out of Kiya's grasp. "We're as private here as anybody can be in Egypt. Now tell me, girl: what is going on?"

"Sitamun plans to kill the Pharaoh."

Tiy's heart lifted high in her chest, then stopped, seized by a hand as cold as bronze. "Why?"

"She believes Nebetah to be in danger. She thinks the king might put the girl into the harem."

"And so he might," Tiy said. "So he *will*, sooner or later. When does she plan to do it? The foolish girl!"

"I don't know," Kiya said breathlessly. "I told her we should talk more tomorrow night, but—"

"I must put some sense into that child," Tiy said. She turned and stalked back down the path to where the boats bobbed in the current, moored against the stone walkway.

Kiya stumbled along behind, panting in her excitement. "I thought you might be able to—to convince her the plan is folly. And dangerous! What if she's caught? What if Akhenaten realizes—"

"Hush, now," Tiy snapped. "Remember your guards."

They made their way silently onto the quay, and Tiy reached one hand out abruptly. One of the guards took it and helped her step down into the boat. She sat calmly on the low, carved-back seat that spanned the breadth of the rowing boat. Kiya and Nann scrambled down into the boat with less grace, rocking it violently, and sat on either side of Tiy, both of them trembling and staring about at the darkness.

"Be calm," Tiy said brusquely as the guards cast off the lines and pushed the boat into the current. "I can't think if you two flutter about me like a couple of netted birds."

She *did* think as the boat returned to Akhet-Aten, slipping quietly through the darkness. But although Kiya and her servant held themselves still—with obvious effort—Tiy's thoughts were a dark jumble, and they tangled and tripped over themselves within the confines of her heart.

Sitamun. What can *the girl be thinking?* She had always been a timid child, lacking the confidence of her elder sisters and the grasping ambition of Akhenaten. The Pharaoh, coolly observant and patient as a leopard in the trees, was much too dangerous a foe for quiet, sad Sitamun. *If Akhenaten sees what she intends—if he thinks he's in danger—the poor girl's life will be forfeit.*

The king had only grown more cautious since the rise of his golden city. Mahu and his soldiers hung about the

Pharaoh like dogs hoping for scraps, and their presence fed into the king's anxiety, reinforcing his suspicion that he *needed* constant protection. *From what—from whom—I surely cannot say.* Akhenaten was the very *ka* of the City of the Sun, its only reason for being, and the one force that held the nobles of Egypt to this dry, hot valley, imprisoning them like birds in a cage of reeds. Yet still, as powerful as he was—in this place, at least—Akhenaten was never without his protectors.

He and Mahu are always alert for threats. He will not suffer an attack from any quarter—not even from his sister, his King's Wife. If Sitamun moves against him, she will die.

Though she held herself as immobile as a statue of Iset, watching Akhet-Aten grow larger and brighter through a mask of thoughtful calm, Tiy could puzzle out no solution to this dilemma. None, save that she must reach Sitamun before the girl could act on her mad impulse, and convince her not to be so damnably rash.

They reached the eastern quay, and Tiy glanced up at the palace walls towering above. They were dim and gray in the night, with here and there the ripple and stir of weak golden light reflected from the mobile surface of the river. The light writhed over bold glyphs of the sun-disc, which stared down like sentinels from either side of the palace's gate. Deliberately, she turned her gaze away from the sun-discs and climbed onto the quay.

"Come," she said shortly to Kiya, and set off for the gate without waiting to see whether the Hurrian would follow.

Inside the palace, Tiy found a few servants going about their late duties. She sent them scattering with a glare or a jerk of her head. Soon the pillared halls were truly deserted, and when Tiy was satisfied that no one was close enough to see, she hitched up her skirt and rushed to Sitamun's isolated chambers.

She was out of breath by the time she reached her

daughter's door. She did not knock or wait to summon a servant who might announce her presence, but pushed her way inside, and she heard the rustling of Kiya and Nann close on her heels.

The little entrance hall of the secluded apartments stood dark and silent. Tiy paused, lowering the hem of her skirt slowly, listening for movement or voice—for anything that might indicate Sitamun's whereabouts. But the chambers were as still as a tomb, and a prickle of foreboding crept up Tiy's back.

Light, shuffling footsteps sounded from the depths of the hall and a moment later, a servant appeared from the gloom, her white tunic a pale smudge in the darkness. The woman drew a few steps nearer before she noted Tiy and her companions, lurking like spirits around a shrine. She threw up her hands in sudden panic, and Tiy moved quickly to seize the woman's shoulders, stifling her shriek of alarm.

"Quiet, you! It is I, Lady Tiy. You know me. Where is Sitamun? Take me to her."

The servant, shuddering, clutched at her heart. "I cannot take you to her, Lady. She is not at home."

"Not at home? Where has she gone, at this hour?"

"She has gone to see the Pharaoh."

From the darkness behind Tiy, Kiya gave a low, strangled moan. The shiver in Tiy's spine turned to a flood of cold, rushing along her veins faster than the Iteru's current. She let go of the servant's shoulder, dazed by defeat, by the cruel whim of the gods.

"Leave us," she said to the servant.

"But Lady, I—"

"I said, *go*."

The servant turned and fled back down the hall, melting

into the black depths of Sitamun's still, quiet home.

Tiy glanced at Kiya. The Hurrian and her serving-girl were clutching one another like two children cowering from demons.

"We're too late," Kiya muttered. "I thought I would have more time to convince her..."

"It may not be as bleak as it seems," Nann said. "Perhaps Lady Sitamun has not yet decided to strike. Perhaps the Pharaoh only summoned her to his bed, and—"

Tiy cut her off with an abrupt gesture. "If Akhenaten realizes what she's about, his paranoia will only increase. And how can she possibly succeed? The girl is no assassin."

Kiya shifted uncomfortably, glancing over her shoulder, but said nothing.

"The fool," Tiy spat. "I never would have guessed Sitamun, of all my children, to be an impulsive, thoughtless blunderer!"

"Grandmother? Is that you?"

Tiy spun, stifling a gasp. Little Nebetah stood in the arch of a doorway, leaning against its jamb, her smooth cheek pressed against the stone. The child's hands fidgeted with the hem of her light linen night-dress, but Nebetah's eyes watched Tiy's face with quiet deliberation, with a sharp, observant wisdom that gave Tiy pause.

"Where's my mother?" Nebetah asked—not plaintively, as most girls of eight years would do, but with a mild, detached curiosity.

"Gone," Tiy said quietly. And as she spoke that word, she knew, with the gripping certainty, the totality of loss that only mothers can know, that it was true.

Nebetah blinked, furrowing her brow in dawning comprehension.

Tiy held her hand out to the girl, extending the edge

of her shawl like the protective wing of the sacred white vulture. Nebetah stepped away from the doorway and walked calmly into Tiy's embrace, tucking herself beneath the folds of the cape. Her little body was warm against Tiy's side, and tense with alertness.

"There must still be time to stop her," Kiya said rapidly. "We can go to the king's chambers, and—"

"There is no time," Tiy hissed. "If the gods are good, they'll protect Sitamun. But I fear the foolish girl has already damned herself."

Kiya went pale at those words, her face a spot of white in the black hall, like a moon standing out, stark and cold, in a starless sky.

"We must think of Nebetah now," Tiy went on. "With her mother gone, there will be nowhere for her to go—except into the harem."

"Sitamun did not want that," Kiya said faintly.

"I know. She will come with me—now, while she is still a creature of the shadows—before the king can recall her and fix her in his eye. You will tell no one, Kiya, nor you, Nann, where Nebetah has gone."

"But Sitamun's servants—"

"I will have my steward, Huya, dismiss them all at dawn. I'll send them back to their families in the city with fat pensions. They'll have no reason to return to the palace, and no reason to wonder about their mistress or her child."

Beneath her cloak, Tiy pressed one hand firmly against Nebetah's back, guiding the girl down the hall, toward the garden—and beyond, the boat; the river. Nebetah was as thin and small as a songbird; the little, knobby bones of her back felt as fragile as glass beneath Tiy's palm. But she stepped quickly enough at Tiy's directing, and she did not look back at Sitamun's chambers as they left.

Outside, in the tangled, blue-gray garden, a thin film

of moonlight settled on the world, raising a strange, glittering sheen on leaf and path, on Kiya's hands as she pressed them against her face, as if trying to drive away her own sight—her own bleak certainty of Sitamun's fate.

"All will be well," Kiya said rapidly. "Sitamun has only gone to the Pharaoh's bed, and will return at dawn. She will look for her daughter. She will want to know where Nebetah has gone."

Nann took her mistress's arm in silent pity, and held Tiy's gaze for a moment. Fear widened those green, Hurrian eyes.

"If Sitamun returns," Tiy said coolly, "then I shall bring Nebetah back to her. What harm can come to the girl in her own grandmother's care?" Her hand crept up to the back of Nebetah's neck and tightened there protectively. "But until I see my daughter again with my own eyes—*unless* I see her—I will not risk this child. Hers is the purest blood in Egypt—a valuable commodity."

They parted ways at the long stone dock—Tiy seating herself once more in the little rowing-boat with Nebetah beside her, the girl still sheltered in the warmth of the cloak. Kiya and Nann swore to wait for the return of their guardsmen, then to go back to the northern palace. They promised to tell no one what had transpired.

Gods grant that soft-hearted Hurrian goose the wisdom to keep her vow, Tiy thought drily as the guards pushed the boat away from its mooring.

The boat crept slowly out into the current, the oars pulling and dodging against the force of the Iteru. With a pang of bitter loss, Tiy remembered another silent crossing on a night not unlike this one, with another young girl for company. She recalled the bright, glowing eye of the crocodile that watched her schemes unfold across the dark expanse of the river. There was no avatar of Sobek to watch Tiy now, and the only lights that flickered in the darkness were the few lamps of Akhet-Aten that still burned against the lateness of the hour—the lamps of the city and the torches of Mahu's soldiers that ringed the palace walls.

Sitamun was somewhere in that palace, traveling on her fool's errand. Perhaps she was already apprehended, caught up in Mahu's fist—or worse.

Tiy's mouth turned down, and the taste of bile rose in her throat. Iset and Henuttaneb—her two eldest daughters—had never returned to the royal palace, preferring the sequestered lives of priestesses in far-off temples. Tiy could not fault either one. Might her own life, she wondered, have been happier if she, too, had been sent off to serve the gods rather than married to Amunhotep to suit her family's ambitions? She could not fault her daughters, but she was certain she would never see them again. And now Sitamun was as good as gone—if not dead already—carelessly throwing her life away on a mad and dangerous gamble, the gods alone knew why.

Akhenaten will destroy her, Tiy thought miserably. She remembered the sight of Sitamun on the docks in Waset, bending to kiss Smenkhkare good-bye, the dark cloak falling away to expose the terrible, obscene swell of her belly. She remembered Sitamun on the throne of the King's Great Wife, silent and still, with a single tear sliding down her cheek.

And she thought, *It was I who destroyed Sitamun. It was I.*

Nebetah seemed to sense Tiy's bleakness. She looked up from where she sat huddled in the cloak, her eyes round and dark and solemn.

The gods have given me one final chance, Tiy realized with a sudden thrill—part fear, part desperate, surging gratitude. *They have delivered this girl into my hands—this small, delicate, sharp-eyed child.*

In their mystery, their incomprehensible, knife-sharp

caprice, the gods had placed Nebetah in her care. And Tiy knew, with a shiver of certainty as deep-rooted as her own *ka*, that when she stood before Anupu on the day of her judgment, it would be Nebetah's fate that balanced Tiy's heart on the divine scale.

Tiy pulled the girl closer. *Through you,* she told her granddaughter silently, *I will change the world for the better. Through you, I will right my wrongs, atone for my sins. Through you I will redeem my* ka.

Sitamun

*Year 8 of Akhenaten,
Beautiful Are the Manifestations,
Exalting the Name,
Beloved of the Sun*

THE PILLARS OF THE ROOFLESS palace hall were awash in pale, silver light. As Sitamun passed beneath them, they seemed to her a forest of great knives, sheathed in cases of starry electrum. They were the bars of a cage, hemming Akhenaten in, holding him against the coming of his judgment.

She crossed a small courtyard fringed with shaggy palms. The edge of the low-slung moon peeked over the wall, a sliver of golden-white like the paring of a nail, barely visible above the pale brick of the palace. Sitamun paused and lifted her hands in the narrow shaft of moonlight. Her skin seemed to glow, gold-tinted and warm.

Like a god, she thought. *The gods are with me now, after all.*

The realization surprised her. Her sins were many, and vast. Yet she could feel divinity drawing near, descending upon her, filling her—and cooling the fever of self-loathing and doubt that had burned within her heart for so many years.

What I do is right. I am the gods' instrument, acting as they will.

Even here, in the Aten's city—in the very stronghold of Akhenaten, who had pushed away all gods but one—Amun-Re's truth descended upon her, and Sitamun felt the wings of Mother Mut enfold her.

She flexed her fingers in the moonlight. They curved like a lioness's claws. She would not fail. She knew it with a rush of certainty that straightened her spine and lifted her chin. She *could* not fail—not with the old gods of Egypt lending their strength.

Sitamun raised both her palms to the moon, a gesture of obedient worship. *I named my daughter for thee, Iah, Lord of the Moon. And night is thy time of power. Night is when the Aten sleeps, fallen below his black horizon. Light my way now. Deliver me to my task. And if I should not survive, grant Nebetah a life of peace and freedom. Give her what I never had.*

Sitamun strode on, moving with the confidence of a King's Great Wife. But as she approached the hall that led to Akhenaten's private palace, her steps faltered and slowed. A pair of Mahu's soldiers guarded the entrance to the king's estate. The distinctive kilts that marked them as the Pharaoh's watchmen rippled in the starlight as they patrolled among the pillars, emerging from the shadows, moving through the gray corridor as tense and wary as a hunter's hounds, then vanishing again into darkness.

The gods are with me, Sitamun reminded herself, and swallowing her fear, she pressed on toward the king's hall.

"Halt," one of the men called as she entered the corridor.

But Sitamun did not pause. "The king has summoned me," she told him sharply. "Don't you recognize the King's Wife?" She breezed past both the men, and they bowed, murmuring their apologies.

Sitamun found the great double doors of Akhenaten's apartments, emblazoned with his personal device: the Aten sun-disc, round and faceless, each of its long, slanting beams bearing a small hand that reached greedily down toward the earth. Some broad, dark shape moved in the umber shadows beside the door, and Sitamun checked, staring.

"King's Wife." The voice in the darkness was thick and

rasping.

Sitamun recognized it at once. "Mahu. You have drawn late duty tonight, I see."

The chief of the Pharaoh's soldiers stepped from the base of the pillar where he lounged, his tall, blocky form taking shape amid the gloom of the night-time palace. His small eyes, as hard and glittering as flakes of obsidian, stared down at Sitamun from his superior height, and his jaw clenched, the sinews of his cheek standing out for a moment in sharp relief against the shadows that surrounded him.

Mahu chuckled, a dry, humorless sound. "I find it expedient to take the same watches my men take. It allows me to keep my eye on all the king's guards."

"Wise."

"What brings you here, Lady?"

Sitamun lifted her chin. "The king."

"He summoned you? I heard nothing of—"

"The king does not always share his private desires with you, Mahu, close to his heart though you may be. Would I be here now, at an hour so late, if Akhenaten had not called for me?"

Mahu's brows lowered, and Sitamun could feel the doubt rolling from his towering body like heat waves emanating from the walls of the sun temple.

Stiffening her spine, Sitamun stepped around him. "I will not be with the Pharaoh long, I am sure. He is easy to satisfy late at night."

Mahu's suspicion was a palpable wall, a dense barrier that dragged at her like the river's current as she passed. But once he was behind her, Sitamun found that she could move with greater ease. She leaned into the huge cedar door, pressing her shoulder against its gilded smoothness, and pushed her way into Akhenaten's chamber.

Beyond his empty, silent anteroom, in the depths of the king's bed chamber, Sitamun could see a flicker of lamplight dancing on the walls, playing in patches of orange and yellow that flared and receded, revealing here and there the details of a great, many-hued mural: all the creatures of the sun's creation, worshiping the Aten's light and warmth beneath the turquoise of a cloudless sky.

His lamp is burning. He is still awake.

No matter, Sitamun told herself. It would be easier to carry out her divine task if Akhenaten slept—or was on the point of unconsciousness, as her father had been when she'd pressed the cushion to his sagging, pale face. It would be easier—but whether it was simple or difficult, Sitamun was resolved to do her night's work, and do it well. The gods would present her with an opportunity, clearing all obstacles from her path when the moment was right. She need only remain alert and confident... and watch for her opening.

She strode across thick winter carpets, strewn over the tiles of the floor, and slipped into Akhenaten's bed chamber without pausing to announce her presence.

At the sound of her footsteps, Akhenaten glanced up from his long table. Its surface was scattered with scrolls and stacks of papyrus sheaves. A writing brush stood upright in a pot of ink beside the clay lamp with its dancing flame. Akhenaten's long, narrow face, almost feminine in its refinement, folded at once into a frown. His eyes sharpened on Sitamun, passing from her head to her foot and back again, and darkening by the moment with irritation.

"What do you want? Why have you come? Can't you see I'm busy?"

She smiled lightly and drifted toward his table, clasping her hands together in the long, loose sleeves of her winter robe. "What are you working on?"

He gestured toward the papers, some of them held in place with sample bricks of limestone. "Plans for my tomb. But what business is it of yours?"

Your tomb, Sitamun said silently, laughing within her heart. *Oh, Brother, your tomb is closer than you think.* But she only peered down at the papers with a quick tilt of her head, her gaze as benign as a springtime morning.

"Akhet-Aten has grown," she said. "It has become all you dreamed it would be. Do you remember when we first saw this valley?"

"Of course I do."

"And do you remember now I tried to convince you to dwell apart with me, to trust your madness into my hands?"

He glanced up at her sharply, his lips parted in silent outrage.

"Akhenaten, my brother—what sorrows you might have prevented if you'd only listened to me then!"

"What are you speaking of?" His voice rose in pitch, edging near a shrill, womanish cry. "You shouldn't be here, Sitamun. Get out!"

She smiled again and stepped around his table, so close she could feel the heat from his bare chest and arm—just for a moment, before he flinched back and dodged away, unnerved by her boldness, the confidence she hadn't shown since the court had vacated the West Bank.

"What do you want from me?" he demanded. "Why are you here?" And the flash of fear in his eyes made Sitamun's heart leap with surety of her victory. "I'll call Mahu if you don't leave at once. He'll arrest you! This audacity is unacceptable, and I won't hesitate to—"

"I won't be arrested," Sitamun said with cool assurance.

"And Mahu will do nothing to me."

"Sitamun…"

She moved close to him again, and once more the Pharaoh backed away. His hip collided with the edge of the table; he hissed in pain, and the lamp rocked. Its light danced over the walls and floor in patterns of dizzy chaos.

"Get out!" Akhenaten cried. Spittle flew from his lips, and his eyes glazed with panic.

The knotted cord was wound around Sitamun's wrist, as tight as a serpent claiming its prey. She loosed the cord deftly. It dropped from her sleeve, swinging at the ends of her fingers.

Akhenaten's stare was drawn down by the motion. When he recognized what Sitamun held, he stumbled backward, flailing his hands, and a high, harsh scream ripped from his chest.

Mahu will have heard that, she thought calmly. *I must move quickly now.* Her heart beat fast and hard, knowing the window of her chance was closing. But she counseled herself to composure. *The gods are with me. All I need do is this one task—their holy work—and when it is done, I shall be redeemed. There is nothing to fear. There is nothing to fear.*

She stretched the length of the cord between her hands, grasping it tight by the endmost knots, and moved decisively toward her brother.

His hands rose defensively, as if they were a wall between the Pharaoh and the King's Wife. "Sitamun, no!"

"I will do what I must."

"You don't have to—"

"It's the will of the gods."

That word—*gods*—stunned Akhenaten to momentary inaction. His teeth clenched in a grimace of wild fear as his hands lowered slowly, all his defenses—all his power—

melting away.

Now, said a voice in Sitamun's heart. She flicked the cord, seeking Akhenaten's throat, but his arm flashed in the lamplight, reaching for something on his table—and he screamed again, harsh and loud, a piercing shriek of pure terror, like a small, twisting animal caught in a trap.

Sitamun never saw the blow coming. An explosion of terrible white light burst across her vision, and on the instant she toppled sideways. The left side of her head was a flame of pain, crackling and flaring. She hit the ground hard and lay there, fighting for breath, struggling to curl feebly around herself, to escape from the pain in her head.

"Oh, Aten!" her brother cried. He sank to his knees beside her. A hard, hollow crack reverberated across the tiles as a brick of limestone—one of those that had been scattered across his table—dropped from his hand. Through blurry eyes, Sitamun blinked at the brick. Its end was painted, red and slick, with blood.

Akhenaten scooped Sitamun up in his arms. She tried to protest against the agony, but nothing would come from her throat but a hoarse, wordless rasp.

"Mahu!" Akhenaten cried. "Mahu, come quickly!"

Almost before the king had stopped shouting, Mahu was there, a shadow flitting through a world that grew darker by the moment. He leaned over Sitamun. "My lord, what have you done?"

"Go and get a physician!" Akhenaten shouted. "Now, Mahu!"

Sitamun turned within Akhenaten's embrace, trying to look up at him, trying to speak. He rocked her gently.

"Sitamun, I didn't mean it," he said. And to her surprise, he was weeping. One hot tear dropped onto her cheek, then another, mingling with the blood that flowed there. He bent over her, and she could just make out his features—but it was not Akhenaten who stared anxiously into the ruin of her face. It was Thutmose.

"I'm sorry," Sitamun told him.

"No," her brother said. "No, it's I who am sorry. I didn't want this to happen, Sitamun. I have loved you—I *have*."

He pulled her tighter to his chest, rocking, keening, his mouth distorted by fear and grief.

Sitamun tried to speak again, but her throat was like an empty vessel, hollow and dry. She sent the words up from her heart, and hoped her brother—Thutmose or Akhenaten—could hear them.

Now I will go down into the Duat, and face my judgment.

Her body shuddered, wracked with pain and fear—and the fear was the greater agony. She waited for the mouth of the underworld to yawn before her. She braced her weak body and quailing *ba* for that impossible, unending blackness.

But her brother went on rocking her, crying out his regrets, and no cavern of the underworld revealed itself. There was no pit of despair. The arms around her held her tight, and did not cast her into the Devourer's maw. Her sight faded into nothing, and like a soft, well-worn cloak, a soothing calm fell over her. The pain receded and vanished. Death was a pleasant surprise to her, in the end—and welcome.

Ankhesenamun

Year 1 of Horemheb
Holy Are the Manifestations,
Chosen of Re

IT WAS AKHENATEN HIMSELF who told me how Sitamun died. Even after many years had passed, the memory still brought tears to his eyes. I recall him sitting beside the garden lake, trying to speak of what he had done—attempting to unburden his heart by pouring out his grief into my own tender *ka*, although I was only a child. I remember how the sun sparkled in his wet eyes, and how a single tear hung, round and heavy with the weight of his sorrow, from his long, pointed chin.

I believe he loved Sitamun, as truly and deeply as he loved Kiya, though perhaps he did not realize it until she lay broken and bleeding in his arms. Sitamun's death seemed to crack something loose inside the Pharaoh. Forever after, a hard, sharp stone rattled inside him, quaking his thoughts and dogging his every step with the ceaseless roll of its drum. I do not believe he had a single night of rest from the time he consigned Sitamun's body to the embalmers. Was it her *ka* that haunted him, her *ba* that whispered accusations in his ear? Or was it some older ghost, one wrought not by Sitamun's death, but by the strange, bleak fate the gods had made for him?

As Akhenaten sank into his own dark depths, Egypt's allies to the north—those city-states that had been conquered and reformed by Thutmose the First—came under attack, one by one. Their traditional enemies, disorganized bands of mountain raiders and seafaring marauders, were not yet so strong that they could strike a devastating blow against the Two Lands. But the battles were serious enough that any king whose thoughts were sound should have been concerned, and should have rushed to the aid of his loyal client-kings.

Tiy was the last recourse for the northern kings; their final, brittle hope. She received their letters, one by one—their pleas for succor from the Pharaoh—for Akhenaten himself dismissed the letters, and would not read them, nor have them read aloud by the stewards.

It must be said that although Tiy knew the situation was quite hopeless, she made every attempt to interest the king in the fate of his nation. She brought petitioners from the northern states down to Akhet-Aten, to plead their case before the throne. She even managed to convince her brother Ay to prod, in his dry, careful manner, at Akhenaten's wall of indifference on behalf of the client-kings. When all of Tiy's attempts failed, she fell on her knees before the court, debasing herself at the Feast of Wag, to beg the king's aid on behalf of the north.

But all Tiy's efforts, all her sacrifices, were in vain. Akhenaten listened, now more than ever before, to the voices inside his heart, and to no other sound. Nothing was real to him save for his god—save for the godhood he felt growing within, burgeoning on the point of bursting forth, like an over-ripe melon ready to split and spill its cloying insides on the fly-speckled ground.

He spoke only of his temples and rites, listened only to the hymns he wrote himself. He worked for the Aten, which is to say that he worked toward his *own* ends. Everything outside his city—all that lay beyond its boundary stelae and the walls of its high, curving cliffs—the entirety of the Two Lands, and every land beyond—ceased to exist for the Pharaoh.

During this dark time, when Nefertiti most needed

to solidify the unstable, friable power she held over the Pharaoh, she gave birth to the last two children she would ever bear. Twins—and, in a crowning insult from the gods, both of them were female. The High Priestess of the Sun, with her tenuous grasp on the king, was left with six daughters and, all the midwives and physicians agreed, a womb that could certainly bear no more children. To keep the king within her thrall and her father at a distance, Nefertiti had nothing but a flock of little girls—very common birds in Egypt—and whatever pious bleating she could wring from her own throat within the Aten Temples.

The twin girls were a defeat to Nefertiti, yet Akhenaten took them as a charm, an omen—a sign that he was doubly blessed, that his power of creation grew in leaps. After their birth, he raised Nefertiti to the throne of the King's Great Wife. But she never sat easy in that office. I believe her strange, roundabout path to the throne only made her feel less secure with her position. Nefertiti's hold on her own autonomy was so tenuous and frail that I find I can forgive her easily for the things she did in those four years between Sitamun's death and the Tribute Festival. I might have done the same, if I'd stood in her place.

Akhenaten made few pronouncements in those days that carried beyond the City of the Sun. But the demands he made of Egypt caused the very bones of the earth to shudder. He declared the gods of Egypt dead. He called them fabrications, lies—and claimed that they had never truly *been*. He set the Aten in their place—one god to replace a multitude—and declared that all men and women must worship as the king demanded, and should pay homage to his lone, faceless god—the Aten, and no other.

Nefertiti did not oppose him. In fact, she gave every appearance of welcoming this stunning proclamation with open arms, declaring a new era of light and wisdom for the Two Lands. She seemed to discard the true gods of Egypt with as little thought as a bloom sheds its petals when the heat of Shemu comes.

Can you say that you would have acted differently if you had lived alongside Nefertiti? If your prison was the walls of the Aten Temples, if its bars were the hands of the Pharaoh, his rash words and his dark impulses, *could* you have chosen any differently?

I do not blame Nefertiti for any choice she made during those four years, no matter how her actions shook and remade Egypt.

But what she chose after—that is another matter. I shall take on her sins when I stand before Anupu, because the gods may leave me with no alternative. But will I forgive her...?

As the priests revolted and Mahu's soldiers rose up, as the ancient cults that had made Egypt live for centuries fell, one by one, Tiy took her leave of Akhet-Aten. No one in the city saw my grandmother again for many years, and while she was gone, none spared the smallest thought for her well-being. Undoubtedly, this suited her well. Like a mist dissipating with the dawn, Tiy vanished from the City of the Sun, and from her farm on the western bank. The anonymity into which she faded was both shelter and disguise to her.

But Tiy was not idle in her absence. From the remoteness of her private sanctuaries, she worked unceasingly for Smenkhkare, minutely alert for the right connections, the best supporters to usher the young heir to the throne without destroying the sacred balance of Egypt—the sovereignty of the Pharaoh, which makes the river rise in its season and brings life to the land. But all her old power was long gone. Ay, more a presence than ever before, held the nobles of Akhet-Aten in his hands, and his fists were too tightly closed for Tiy to salvage a clandestine grip.

The gods had left Tiy only one recourse—one tool with

which to carve out her niche, that shallow, precarious hold over the smooth and towering monolith that was Akhenaten's reign. It was a small, rather fragile tool. But by the grace of Amun-Re, Tiy wielded it well.

Baketaten

*Year 12 of Akhenaten
Beautiful Are the Manifestations,
Exalting the Name,
Beloved of the Sun*

LONG BEFORE THE BOAT LANDED at the long stone quay, Baketaten could see that the city had changed. She stood still and alert at the railing as the small, agile boat moored, taking in the sight of Akhet-Aten. To set eyes on the place once more gave her a curious feeling, a deep, quivering, half-chilled satisfaction, like slaking a long thirst with cold, clear water. The City of the Sun was golden, dense, filling the bowl of the valley and bouncing its piercing, brilliant light up to the crags of the red cliffs, so that even the towering stone seemed to sparkle beneath the Aten's disc.

Four years had passed since she had last set eyes on the City of the Sun. She had left it in the dark of night, sheltering beneath her grandmother's cape, with a bitter flavor on her tongue—sharp and acidic, prickling in the back of her throat. She hadn't recognized the taste of fear then. But she was older now; she had grown. She had learned, and become much more than the small, helpless child who had fled from one shadow to the next, tucked under Tiy's arm. She had left Akhet-Aten as Nebetah, motherless and forgotten. She returned now as Baketaten—her true self, her heart's identity—and she had come to the City of the Sun to do her duty to the gods.

Tiy, silent as a mist but moving with her customary

directness and cool, natural command, joined Baketaten at the boat's rail. The old woman's gaze fixed on the high, square-topped walls of the palace and held there, glittering and dark, a falcon's stare.

"It's larger," Baketaten observed. "I am correct—the city has grown."

It was not a question. Baketaten knew she was not wrong. Tiy had taught her well, schooling her in observation, in careful thought, in assessment. She was even adept now at picking through her own memories, sorting and weighing them like a fig-seller in a marketplace, discarding the worthless and keeping those that were fat with possibility—with information and use. She trusted her own judgment, and knew that she could do so, because Tiy trusted *her*. Tiy was the only tutor Baketaten had ever required.

"You are correct, of course," Tiy said. "I would estimate that Akhet-Aten has grown by not quite half." The old woman's voice dropped to a murmur. "How the Pharaoh has managed to lure more people to his city, only the gods can say. If I hadn't you to deliver, I would have sailed on past this place. I can feel its sickness in the air. *Pah!*"

Baketaten smiled. "So many people. They crawl about the streets like ants on a hill! How many, do you think, are only here for the Tribute Festival?"

It was the twelfth year of Akhenaten's rule, and in celebration of his long reign, the Pharaoh had invited the people of his vassal states to visit the golden city, offer pledges of wealth to seal their loyalty, and prove their allegiance to his god.

"I cannot say how many." Tiy's mouth turned down even more than it usually did, the stark lines of her permanent frown deepening around her mouth like the gouges of a wood-carver's chisel. "But I have no doubt that all of them—all those who are not Egyptian, at least—have come in futile hope."

They made their way down the boat's ramp to the shore. Baketaten, following close behind the drifting tail of Tiy's sheer sun-cloak, had no need to ask what her grandmother meant by *futile hope*. Before they'd even reached the end of the quay, they passed at least a dozen men whose clothing and style—long, curling beards; hair clipped short without wigs to cover sun-reddened pates—spoke plainly of their distant homelands. The docks rang with a cacophony of tongues, sibilant or slurred, lilting and musical, and none of them Egyptian. Bodies, ripe with the smell of sweat inside heavy woolen robes, pressed all about, and nearly every face Baketaten saw had the look of the north: eyes of green or turquoise-blue; sharp, hawk-like noses; thin lips and pale cheeks. Every face, too, seemed gaunt with a quiet desperation. Whether an ambassador sent by a distant king or a noble come on his own terms, the men from the far-northern reaches of the Two Lands sought the aid of the Pharaoh. They hoped to buy Akhenaten's interest—the security of their homelands—by heaping treasure at the Pharaoh's feet. As she twisted and dodged through the crowd, never more than two steps behind her quick-darting grandmother, Baketaten couldn't help but wonder: did these foreign men know already that they had traveled to the City of the Sun in vain?

Tiy and Baketaten made their way up the crowded waterfront lanes. They shouldered through a marketplace, each stall made of coarse linen panels stretched between short, rough-hewn posts. The sellers barked over their wares in a language unknown to Baketaten. The syllables struck her ear almost painfully, beating into her head with a rising pulse that caused her heart to leap with excitement. One seller, a fat man with a great, black beard that spilled down his chest in waves, haggled with a veiled woman over a basket of beads. As he shouted, his hand lifted high in the air, punctuating his words with short, hard jabs of his fingers. His manners were distinctly un-Egyptian, and Baketaten grinned as she passed his stall, craning as she walked to watch the bearded man's wild gesticulations.

A dancer spun out from behind a knot of chattering shoppers, nearly colliding with Baketaten. She sprang back, and watched for one awed heartbeat as the dancer whirled in the midst of heavy, tasseled skirts that lifted like banners on a breeze. The woman's fingers flicked as she danced, clashing together the metal discs she wore like rings upon her fingers, beating out a rapid, ringing counterpoint to the rhythm of her footsteps.

"Come!" Tiy's imperative call cut through the din of the dancer's music, and Baketaten dodged around the flying skirts, lifting the hem of her own long dress to hurry after Tiy.

Together they pressed through one final pack of shoppers and found the street beyond the marketplace somewhat less crowded.

Tiy sighed in relief as the press of bodies, the smell of wool and sour sweat, receded. "Stay close, child. And don't touch anything these foreign hawkers might offer you. Don't eat or drink anything from their stalls."

"Why?"

"Some of them look ill. Did you not see?"

Baketaten's face heated with shame. She hadn't seen—but she ought. Tiy had taught her better than to be distracted by a spectacle—to be blinded by the enchantment of a dancer or deafened by the clamor of foreign tongues.

"I'm sorry," she said.

Tiy waved her hand in dismissal. "Just keep away from them. The gods know—" With a twist of her lips and a darting glance up at the palace, Tiy amended her comment—"the *god* knows what fevers and afflictions these northerners may carry."

The god. Baketaten peered about her, at the wide, uncurving lane and the walled villas that lined it, at the towering façade of the Pharaoh's palace rearing above the city, watchful and still amidst the bustle of the Tribute. Here, in the City of the Sun, there was but one god, and any man or woman who dwelt here would do well to remember it. Since spiriting Baketaten away, Tiy had kept moving from one modest, secluded estate to the next, never spending more than two seasons in one place. But wherever they went, messages from the loyal steward Huya found their way into Tiy's hands. As the years passed, the Pharaoh's reactions to any perceived slight grew more unpredictable and extreme. And there was nothing that could upset the king more than reminding him that in the hearts of his subjects, more than one god still dwelt in the Two Lands.

The palace's high walls cast a long, pale-blue shadow down the length of the street. Baketaten shivered at the sudden coolness when she stepped within its reach. The air was suddenly crisp and bracing around her; the sweat that had formed beneath the fringe of her wig was like a cold hand upon her brow. She squinted at the foreign faces she passed, sharp-eyed and alert now, determined to remain observant.

Two men, each with a beard the color of old copper, stood close with heads together in low, urgent conversation. Even for northerners their faces were pale, as sallow and damp as half-mixed bread dough. Their shoulders and hands trembled faintly, though they did nothing more strenuous than standing in the palace's cool shade.

A woman in Canaanite robes crossed Baketaten's path, dull-eyed, panting as if the basket of fruit she carried were as heavy as a load of bricks. Sweat beaded on her brow, but did not run. It remained on the woman's skin, persistent as a pattern of beads, and she made no move to wipe her brow as she stumbled across the street. It was, Baketaten thought, as if the woman had grown used to the dampness that plagued her—or was no longer aware of any sensation at all.

What Tiy had said was true: illness moved through the streets of Akhet-Aten. And not the sickness Tiy had sensed from the ship's railing—that slow, insidious reach of the Pharaoh's influence, that dark disturbance spreading from the king's throne like ripples through an oily pool, infecting whomever it touched with the seeds of the king's madness. What walked the streets of Akhet-Aten was an illness of a more visceral and immediate kind.

The gods alone know what pestilence might thrive in the northern lands. Baketaten pulled her sun cloak tightly about her shoulders, gathering herself in, careful to prevent even the hem of her skirt from brushing the sweating woman's clothing.

They passed the final row of waterside villas, and the shadow-cooled lane opened out onto the broad, flat stretch of the Royal Road. Wide enough for two chariots to proceed abreast, with plenty of room for crowds of spectators to gather on either side, the Royal Road extended from the heart of the palace in a line as straight as a knife's blade, into the belly of Akhet-Aten and on to the site of the lesser Aten Temple. There were no assembled crowds today, no procession of the king and his family. Even so, a few servants in plain linen smocks moved in pairs down the length of the road, sprinkling water from the jugs they wheeled in hand-barrows. Not a puff of dust rose from the golden expanse of the road. It stretched perfect and true beneath a high, brickwork bridge that led from the palace to the king's private quarters. There, on the bridge's ornately carved balcony with its wide, shadow-dark window, Akhenaten and his family would appear to the courtiers and ambassadors gathered below. There the king would bestow upon his followers judgment or favor, tossing down bangles and ornaments of gold. There he and his King's Wives would stand high above all other men, as superior as the sun in the sky.

The Window of Appearances was empty now. As Baketaten followed Tiy down the Royal Road, she peered up at the span of the bridge, trying to imagine the king looking down on her, watching her. She could not recall Akhenaten's face—not with any certainty—and in her imaginings he had the small eyes and long, exaggerated aspect of a lion. He had the lazy, contented gaze of a lion, too—an expression of gloating self-satisfaction, of security in his own great strength.

Tiy strode confidently through one of the three arches that supported the Window of Appearances. Baketaten tore her gaze from the balcony and rushed after the old woman. Beyond the great bridge of mudbrick, the Royal Road bent square, swinging abruptly to the west and the palace gate. A man stood in the center of the road, waiting in a posture of supreme patience with his hands clasped at the small of his back, his blunt-cut wig neatly framing an intelligent, sharp-eyed face.

Baketaten recognized her grandmother's steward at once, though she had hardly seen the man himself—only his letters, more often than not—for most of the years of her seclusion. "Huya is here!"

"Of course," Tiy said. "He has been in the city for two days now, awaiting our arrival."

Huya bowed low as Tiy approached. The red sash of his kilt swung down to the road, and he twitched at it with one hand as he straightened so that it hung as neat and tidy as ever.

"My lady," Huya said to Tiy. Then he smiled at Baketaten—only a small, tight curving of his lips, but it was as much pleasure as Huya ever showed. "I must call you 'my lady' now, too, it seems. When I saw you last you were still wearing a child's sidelock."

Baketaten held herself up straighter, smoothing her hands over her pretty, red-linen gown, over the slight curve of her newly sprouted hips. "I have been a woman now for three months." As soon as the words left her throat she realized how childish they sounded, and fought back a flush of embarrassment. She was not a child any longer. No one whom Tiy had trained so meticulously could ever be called a child. Silently she cursed herself for sounding like any common girl of almost-thirteen. She refused to look at Tiy for fear she would see disapproval on her grandmother's face.

But although the old woman's response was wry, Baketaten could detect no irritation or disappointment in her voice. "For three months," Tiy said, "and not a moment too soon."

Huya ducked his head in agreement. "And the timing of your arrival today couldn't be better. The Pharaoh has just sat down with his wives and daughters for an early supper."

"How quaint," Tiy said.

Baketaten had studied every letter Huya had sent to Tiy's various estates for the past four years—every note and tablet, every tally and figure, each detailed report of the most mundane and expected events. Such study was a necessity, of course, if she wished to be prepared for her life in the palace. And so she knew already that the king placed unusual emphasis on his family, and knew, too, that Akhenaten insisted with increasing frequency that all the women of the royal blood—all those who still dwelt in the City of the Sun, at least—gather close about him at his meals, at his leisure, and certainly before the eyes of the court and Egypt's assembled subjects. Akhenaten's fixation on his female relations was the pawn which Tiy and Baketaten held within their hands. It was their greatest advantage over the king, and Baketaten was determined to use it well.

Huya stepped to the side, ushering them toward the

palace gate with the sweep of his arm. Baketaten permitted herself a tingle of awe as she looked up at the soaring pylons, flat-topped and towering. Through the years of Tiy's guidance, all the many times she had sat on the warm earth with her head resting on her grandmother's knee, listening to Tiy speak of the Pharaoh's great house, never had Baketaten pictured it like this: stern and imposing, austere in its beauty, so bright in the light of the sun that it stung her eyes and left echoes of its own image dancing behind her eyelids when she blinked.

She had lived in Akhet-Aten as a child, but she could recall little of the palace, save for its quieter gardens and the courtyards and corridors of its least-used wings, where few ever ventured save for the hard-working servants. Her memories of the City of the Sun were all of seclusion, of the coolness of leafy shade, of quiet hours whiled away at her mother's side, reading beside the pond or playing simple games amid the sweetness of roses and the hum of insects in flight. Somehow, as she had absorbed Tiy's lessons, Baketaten had failed to picture the palace as it truly was. Now, walking between the steep white mountains of the pylons, her memories of garden idles—of her mother—wavered. Fine cracks appeared in the soft luster of memory's surface. Faced with the reality of the king's great house, Baketaten wondered whether any treasured remembrance of her mother could still be trusted, or whether those faded pockets of warmth and simple joy had only been illusions.

Four guards stood at attention below the pylons, wearing the blue-and-red striped kilts and wary expressions that marked them as Mahu's men. They called out a brusque challenge.

Huya's response was ringing and unafraid. "I escort the King's Mother, Lady Tiy. This is her ward, Lady Baketaten."

Mistrust was plain to read in the guards' slow glances and down-turned mouths.

"You all know me," Huya said rather scornfully. "I've served the king's family for nearly twenty years."

One of the guards edged close to Tiy, examining her face carefully. The old woman lifted her chin and stared until the hulk of a man lowered his eyes, then his head, in a bow of apology.

"I beg your pardon, King's Mother. It's only that you've been away from the city for so long. Otherwise I would have known you on sight."

Tiy jerked her head in dismissal, and the guard returned to his post. Then she beckoned for Baketaten to remain close, and together they followed Huya past the gate and into the palace.

The familiarity of the grounds sent a strange thrill racing up Baketaten's back—half nostalgia, half disorienting fear. Her feet found the correct paths and corridors without the need to pause and consider. But trees that had been little more than saplings when she had left Akhet-Aten now stood tall, their broad trunks casting ample shade—and courtyards that had stood hot and bare beneath the sun were now lush and thick with dense screens of shrubbery and vine.

"It's so like I remember it," she said quietly as they passed a pool where she had once splashed as a child. The water was barely visible through a tangle of purple-flowered creepers. "And yet...so *not* as I recall."

"Akhenaten has succeeded in making the place thrive. I cannot deny him that bit of praise." Tiy sounded as if the concession might choke her.

"It's strange to think that this is where I last saw my mother—here in these gardens."

Tiy's glance was brief, but Baketaten caught the flash of sympathy in the old woman's expression. A display of compassion from the staid, sensible Tiy was never more than a fleeting thing, apt to go unnoticed by anyone who hadn't been trained in quick observation and instant interpretation, as Baketaten had. The flicker of kindness from Tiy warmed Baketaten like a wide brazier beating back the chill of night.

"There's the supper hall," Huya said, pointing to a nearby portico. Two great doors, painted with the sun-disc of the Aten, stood in deep, cool shadow beneath the pillars. "Are you ready?"

Tiy turned to Baketaten, and assessed her from head to foot with one sweeping gaze. She twitched the braids of Baketaten's wig with her fingers, settling them straight to better frame her face, then chased away a speck of dust on Baketaten's thigh with a quick tap of her bony hand. Another girl might have felt rather dismissed by Tiy's brusque ministrations, but Baketaten saw the subtle lift of her grandmother's brows, the tightening of her age-thinned lips, as if Tiy were fighting back a satisfied smile. Baketaten drew herself up, watching her grandmother serenely, buoyed by the confidence Tiy clearly felt in her appearance—and, more importantly, in her ability.

"I'm ready," Baketaten said.

Huya led the way under the portico, striding directly for the hall's doors. He shoved one open with a loud squeal of its hinges and stood aside as Tiy swept into the room.

The royal family, gathered around a single long, low table, halted in their conversation. Baketaten's scalp prickled beneath her wig as she recognized faces she had not seen in four years. Kiya, the Hurrian wife, gasped at sight of Tiy; her soft, green eyes lost their remembered timidity and widened in shock. Nefertiti's full lips fumbled the words she had been speaking, and her face—fiercely beautiful, far more arresting than Baketaten remembered—seemed to tighten slowly into a mask of ready calm, like damp linen shrinking in the sun. Her three eldest daughters sat arrayed to her left, each one with goggling eyes and round, startled mouths, their sidelocks whipping as they looked frantically between Tiy and their mother. The nurses, tending the littlest girls on the near side of the table, turned and craned their necks to see the reason for the family's sudden discomfiture.

The Pharaoh held Tiy's gaze for a long, silent moment, his dark eyes keenly assessing, his long, sharp-featured face just as leonine as Baketaten had imagined. His mouth—curiously full, as soft and highly colored as a woman's—tightened in disapproval, and then, as Baketaten watched with a tremor of caution, it curved into a slow, welcoming smile.

This is the man who killed my mother, she told herself. And her heart was steady and calm, prepared for the work she must do.

Akhenaten placed his hands, palms down, on the table, as if at any moment he might push himself up, spring to his feet like a leopard ready to pounce on its prey. But he made no further move to rise. His smile remained, as did the watchful glitter of his stare, but when he spoke his voice was light and carefree. "Mother. What a surprise this is."

Tiy bowed her head in greeting, lowering herself to the precise degree required of a King's Mother, and not a finger's breadth more.

Nefertiti did not bother to force a smile. "What brings you back to Akhet-Aten, Lady Tiy? We have not seen you here for many years."

"I've come with a gift for my son."

Tiy stepped to the side, revealing Baketaten to the assembled royal family. The Pharaoh eyed Baketaten with a pinched brow, a frown reminiscent of the one that had permanently marked Tiy's face. Then, slowly, his expression softened.

But it was Kiya who spoke first. "Nebetah?"

Baketaten stepped forward, leaving Tiy behind, and stood before the scrutiny of the Pharaoh and his wives, alone and unafraid. "That is not my name. Not any longer, King's Wife Kiya. I have given up my old name, and now I am Baketaten."

The king's hands slid from the tabletop, back into his lap. He smiled with a sudden warmth, an expression of gratified pleasure that leapt so forcefully into his face that it caught Baketaten up short. She swallowed hard, resisting the urge to step back from him, to retreat behind the safety of Tiy's cloak.

"A fine name," Akhenaten said. "This pleases me greatly. Baketaten—yes."

A man entered the room from an adjoining hall. Thin-skinned, with an unreadable face and a habit of glancing carefully around the room, he was somewhat older than Tiy, but carried her same air of able self-reliance and constant, keen-eyed assessment. When he saw Tiy standing just beyond the great double doors, his steps slowed and one corner of his mouth turned up in an easy, darkly amused grin. Baketaten recalled him—his sudden appearance in the garden one day when she played, carefree, with Sitamun. His knowing smile, and the way it had chilled her to her core, even when she was a child.

Baketaten addressed the Pharaoh. "Tiy has taught me much about the greatness and worthiness of the Aten. Even outside the City of the Sun, we recognize the god's power."

The old man huffed a dry laugh as he sank down onto his stool. That rattle of arrogant amusement brought his name bubbling back to the surface of Baketaten's memory. *Ay, the father of Nefertiti.*

"Recognize the god's power?" Ay said, pinching a bit of bread from the small loaf that lay in his supper bowl. He dipped the bread into his stew. "Are we truly to believe that you've become an Atenist, Tiy?"

Tiy eyed the hallway from which Ay had come. "Gone to the privy, old man? Can you not hold your water through a single meal these days?"

"Gently, Sister. You are not so many years my junior, after all." Ay popped the bread into his mouth, then turned to Akhenaten. "Pharaoh, my sister has always been a schemer, and fancies herself sly. No one knows this better than you, her own son. I hardly need to beg my lord not to believe her assertion that she has seen the light and power of the one god. Surely it is only a ruse, meant to secure your compliance with whatever traps she has laid for you."

The tension in the room raced like a chill breeze along Baketaten's skin. The fine hairs of her arms raised, and her heart beat fast in her breast. Heightened as her senses were, she felt Tiy shift minutely, gathering herself to speak—but Baketaten lifted her chin, faced Ay's self-congratulatory sneer, and spoke on her own behalf. "My allegiance to the Aten is not for the likes of *you* to question, old man. How dare you suggest I do not truly worship the one god? I am a true woman of Egypt—a true disciple of the Pharaoh—and my heart belongs to the sun."

Ay leaned back on his stool, his graying brows rising. His hand stilled in his supper bowl. Baketaten did not need to look around to know that Tiy wore a mien of quiet satisfaction. She could feel the old woman's delight beaming from her like the rays of the sun itself.

And the Pharaoh—he stared up at Baketaten in frank awe, a strange flush darkening his chest and neck, his unblinking eyes fixed on her face. Baketaten did not meet the king's eye, but stared steadily past him, gazing regally into the distance—and feeling, with a coil of anxiety deep in her stomach, the palpable intensity of his presence.

"I may be on the verge of disintegrating into mummy-dust," Tiy said to her brother with marked irony, "but even I have not yet gone blind. I can see which way the wind blows—have seen it, these past four years, while young Baketaten has lived under my care. The Aten is the only god in Egypt now, by the will and decree of the king. And I have raised my granddaughter to be true to the Pharaoh."

Akhenaten spoke. His voice was low and thickly sincere, as if tempered by some great, choking effort. But his eyes held steady on Baketaten, their singular force driving into her gut, her heart. "And what is your purpose in returning to my city, Mother? Did you merely wish to present this... *remarkable* young woman to the court? If so, we are pleased to host her. Will you stay for the duration of the Tribute Festival? There are games and feasts and ever so many ceremonies at the Aten Temples. Happier times were never seen in Akhet-Aten."

Baketaten bowed low, dropping her gaze in humble acceptance of the king's invitation. "I am pleased to return to Akhet-Aten, my lord, and more pleased still to remain. I have come back to your city—*my* city—to do my divine work."

Nefertiti tossed her head; the heavy golden beads adorning her wig made a sudden, startling clatter. "What do you mean, child? Speak plainly."

"Sitamun was my mother," Baketaten said, noting smoothly how the Pharaoh's face twitched at sound of the name. "I was born of the divine blood, the royal line. I have come to the City of the Sun to wed my king and bear him a son—the heir to his throne, the pinnacle of his achievements."

Silence shrouded the room, as thick as Iteru mud. Baketaten kept her gaze fixed coolly on the wall between Nefertiti and the king.

Ay, his mouth full once more of bread and stew, barked a harsh laugh. "Many times I've watched you crawl upon your belly, Tiy, writhing in your schemes for ever-greater power. But never did I imagine you would sink so low." He indicated Baketaten with a brisk wave. "Look at her! She is a child!"

"She wears a woman's garb." The Pharaoh's words were silken-smooth, and tense with eagerness. Baketaten suppressed the shudder that was building in her middle.

"But still too young," Ay insisted. "And what does Tiy care for that? Look at the King's Mother—all too eager to sell a defenseless girl, so long as the price is high enough. And make no mistake, my lord: this is a sale. A transaction. Tiy will exact a price for the goods she delivers you today."

"What, Father," Nefertiti said coolly, "have you grown soft in your old age? Now *you* balk at using children for one's own ends? I never thought I'd see the day."

Nefertiti turned her black eyes up to Baketaten's face, and the girl could not help but meet the stare of the King's Great Wife. Nefertiti's paints were artfully applied, emphasizing the enchanting depths of her gaze and the languid slowness of her blink. But behind the glittering paint, behind the arresting beauty, Baketaten read speculation in Nefertiti's face. *I must be careful of this one, above all the rest. Nefertiti is dangerous.*

But she was prepared for danger. Tiy had seen to that. Young she may be, but Baketaten was no fool. She knew the work that lay ahead of her—understood its import, its vital and delicate nature. She understood, too, that there was no one better prepared than she. Tiy had honed her well, and made of her a sturdy, useful instrument. Baketaten was in the gods' hands now, and they would use her for their own ends. She would not bend, nor snap, nor fail in their divine wielding. Tiy had tempered her, and Baketaten felt her own secret edges and points singing with readiness, reverberating with the hiss of a sword drawn from its sheath.

She was ready. The City of the Sun may be a nest of vipers, but Baketaten did not fear to set her foot amid the snakes. With the supreme confidence trained by Tiy's steady and patient hand, Baketaten went calmly toward her fate.

She bowed low before the Pharaoh. "If you will have me, my lord, I shall do my duty to the Aten most joyfully."

The Pharaoh's smile was all the answer Baketaten required.

Horemheb

*Year 12 of Akhenaten,
Beautiful Are the Manifestations,
Exalting the Name,
Beloved of the Sun*

THE FARTHER HOREMHEB WENT from the palace gates, the lighter his feet became, until, by the time he and Djedi reached the three high arches that supported the Window of Appearances, they were all but running. Some very undignified hoots—expressions of the pure bliss of liberty—formed deep inside Horemheb's chest as he bounced on his toes down the Royal Road, and he was obliged to stifle his shouts of pleasure. Mahu would not be impressed if word made it back to the hulking, hard-eyed general that his soldiers were behaving like schoolboys out on a festival frolic.

But Horemheb still felt like a schoolboy most of the time—and how not? Only a few years ago he had been a lad reciting his lessons at the School of the Barracks, honing the rudimentary skills with letters—and the far more important command of numbers and sums—that any man with serious military aspirations required. At seventeen, with the promise of a brilliant career spread before him and a pretty wife of noble birth keeping his small but respectable home, it seemed the whole world expected Horemheb to be the man he was in body. But he was still a boy in his heart, and today, unexpectedly freed from guard duty in the Pharaoh's tedious palace, he had never felt more inclined to fill the air with whoops of laughter.

"Come on," Djedi said.

He veered past a group of women, who herded their naked children toward the riverside bathing pools like shepherdesses tending a flock of unruly goats. Horemheb followed his friend closely, and once they were clear of the children, Djedi dodged up a narrow alley between two white-walled villas.

The sounds of foreign music and the shouts of haggling sellers drifted down the alley, a steady flow, and Horemheb pushed into that current with an eager smile. The Tribute Festival had drawn more visitors to Akhet-Aten than the city had ever before seen. Day and night, the streets and courtyards rippled with the excitement of strangers mingling, of novel sights and stimulating music, and the air, held captive in the valley by the high eastern cliffs, was spiced with the aromas of unknown delicacies. For five days, Horemheb had done his duty at the palace, serving long, back-to-back watches on walls and gates while the Tribute Festival with all its lush temptations grew and flourished in the streets outside. He hadn't even had the leisure to return to his little house on the southern edge of the valley, let alone to explore all the fresh thrills the Tribute brought to the city. Only five days of the festival remained, and Horemheb had begun to fear that he would miss out on the excitement entirely.

As he and Djedi drew nearer to the sounds of the marketplace—the twanging, plucked notes of some stringed instrument pulled at him with a particularly compelling hand—Horemheb nearly collided with three young women as they spilled, giggling, from the mouth of an intersecting alley.

"Steady, fellow!" Djedi caught him by the shoulder before he could bowl the girls over.

The girls shrieked good-naturedly and clustered

together like geese in the reeds, blinking at Horemheb with their bright-painted eyes, their smiles flashing white in the alley's cool shade. Then they lifted the hems of their gowns and hurried toward the marketplace, casting glances back at the two young soldiers as they went.

Djedi gave a long, low whistle in appreciation of the view, and Horemheb couldn't help but grin as the girls' curving hips and soft bottoms wiggled away down the alley.

"Don't let me catch you leering like a jackal," Djedi said. "I'll tell your wife, and she'll take her sandal to you and beat you senseless in the street."

"What Mutnodjmet doesn't know can't hurt me," Horemheb rejoined. "But you know I'd never be unfaithful to her. Still, a man can enjoy the sights, even if he is married."

"It's lucky for me that you've already harnessed your chariot to a filly. I'm not half as muscular as you are, and although I am far cleverer, I'm not as pretty in the face as you, either. If Mutnodjmet hadn't stolen your heart, I'd still be waiting like a dog under the table, hoping for your thrown-away scraps. Now that Horemheb's an old married man, the rest of the boys of Akhet-Aten finally have a chance at love!"

Horemheb slapped Djedi on the shoulder. "You know what you said isn't *all* true. I'm much cleverer than you are."

Their alley spilled at last into the wide intersection of several streets—a kind of mid-city courtyard, now lined with the ramshackle stalls of merchants and craftsmen, and crowded with men and women. The variety and strangeness of their dress dizzied Horemheb as he turned first one way, then another, distracted by long, loose robes of garish colors, belts of copper bells and silver leaves, and embroidery worked in a hundred unfamiliar patterns.

He had served in the palace long enough to recognize

the earmarks of the various northern city-states, and so he could tell at once that this market catered mostly to Canaanites. At least, the majority of the stalls were run by Canaanite merchants, hawking goods made of wool, beads of silver and turquoise mined in their high, rocky mountains, and wooden boxes—skillfully carved with exotic designs, and quite popular in Egypt, where trees were scarce and small.

But not all those who visited this marketplace were from the land of Canaan. Horemheb noted the tasseled skirts of Hurrians, the vibrant dyes of Tyre, and silk from beyond the land of Kadesh, flowing and shining like water. And there were Egyptians by the score, of course. The courtiers of Akhet-Aten wove through the crowds, sampling the foreign wares, brushing their bare shoulders against coarse wool and bright-stitched silk. All around, the clamor of a dozen different tongues rang like merry music, and Horemheb added his laughter to the song.

He pulled Djedi through the crowd toward a stall where a middle-aged Canaanite woman held up carved-turquoise amulets on strings, shouting to passers-by in her slurred, honey-sweet language. The woman displayed her wares with an eager smile as Horemheb approached. She placed one item in particular into his hands, nodding and chattering on with words he did not understand. But he understood the wry smile on her face well enough, and the way her pale-brown eyes sparkled beneath her fall of graying hair. Horemheb glanced down at the amulet—a crowned man, probably some northern god, with fists on hips, proudly displaying a huge, erect phallus.

He blushed and handed the charm back to the seller.

"Ah," Djedi said. "Our man Horemheb needs no aid where *that* is concerned, Mother."

The amulet seller shook her head, only half comprehending, but entirely amused.

"His wife wants a baby," Djedi told her. "A *baby*." He made an exaggerated gesture over his own abdomen, describing a woman's enormously pregnant belly with the sweep of his hands.

The woman babbled a few words of her tongue, then rummaged in a basket at the rear of her stall. She straightened with an exclamation of triumph and waved her fist in the air. A small turquoise figure danced on the end of its leather cord.

Horemheb examined the amulet. He had expected something as grotesque as the man with the large phallus, but this figure was slender and demure—pretty, with long hair spilling down her back and a sweet, smiling face—the very picture of a virginal girl.

The seller managed a few words of Egyptian. "Put baby in girl—many baby, good baby. Healthy baby!"

Horemheb acquiesced, and rummaged in his belt pouch for an acceptable trade. The woman took an ornate silver cloak pin with a grin and more wishes for Horemheb to sire "many baby, healthy baby." He gave a self-deprecatory chuckle and turned away, tucking the amulet into his pouch.

In truth, the last thing Horemheb wanted now was fatherhood. He'd had hope of a son once already—*Or*, he thought cynically, *threat of a son*. Mutnodjmet's pregnancy had been the reason for their marriage—something not even friends as close as Djedi knew. Horemheb could have left Mutnodjmet to her condition, but she was the youngest daughter of a good family, one with high standing in the Pharaoh's court, and it seemed unjust to saddle her with a child but deny her the comfort of a husband. Although he was only a young soldier, of a status far below Mutnodjmet's own, he had offered to wed her if she pleased.

She had pleased, and they had married straight away,

without her parents' consent. When she lost the pregnancy only a few days later, Horemheb hoped for one brief and selfish moment that she might move back to her parents' house, which after all was much finer and better situated than his tiny brick hut, and set him free again to enjoy the life of a carefree soldier. But Mutnodjmet had made no mention of a divorce. Sometimes at night Horemheb woke to the sound of her soft weeping, stifled against the edge of her blanket, and in those moments he wanted nothing more than to erase the pain he had caused her, to make amends for every ill turn life had done her.

It was unlikely, Horemheb knew, that the Canaanite woman's amulet would give Mutnodjmet the child she longed for—the child, and an excuse to remain at the side of the lowly soldier she loved. But perhaps it would bring a smile to her face, for it was a pretty little trinket, and these days any amulet or carved image was a true novelty in Akhet-Aten. A smile from Mutnodjmet was worth the amulet's price.

Horemheb followed Djedi from one stall to the next, joking with his friend as they examined cedar boxes with stone-inlaid lids, bolts of bright-dyed wool, and bags of exotic spices. At first, Horemheb noticed nothing but the wares on display, and the bustle and press of the crowd. But as they worked deeper into the square, he peered with greater attention into the faces of the men and women who drifted about him in the slow eddy of the marketplace. More often than not, he saw eyes that were red-rimmed from lack of sleep, sallow skin and sunken cheeks, and upper lips coated in a fine sheen of sweat. Men and women alike seemed weak, and some panted as they moved about, as if the market's leisurely pace were more than they could bear.

"Djedi," he said quietly as his friend folded a length of fine wool beneath his arm, "does this market seem strange to you?"

"Full of Canaanites," Djedi laughed. "Is that what you mean?"

"Look around you. Are they ill?"

Djedi raised one brow as a woman pushed past him, dull-eyed beneath the edge of the flat-topped turban that covered her hair. Her cheeks were darkened with a blotchy flush, and she staggered a little as she moved.

"Probably," Djedi finally agreed. "But that's not a surprise, is it? No telling what kind of foul airs linger in the north. Anyway, I've got nothing to fear." He reached into his pouch and pulled out something small and flat, dangling from a thin strip of leather. "I'm protected from disease."

Horemheb caught the amulet in his fingers as it spun at the end of its thong. When he recognized its design, he frowned. "An Eye of Horus? Are you mad? Mahu will skin you alive if he knows—"

"Good thing Mahu won't know, then." Djedi shrugged and dropped the amulet back into his pouch. "Unless you tell him, that is."

"Of course I won't."

"The Pharaoh may have banned all images of the old gods from his city, but that doesn't mean I must go about exposing myself to foreign diseases. As long as I don't *show* my friend Horus here—" he patted the pouch comfortably—"then I need not worry."

"But suppose Mahu does find out. Suppose the Pharaoh learns of it. He won't tolerate such audacity in his personal guard."

"Then I might be banished from Akhet-Aten," Djedi said drily. "Dear me, a fate worse than death."

"Where would you go, if you could?"

"Anywhere," Djedi said, leading the way toward a spice-seller's stall. "I've always wanted to see Ankh-Tawy, and

Annu sounds intriguing. Or one of the towns in the Delta, with a view of the sea. I'd even go back to Waset, if it held any promise for me. But the king shows no inclination toward campaigning, and I can't get a detail at one of the frontier outposts—believe me, I've tried. Where else can a young soldier carve out a life, but here at Akhet-Aten?"

"Guarding the king," Horemheb agreed morosely. "From what, I wonder?"

"Don't let Mahu hear you wondering aloud. Your career will be over like *that*." He snapped his fingers.

"Still, one day I'll take Mutnodjmet north to Ankh-Tawy. I've heard rumors that they still worship the old gods in the northern towns, though no one will admit as much to the king."

"I wouldn't be surprised," Djedi said with a sly grin, "if they still worship the old gods in Akhet-Aten. Though of course *everyone* will deny it, if you pry."

"Of course."

Horemheb sniffed a sample of spice, but whether it was sharp or smoky or sweet, he couldn't have said. His thoughts were elsewhere, his heart suddenly shadowed by the turn their chatter had taken. He returned the sample with a sigh and pushed out into the thick of the crowd. Djedi dodged and wove through the press of bodies to keep pace.

When Djedi caught up to him once more, Horemheb turned to his friend with a sudden fury of passion, a leap of emotion that startled him. "Do you ever think that perhaps Egypt has taken a turn for the worse?"

"*Ha!*" Djedi's raucous laughter burst forth with a shower of spit. He wiped his lip with an apologetic shrug. "Do I ever think it? Come on, old fellow. It's *all* I think."

"Sometimes I wonder whether we're the only ones who notice how strange the Two Lands have become, how un-

Egyptian."

"You and I?"

"The commoners. The low-born."

"We can't be," Djedi said sensibly. "Nobles are all fools, but they aren't fools of *that* kind—blind and ignorant. We aren't the only ones who see it, but what can any of us do to change the world?"

"Somebody ought to do *something*."

"Like what? Kick the Pharaoh off his own throne? Akhenaten may despise the gods, Horemheb, but it was those same gods who put him on the throne. The same gods *some* of us still worship." Again he patted his pouch and the contraband amulet it contained. "You wouldn't work against divine will, would you?"

"No, not I. I've a wife to think of now. If I did something drastic, I'd leave Mutnodjmet all alone in the world. But sometimes I wish—"

"*Ho there, men!*" The Egyptian tongue cut clean and sharp through the clamor of the marketplace. That commanding bark could only have come from a soldier; Horemheb and Djedi both gave a guilty jump, and for a moment Djedi's face went pale. The prominent stone of his throat rose and fell as he swallowed hard.

Are there spies in this market? Horemheb thought frantically, glancing at the pale, sweat-beaded faces of the foreigners that moved, blank-eyed, around him. *Has Mahu heard already of our treasonous whispers?*

No, he decided firmly as he scanned the crowd. There hadn't been enough time for any sneaking eavesdropper to alert the chief of the guards. The timing was only an ill coincidence, a cruel trick of the gods.

Horemheb spotted the white kilt with its blue-and-red stripe bobbing and weaving through the crowd. "There," he said to Djedi, pointing.

They made their way toward their fellow soldier. It was Ranofer, one of Mahu's lieutenants. His blunt-cut wig was disarrayed from shouldering through the marketplace, but he had lost none of his natural command, his no-nonsense air of efficiency.

"You're both on temple duty this afternoon," Ranofer said. "Report at the Great Aten Temple in half an hour, and be presentable. The royal family has business with the god."

Djedi tossed his head in obvious annoyance. "We're on liberty. We've both served for five days straight."

"And you'll serve for one afternoon more," Ranofer said. "It won't be the death of you, so brace up and stop your whining. When temple duty's done, you'll have your liberty again."

"Sir," Horemheb said respectfully, "what happened to Pihuri and Sobekkare? Weren't they assigned temple duty today?"

"Down with a fever," Ranofer said, already turning away and picking his route back through the crowd. "Both of them. Half an hour! Look sharp!"

In silence, Djedi and Horemheb watched their lieutenant go. Then, when Ranofer had vanished among the Canaanites, Djedi cast a look of smug significance at Horemheb. "Fever," he said. "What did I tell you? That's what comes of abandoning the old gods."

"You might catch fever, too, amulet or no."

"Never. Horus's mighty wing is stretched above me. Let these Canaanites, and all the rest of the dirty foreigners, do their worst. The gods of Egypt are great, even when they're outlawed." He sighed abruptly. "Ah, well. Temple duty. Come on, old fellow—let's get it over with. If the gods are good, we'll have our liberty when the sun sets."

IN THE TWO YEARS of his service to Mahu and the throne, Horemheb had served temple duty often enough to know that he preferred any place in the city to the Great Aten Temple, and the place was at its foulest, its most fearsome and hostile, at midday. The sun beat down from its pinnacle, where its fire paled the blue of the sky and spilled through the temple's open roof to scorch the deep-piled sand of its floor. The high walls reflected the sun's violent heat, amplifying it until the air within the temple shimmered and swam, distorted by the power of Akhenaten's distant, faceless god.

Horemheb stood at attention, as near as he could manage to the thin sliver of shadow cast by one of the king's giant statues. The thick, suffocating warmth made him drowsy, but the sweat running down his back and chest in thin, constant rivulets tickled and itched, keeping him passably alert. Across the temple's gateway, Djedi wavered on his feet, as affected by the heat as Horemheb was. Both of them drew themselves up, fighting against the sun's onslaught, when the tinkling of metallic chimes drifted down the walkway outside the gate.

Gods, Horemheb prayed, *let this ceremony not last long*. Mutnodjmet was waiting in the coolness of their little home. She would have a cup of chilled beer waiting for him, and would soothe away the memory of temple duty with her soft, graceful hands. *I can last until the ceremony's end*, he told himself. *My liberty is just around the corner*.

The chimes came louder, their bearers drawing closer— but not quickly enough for Horemheb's liking. He caught Djedi's eye across the broad walkway, and Djedi gave a quick, wide-eyed grimace of impatience, his head rolling on his neck. Horemheb bit back a laugh, forcing the humor from his face with an effort that came slow and hard beneath the dizzying blows of the sun. He concentrated fiercely on remaining stoic, unmoved by the heat or by

Djedi's subtle antics.

After what seemed an endless interval of heat, the royal family appeared from the outer corridor, proceeding between the gate—and its two swaying guards—at a stately, measured pace. Akhenaten and Nefertiti, clothed in the flowing robes of priest and priestess, walked side by side. Their hands were joined, their faces lit with serene smiles. The white of their robes was so intense in the unfiltered sun that Horemheb squinted as they passed. He wrestled with the urge to sneeze in response to the fiercely brilliant light. Behind them, the king's daughters walked in pairs, naked and browned by the sun's rays; the smallest were carried in their nurses' arms, but each of the children was hung all about with chains of tiny bells—gold and electrum, silver and copper, the ornaments shimmered in the sun, glinting from the girls' necks and wrists, chiming on their ankles with every step.

Lady Kiya, the Hurrian wife, brought up the rear. She wore a robe of linen so finely woven that her body was exposed to view, and Horemheb—a young man, after all—allowed himself one surreptitious glance at her small, round breasts and curving hip as she drifted past. He noted that her sheer gown was already darkened by sweat beneath her arms, and a ring of dampness stuck the collar of her dress to her pale, freckled shoulders.

Ordinarily, the temple processions ended with Kiya. But today, a small, slender figure followed in Kiya's wake. She was a newcomer to the Great Aten Temple, as far as Horemheb could recall. He stared at her frankly as she passed.

She looked young—newly entered into womanhood, but her flowing robe and full wig marked her as a woman in truth, no longer a girl. Beside Nefertiti, her face and form were almost plain. But then, what woman could shine as brightly as the High Priestess of the Sun? The new young woman's face was long, and her narrow, elegant features held a solemnity and focus that were unusual in a person of her age. As she passed, her painted eyes lifted from the sand and gazed into Horemheb's own. That searching stare, its forceful, unexpected intimacy, tightened a noose around Horemheb's heart.

Some relation of the king? Or one of the King's Wives? Horemheb wondered. He could not recall having seen the young woman before, at court or in the districts of Akhet-Aten. *Did she come from the West Bank, opposite Waset?* A few families still scratched out an existence there, he knew.

The ceremony to welcome the Aten opened with a clamor of iron rattles, shaken by the Pharaoh's small, naked daughters. Nefertiti lifted her voice in a rhythmic chant of praise. It was the same ceremony Horemheb had witnessed every day he'd served on temple duty, long and monotonous, a trial for the body and the heart. But today, as he watched the new young woman with cautious glances and—as his fascination grew—with lingering stares, the rote words of worship raised a thrill along his spine and sent a throb of anticipation racing along his limbs.

She was beautiful, intoxicating in her mystery, and by the time the ceremony was finished, Horemheb could barely tear his gaze from her face.

"AT LAST, YOU'RE HOME!"

Mutnodjmet came running from the cool back room of their little house when she heard Horemheb shut the door. Her small feet, pale and bare, stepped with quick, eager grace, pattering over the hard, flat-woven rugs that covered the dirt floor. She held up the hem of her dress with both hands, and the linen floated around her knees as she ran. Mutnodjmet was as lovely as an open flower, and the sight of her made Horemheb's heart twinge with guilt.

He always felt vaguely remorseful whenever he saw his wife flitting about the little house, bubbling over with gaiety, smiling with gladness—a joy he could never feel quite certain was real. She had married well below her status, giving up life in her family's large, well-appointed villa to keep house in the dusty outer district of Akhet-Aten—the best a young soldier like Horemheb could afford. But today, the memory of the new woman in the king's household still burned vivid and insistent on the backside of Horemheb's eyelids. Baketaten—that was the new woman's name; he had heard one of the children call out plaintively to her when worship was through, and the sound of it still echoed sweetly in his ears. Mutnodjmet's cries of delight and welcome could not chase away his remembrance of Baketaten's voice, and his own wife, as beautiful as she was, seemed disappointingly plain beside the repeating memory of Baketaten's face, her narrow shoulders, her graceful hands and slow, thoughtful smile. His guilt surged and howled inside like a fierce wind among the cliff-tops.

He opened his arms wide; Mutnodjmet threw herself into his embrace, covering his cheeks with kisses as he lifted her from her feet and spun her around in their small living quarters.

"Five days!" she chided playfully. "You left me alone for five days! Shame on you."

"I had no choice," Horemheb said, laughing. He eased her feet back onto the floor. Her breasts, firm and round through the thin linen of her dress, slid down his bare chest, and Horemheb felt eagerness build for more than just kisses and embracing.

Mutnodjmet affected a pout.

"But I brought you a gift," he said, and fished in his leather carrying pouch for the small turquoise amulet.

Mutnodjmet exclaimed over the bauble and carried it

closer to the lamp to examine its workmanship. Then she held it up against the dark square of their front window, admiring the figure against the sparkle of early stars.

"It's so pretty," she said. "Where did you get it?"

"From a Canaanite woman. Or I believe she was a Canaanite. I can't be sure anymore; there are so many outsiders in Akhet-Aten these days." He slid one arm around Mutnodjmet's waist and laid his other hand low on her belly. "The Canaanite said it's a charm to bring children."

Mutnodjmet gave him a warm smile of gratitude, then kissed him again, this time on the mouth. "You're sweet," she whispered.

Then she stepped from his embrace, business-like, and crossed to the far corner of the room. Two supper bowls waited on the chipped and battered table. "Come and eat," she said. "The stew is still passably warm, but I'm afraid it can't be called hot anymore."

"That's all right by me. I've had enough heat for today. Djedi and I pulled temple duty again."

As he sank gratefully onto his stool and tucked into the meal, Horemheb considered spilling all the woes of temple duty—and the monotony of Aten-worship—into Mutnodjmet's ear. But he quickly discarded the idea, pushing the rash impulse away. As loving and earnest as Mutnodjmet was, she was very young—hardly more than a girl—and she had a good deal more charm than sense. She had never understood Horemheb's distaste for temple service, or for the Aten in general. As the daughter of a noble family, she had known nothing but a life of complacent obedience to the throne, and Mutnodjmet clearly thought it was wiser to go along with the Pharaoh's religious whims than to cling to the old traditions or waste energy on resentment of the Pharaoh's lone god. For the sake of marital harmony, Horemheb had resolved to keep his opinions of the king and the Aten quiet within the walls of his own home. For harmony—and for safety. He knew Mutnodjmet loved him, and would never wish him harm. But she was young and flippant, and if she repeated her husband's frustrations during casual gossip with her friends, Horemheb might find himself called in for questioning by Mahu—investigated for treason. Accusations of treason hadn't ended well for those accused in Akhet-Aten.

Mutnodjmet slipped the turquoise amulet over her head, settling the small figure of the virginal woman between her breasts. She cast a suggestive smile at Horemheb over her bowl of stew. "Perhaps we ought to test this amulet's power tonight."

He dipped his bread in the broth, watching Mutnodjmet's amulet shift between her breasts with the rhythm of her breathing. "You didn't think I'd go right off to sleep, did you? It's been five days, my delicious fig! I'm hungrier for you than I am for this stew."

She pushed herself back from the table and rose with a noblewoman's inborn grace. "Then take me to bed. Your stew will be cold by the time we're finished, but—"

Horemheb was around the table in three strides. He swept Mutnodjmet into his arms and buried his face in the locks of her wig, breathing in the scent of lotus and myrrh. "But I don't care," he finished for her.

The room where they kept their bed was small, but at least it was cool. Even so, when Horemheb shed his kilt and kicked off his sandals, the heat from the Great Aten Temple seemed to follow him, clinging to his skin, embedded in his flesh. Mutnodjmet was eager, and moaned enticingly beneath him—but again and again, Horemheb imagined it was Baketaten's voice he heard crying out in ecstasy so close beside his ear. He stared into Mutnodjmet's face as they rolled together on the mattress, trying to force the memory of Baketaten from his heart. But it was no use. Guilt assailed him, and twice his manhood failed.

He was obliged to blame his embarrassment on exhaustion, but Mutnodjmet was persistent. She used every trick she had learned in her gossip circles, but what finally roused him enough to finish his task was not Mutnodjmet's hands, nor her hot, soft mouth, but rather the thought of Baketaten, bared and writhing beneath his hands, watching him with her silent, knowing, intimate smile.

Later, when Mutnodjmet drifted off to sleep, Horemheb eased himself from beneath the bed's light sheet and padded across the house. The lamp had burned out. In the darkness, Horemheb found the remainder of his bread and carried it outside, shutting the door quietly behind him. A rough staircase led up the house's western wall, and he climbed it with automatic steps, chewing thoughtfully on the bread—which, by that hour, had gone half stale.

A short bench stood on the rooftop beside the pale mound of the brick oven. Horemheb lowered himself onto the bench with a long, despairing sigh. To the west, the flat roofs of the outer district, gave way to the vast expanse of the river. The sky was awash with stars, streaked across the dark of night like a great stroke of a painter's broadest brush. The river reflected that mass of silver, and all the world seemed to glow.

Horemheb turned away from the brilliance of the water. Northward, the Great Aten Temple and the Pharaoh's palace rose together, pale twins towering high above the streets and villas of Akhet-Aten. Horemheb frowned at the distant palace walls. Somewhere in that great monolith, that island of wealth and power, Baketaten was sleeping. He pictured her in repose, her face peaceful as she dreamed, but still touched by that air of mystery, her mouth still sweet with that knowing smile.

I do not love Baketaten, he told himself firmly. *She is only an idle curiosity. She is new to the city, and anything new in this place is fascinating. She is no more to me than the Canaanites and the Hurrians in the marketplace—a novelty, a distraction from the monotony of this place, with its single god and its unending, ever-the-same routines of worship.*

Indeed, Baketaten's distant beauty and strange, untouchable nature had made her seem more godlike than the Aten, with its featureless disc and unchanging rhythm of rising and setting in the sky. She seemed more divine than Akhenaten or Nefertiti, for they, too, had become a part of the city's routine.

Her novelty will soon wear off, and then I will think no more of her. Again and again Horemheb soothed himself with that thought. And he prayed fervently that it was true.

But all too soon, his few days of liberty were over, and Horemheb kissed his wife good-bye on the threshold of their little home. He would return to service at palace and temple for several more days, working whatever shifts Mahu ordered, back-to-back, if necessary—the plight of a junior soldier. As he crossed the city on foot, turning his face away from the glare of the rising sun, Horemheb prayed that he would encounter Baketaten no more—and felt a pang of nausea at the thought that the gods might answer his clandestine prayer, and he would never see her delicate beauty again. By the time he reached the palace gate and reported for duty, he did not know what he feared more—that Baketaten might be within the palace, or that she might have vanished forever, gone back to whatever distant estate she called home.

The gods were both kind and cruel. Horemheb was placed on perimeter duty, and that very morning as he walked the high circuit of the palace's wall, he gazed down from that height into the women's garden and saw Baketaten sitting alone on a stone bench, sheltering beneath the blue shade of a sycamore, toying with a roll of papyrus in her lap. Even at a distance, he recognized her—the slender, richly dressed frame, her long but lovely face, the slow, thoughtful turn of her head when some sound in the garden distracted her from her reading. Horemheb's heart beat in his throat; he didn't know whether to thank the gods or curse them. He stood for a long time, gazing down at her. He felt her every movement as a hot throb in his heart, and each gesture raised a flush on his skin. She flipped her scroll over to examine its backside, and absently brushed the braids of her wig from one shoulder. Horemheb's chest constricted. He only continued pacing out the dull route of his watch when his longing to draw closer to Baketaten seared him so badly that he nearly whined aloud like a dog begging for scraps in an alley.

The weeks of duty that followed were pure torment. He tried everything he could think of to drive his desire for Baketaten from his heart. He wrote notes to Mutnodjmet professing his love, and paid messengers to carry them all the way across Akhet-Aten to the south of the valley. He fasted, and then, when physical hunger only seemed to make the longing in his heart all the more poignant, he gorged on all the rich meat he could find. He returned to the marketplace, where some foreign merchants still dwelt even though the Tribute Festival was over. There he found an amulet to ward off evil thoughts, and kept it in his carrying pouch. He dared not wear it against his skin, as the merchant instructed—not where Mahu or the king might see.

But the amulet, like all other tactics, was of no use. Baketaten had worked her way deep into his heart, embedded like a thorn in his flesh. And Horemheb soon realized that whatever his feelings for the mysterious young woman—whether he loved her or was only the victim of some strange spell—he could no more forget Baketaten than he could command his blood to stop flowing through his veins.

After two weeks of patrolling the palace wall—and several nights of liberty, spent in the embrace of Mutnodjmet's arms and the grip of stifling guilt—Lieutenant Ranofer ordered Horemheb and Djedi to take to the temple once more.

"Brilliant," Djedi muttered drily as Ranofer left the barracks. "I ate half a roasted goat last night at the wine shop. I was in danger of becoming too plump to impress the women, but a good sweat in the Aten's name ought to slim me down again."

Horemheb could not muster any sarcasm. He tied on his striped kilt eagerly, fairly bouncing with impatience while Djedi dressed for duty.

"Have you become a true-believing Atenist?" Djedi asked. "What else could make you so gleeful over temple duty?"

"I just want to get it over quickly," Horemheb replied, struggling to temper his wild joy.

"Alas, old fellow, there's no rushing the adoration of the sun. Well, let's go to it. Ranofer will cite me again if we're not on time."

The sun's violent heat almost seemed inconsequential as Horemheb waited beside the temple's massive pylons. He stood at precise attention, and in his excitement he barely felt the sweat that slid down the back of his neck and trickled between his shoulder blades. His eyes flicked to the side as the royal family appeared, pacing slowly through the ankle-deep sand, announced as always by the tinkling of the little girls' bells. He struggled to catch sight of Baketaten without turning his head. It was the first time he'd been so near her in weeks, and yet she seemed leagues away. When he saw her, a blurred form in the corner of his straining eye but unmistakable in her dainty, confident grace, his heart gave a hard, giddy leap.

Who are you? he wanted to shout as she drew closer. *What brought you here to the City of the Sun—to my life? Are you a cousin of the Pharaoh, a niece of Nefertiti? Speak to me, sweet lady—tell me who you are!*

The procession made its methodical way past the gate, and Horemheb chewed his lip, impatient for the mysterious beauty to pass so close to his own body. The little girls chimed past him, their wrists and ankles glinting with bells, and then Lady Kiya, shy and reserved. And then—yes!—Baketaten moved with unconscious grace, head high, stepping across the deep sand as easily as if it were the smoothest palace floor.

Horemheb's eyes fastened hungrily on Baketaten. She gave a tiny, secretive smile, as if she sensed his stare, then turned her face away from the depths of the temple and looked full into his eyes. Her smile widened.

Gods, Horemheb nearly gasped aloud. The force of her presence was like a blow to his gut, hard and sharp, but he welcomed that impact with a shiver. Then she breezed past him, and he chased all traces of pleasure from his face, concentrating on the terrible assault of the sun's heat to keep his aspect suitably somber.

The opening hymn of worship began. After a few refrains, Horemheb cut a surreptitious glance toward the royal family, watching the ritual unfold. Nefertiti drifted out into the wide, open sanctuary, stretching her arms up to the white fire of the sun, the linen of her gown glowing like a lamp's flame. Akhenaten eyed the High Priestess for a moment, beaming at her with his usual glaze of zeal.

Then the Pharaoh stretched out a hand toward Baketaten. She went to him with quick obedience, and stood still and accepting while the Pharaoh stroked her shoulder, caressed her neck. His hand trailed down to the swell of one small breast, and he leaned forward, balancing the tall spire of his crown with one hand and kissed her, long and slow, on the mouth.

The breath seized in Horemheb's throat. He wheezed

and coughed, and swallowed the hard, painful lump that sprang up so suddenly in his throat. Gripping the handle of his spear, he forced himself to turn away from the sight, but the image of Baketaten standing calmly in the Pharaoh's embrace still burned hot in his heart, no matter where in the temple he stared.

So that is who you are, he said silently, sick with loathing and fear. *Not a cousin—not a niece. You are the King's Wife.*

Nefertiti

*Year 12 of Akhenaten,
Beautiful Are the Manifestations,
Exalting the Name,
Beloved of the Sun*

THE GARDEN SPREAD ITS CLOAK of green below Nefertiti's window. Long banks of flowering hedges stretched across the garden's breadth, their loose blossoms half-spent, yielding their sweet perfumes into the air with a frantic fervor. Soon the days of dry heat would set in, the long, arid weeks of late Shemu that gripped Egypt just before the floods arrived to cool and refresh the earth. Nefertiti sat with her elbow propped on the window sill, her chin resting on her fist. She watched the sun beat down upon the garden, glaring off the pale flowers. A bird sang a repetitive tune from somewhere across the flower beds. The notes fell in a lazy cascade. It was a rare moment of rest for the King's Wife—a respite from the throne room, the demands of the court, the heat and rote monotony of the temple.

A welcome time of peace, and yet Nefertiti could not enjoy it. She seemed to feel Shemu's impending heat and barren days within her own body, a long misery waiting to reveal itself, to dry her heart and wither her *ka*. The flowers' rich perfumes only taunted her, for soon, she knew, the last petals would drop and the garden would smell of dust. The bird would fly away, seeking a friendlier place, where the gods blessed the land with green shade even during summer's most violent heat. But she would still be here, locked in the dry valley of Akhet-Aten like a goat in a pen.

Movement at the garden's farthest edge distracted Nefertiti from her dark reverie. Something stirred beneath the cool darkness of the portico, a ripple of movement, a tumble of laughter. A moment later Mutbenret came into the garden, herding Nefertiti's six little daughters before her like a flock of thin, brown geese. The girls scampered around their aunt, darting across the paths, plucking the wilting flowers from their stems and chasing butterflies through the grass. Mutbenret ushered the girls toward the garden's small, shallow pond. She settled on its edge as the splashing and squealing began.

Nefertiti watched her sister more than her daughters. She couldn't help it; she always cast surreptitious glances at Mutbenret whenever she was near, and no matter the expression on Mutbenret's face—sorrowful or vacantly beaming—Nefertiti couldn't look at her without feeling a stab of regret and self-loathing. Today, Mutbenret smiled as she tended the girls—and not the distant, defensive smile she used at court or around the king. It was a rare thing, to see Mutbenret smile, but the time she spent with her nieces seemed to be the only time she was truly happy. Nefertiti could have hired any woman in the city to tend her children—the most elegant and erudite lady of the court. It would have been an honor no one would refuse. But minding the girls was Mutbenret's only joy, and so Nefertiti left her to it. She had left such a weight of sorrow in her sister's heart. Giving Mutbenret some small happiness was the least she could do to make amends.

In truth, Akhenaten himself may have contributed in a roundabout way to Mutbenret's present state of happiness. With Baketaten's arrival—young, tender Baketaten—the Pharaoh had finally tired of Mutbenret, and now left her entirely alone. Even when Mutbenret was set before his eyes, minding the children at temple ceremonies or festivals, Akhenaten paid her no more heed than he did the other nurses and tutors who saw to the basic needs of the King's Daughters. Surely Mutbenret's invisibility to the king was a delight to her—no doubt, the very thing Mutbenret had prayed for.

Nefertiti was relieved that her sister no longer had to face the odious duty of answering the Pharaoh's summons—the very task Nefertiti herself had burdened her with. Yet this sudden change in the king's behavior disturbed Nefertiti. It shocked her, how quickly Akhenaten could discard one of his playthings. Mutbenret was like a bone tossed aside at a feast, dropped and forgotten, as if the king had never embraced her at all. Caution swelled and tightened within Nefertiti's chest. She thought of Kiya in her beautiful palace to the north, and Nefertiti knew that even as the King's Great Wife—even in her guise as Nefer-Neferu-Aten, the zealous High Priestess of the Sun—she was less secure at the king's side than ever before.

Nefertiti watched Mutbenret splashing and laughing with the girls in the pool, and she frowned. The wariness within her rose; a sour taste filled her mouth. *How long will it be before he discards me, just as he has done to Mutbenret?*

Surely not long. And when that happened, where would she go? There was nowhere she might turn when the Pharaoh cast her off. She could not stand the thought of returning to Ay's household—she *would* not, even if it meant lying in the alleys like a broken beggar. Ay would treat her worse than ever before, and poor, fragile Mutbenret—it would shatter her *ka* entirely, to find herself in Ay's clutches again.

No, Nefertiti told herself grimly. *It will not come to that. I won't allow it.* She knew that if she was to save herself and her daughters—and her sister, too—she must at all costs maintain her tenuous grip on the king.

Nefertiti watched her daughters as they played among

the water lilies—Meritaten, growing taller and prettier by the day; Meketaten, shy and graceful, following her eldest sister's lead. Silent Ankhesenpaaten, standing apart, weaving for herself a crown of lotus blooms. Tasherit bounced amid the flat lily leaves, sending up sprays of bright water with her hands. And the round, pink-cheeked twins, Setepenre and Nefer-Neferu-Re, sat on the pond's wall beside Mutbenret, kicking their feet and laughing. Nefertiti, watching her daughters frolic, heaved a bitter sigh. A son would have been just the thing to bind Akhenaten to her will.

If only Mutbenret had conceived, Nefertiti mused. Was her sister barren, she wondered, or had Mutbenret simply taken herbs to cast the Pharaoh's seed from her womb? That seemed far more likely. *I should be angry*, Nefertiti thought. *I should be livid with her, for defying my command to conceive a son.* But she couldn't summon the rage. All Nefertiti could feel now for her sister was sympathy—and a deep, scalding regret for the role she had played in breaking Mutbenret's *ka*.

Out in the pond, Meritaten spread her arms wide and flopped forward into the water, splashing the other girls with a great, glittering spray. She rose with her sidelock dripping, and the garden rang with laughter.

Six daughters, Nefertiti thought. *All of them perfect and hale, beautiful and strong. But none of them a boy.*

She recalled her visit to Kiya's palace four years ago, and the suggestion she had made to the wide-eyed, scandalized Hurrian. Perhaps after all Nefertiti should be the one to seek stronger seed than the king's. After the birth of the twins, the midwives insisted that Nefertiti would never bear another child. But her womb had nurtured more healthy children than most women ever bore. The midwives might be wrong. The gods might have mercy on her—on the Two Lands—and grant one small miracle.

Kiya had at least been as good as her word, and had never breathed any hint of the treason Nefertiti proposed. For the past four years, Kiya had remained in her little northern palace, secluded and apparently content to be so, cowering from the very king with whom she had once been besotted. The Hurrian only emerged from her refuge when Akhenaten summoned her, appearing at feasts and always present—silently obedient—for the daily visits to the temple. But otherwise she kept to herself—*entirely* to herself, to Nefertiti's dismay, avoiding any hint of impropriety and sidestepping all danger of treason.

I could do it, Nefertiti thought. *I could lie with another man, and gladly, too, if only Ay weren't so often about!*

Ay worked his way deeper into the palace with each passing hour, boring toward the king at its heart like a worm through rotting wood. And while half of Ay's keen, emotionless gaze was always on the Pharaoh, the other half of his sharp attention never left Nefertiti. As High Priestess, Nefertiti knew that she remained above Ay in the Pharaoh's esteem. Nefer-Neferu-Aten still wielded more power at court than Ay. But how much longer could she expect her supremacy to last? If the midwives were correct, and her bearing days were over, would the king discard her? After all, it was Kiya who had that lovely palace, the peace and privacy of favor—not Nefertiti.

Her fall seemed inevitable, if not imminent. *Once the Pharaoh tosses me aside*, she thought calmly, sensibly, *I will be cut off from throne and temples alike. Ay will be closer to the king's heart, higher in his esteem...* And Nefertiti knew that Ay had certainly not forgotten how she had taunted him with her power, those years ago when Akhet-Aten was new, when he had spoken in hushed tones of finding another man to set upon the Horus Throne. Nefertiti had denied Ay her assistance then, when he had exposed his treasonous plan—made himself vulnerable to her strength. She had no doubt that he would revel in watching her fall from the Pharaoh's grace.

Nefertiti ground her teeth together until her jaw ached. *No matter what I do, Ay always gets what he wants in the end.*

And what Ay wanted was power.

Nefertiti rose from her chair and brushed her skirts briskly with both hands. "You'll do yourself no good," she said aloud to her empty chamber, "sitting and thinking these dark thoughts." Outside, at least there was happiness and laughter, and if Nefertiti joined in the day's leisure, perhaps a solution to her troubles would reveal itself.

She made her way down into the garden. Mutbenret looked up from her games with the children as Nefertiti came around the curve of a flower bed. Despite her smile, a haunted, hollow look still clung to Mutbenret's features. It filled Nefertiti with a terrible ache. But the girls came running to greet her and Nefertiti laughed fondly as she bent over them, brushing drops of water from their faces, listening to their lively chatter.

Meritaten was shooting up like a reed, tall for her age, thriving amid the riches and quiet beauty of Akhet-Aten. The girl had inherited all of Nefertiti's beauty. With the exotic addition of Akhenaten's long face and almost ethereal features, she might even surpass her mother in loveliness one day. She lifted the chain of lotus flowers from her shoulders to show Nefertiti how neatly she had woven the stems together.

Meketaten displayed her garland, too—not as tidily made as her sister's, and Meritaten rolled her eyes at the attempt. Meketaten worshiped her eldest sister, and tried her best to follow in her footsteps. She followed too closely for Meritaten's liking. But Meketaten was a sweet child, always willing to please and eager to help care for her younger sisters whenever they became too much for Mutbenret and the nurses to handle.

The three littlest girls, bored now with the pond,

crouched beside the garden path. Tasherit led them in making roadways in the dust with twigs, and the twins squealed with delight as a caravan of ants ran up their little road's length. They barely looked up from their play when Nefertiti exclaimed over their clever construction, but their smiles soothed the darkness from her heart.

Ankhesenpaaten—ah, she was another tale altogether. Of all her daughters, Ankhesenpaaten was the one who sometimes sent shadows of doubt to plague Nefertiti's thoughts. The girl was not exactly retiring—she was often in the midst of things, drifting around the periphery of conversations or activities, observing the world about her in perfect silence. Her eyes shone with a depth of understanding that was almost frightening in a child of eight years.

For many months, when Ankhesenpaaten had been younger, Nefertiti had feared that something was wrong with the girl, for she didn't take to babbling at the age her two elder sisters had. When she should have begun forming her first words, Ankhesenpaaten remained resolutely silent. Nefertiti had grieved, certain the girl was mute—perhaps dull of thought, as well. But when Ankhesenpaaten finally chose to speak, her words were startlingly complete and clear. True, she'd had a child's lisp, a softness and roundness to the sounds that was typical of a tiny girl. But she spoke in complete thoughts, and the things she said—what could pass for wisdom, on the tongue of a child—indicated that she was far from dull. The girl, Nefertiti realized, simply preferred to keep her own counsel, observing the world and piecing together its mysteries within her heart before she freed any words from her lips.

It's wisdom indeed, to think before one speaks, Nefertiti reflected. She embraced her silent daughter, then watched the girl return to her perch on the pond's low retaining wall. Ankhesenpaaten's dark, solemn eyes fastened on her mother; accustomed to the sensation of being watched by the girl, Nefertiti returned her attention to the other children.

The simplicity of the children's games comforted her. The sun was milder in the garden than in the Great Aten Temple. Beside the swaying flower beds, with the laughter of her daughters all around her, Nefertiti could almost believe Akhenaten's insistence that the sun-disc—that same faceless god that reflected its beams from temple walls and sandy floor into a fury of heat and fire—was a benevolent creator after all. She felt its warm kiss on her arms as she played with the children, and wished that her life could always be so. But like Ankhesenpaaten, Nefertiti had acquired her own brand of wisdom over the years of her life, and she knew all too well that fury and heat—*pain*—often hid behind the most beautiful and gentle of exteriors.

A melodious voice called across the garden. "Good day!"

Nefertiti looked up from the children's play and schooled her face to placidity. Baketaten drifted down the main pathway, dressed in a casual, unadorned robe that was nevertheless flawlessly tied, accentuating to perfection the burgeoning curves of her young body. She wore no jewels; the locks of her wig were plain and unbeaded. But even without finery the girl dominated the garden, like a statue created by a most skilled artisan.

Indeed, our Baketaten was created by a skilled artisan, Nefertiti thought. When Tiy had spirited her away on the night of Sitamun's death, no one in the palace had missed Nebetah, the forgotten, inconsequential orphan. But in her new identity, Baketaten was a reflection of Tiy herself—a mirror image of the wily old woman in poise and quiet control, if not in physical appearance. Baketaten even moved with Tiy's same infuriating self-assurance and smiled with Tiy's familiar, slow curl of arrogant confidence. The girl was Tiy come again, but younger and prettier.

Worse still, Nefertiti mused, *the true Tiy still lives. Egypt is infected with a double plague now—the illness and an excess of Tiys—and suddenly, after four years of her absence at court, it's as if Tiy can appear in two places at once.* The realization made Nefertiti shiver. Her aunt was too clever by half, and Baketaten was proof that Tiy had never abandoned her dream of controlling the throne, even as age overtook her—even though Akhenaten's distaste for her was amply evident.

Just another force to contend with. Nefertiti greeted Baketaten with a neutral smile and pleasant enough words. But she told herself, *My enemies gather all around me—Ay, my aunt, and now this girl, her puppet.*

"What did you bring me?" Meketaten, usually content to remain in Meritaten's shadow, skipped to the side of the new King's Wife and stood gazing up at Baketaten eagerly.

"Why ever would I bring you a gift?" Baketaten teased, smiling down at the girl with a patronizing air that grated on Nefertiti's nerves. Baketaten was not so many years older than the King's Daughters.

"You always do," Meketaten said.

Baketaten lifted a small linen bag from her sash and opened its mouth wide. Meketaten reached in, then exclaimed in delight, "Dates!"

"Honeyed dates," Baketaten confirmed. "Extra sweet. Share them with your sisters."

The new King's Wife settled onto the pond's wall beside Mutbenret, laughing fondly over the littlest girls as they smeared their own faces with honey and the sticky brown residue of the dates. In moments, Mutbenret and Baketaten were deep in conversation—inconsequential talk, to be sure, but their chat effectively shut Nefertiti out, relegating her to the world of the children and their idle play. Nefertiti shrugged and returned her attention to her daughters, but she kept one eye on the intimate exchange between Mutbenret and Baketaten.

Ever since her arrival in the palace two weeks earlier, while the city was still humming with the excitement of the Tribute Festival, Baketaten had made a special point of befriending Mutbenret. Perhaps it was only because the two were rather close in years—though in truth Baketaten was much nearer to Meritaten's age. Meritaten, though, was still a girl, while Baketaten had evidently completed her first journey into womanhood—if Tiy's assertion of her physical maturity could be trusted. Perhaps what drew the two so close was only their youth, but Nefertiti suspected that something else about Mutbenret had attracted Baketaten's attention.

The newcomer had taken to her role as a King's Wife with a steady aplomb that seemed unnatural in one so young. Even the best-trained girl had her moments of flightiness, and a wife of Akhenaten was expected to bear especially demanding burdens. Anxiety was certain to plague a young and inexperienced King's Wife now and again. But if Baketaten was disturbed at all by her duties, she never showed it—at least, not where Nefertiti could see. Baketaten seemed to be the type of young woman who had no need of friends at all—and a fragile, broken woman like Mutbenret would hold, Nefertiti assumed, little appeal to this bewildering reincarnation of Tiy.

Perhaps, Nefertiti thought, *this attraction to Mutbenret is simply one of like to like. Baketaten may be too well-trained by her mistress to display her true heart, but somehow poor, broken Mutbenret calls to her. Mutbenret has already faced the responsibilities that Baketaten must now assume. Perhaps I am judging Baketaten too harshly, and doling out suspicion where none is due. Mutbenret has faced the king's lust and survived, as young as she is. Baketaten must draw some grim comfort from that.*

"Ah!" A low, rich voice undercut the peace of the garden, breaking rudely into Nefertiti's thoughts. "All my darlings are here together. How good the Aten is to me, and how lovely is the world!"

The girls looked up from their games at the sound of their father's voice, and all of them save for Ankhesenpaaten tumbled down the path to clutch at his legs and the hem of his kilt, their high, sweet voices clamoring for his attention. Laughing, patting their heads and tugging playfully on their side-locks, Akhenaten staggered as he tried not to trip over the children. He made his way toward the pond, then sat on the wall with a contented sigh, close beside Baketaten. Mutbenret shifted uncomfortably, twitching as if she might rise and scurry away into the garden. But Akhenaten paid her no heed, and Mutbenret settled again, miserable and silent. The smile fled entirely from her face.

The Pharaoh grinned as Meritaten and Meketaten squirmed into his lap. They covered his cheeks with kisses, and the Pharaoh stroked their shoulders, beaming at them with the strange, distant heat of his eyes.

The sight of his smile—of his insistent affection—sent a cold worm creeping into Nefertiti's gut. Of late, his fondness for his daughters seemed to grow more emphatic. Nefertiti had done all she could to distract his eye from those small, vulnerable bodies, throwing herself into her role as High Priestess of the Sun and worshiping the Aten with ever-greater fervor. She joined the Pharaoh at every leisure she could arrange, driving through the streets of his city in his golden chariot, sailing with him on his pleasure barge, standing at his side each day when he took to the Window of Appearances to bestow his favor and gifts of gold on the court gathered in the Royal Road below. She gave him her passion willingly, touching and caressing him, kissing him in view of the court as if she were nothing more than a tawdry whore walking the quays of Waset. She never minded the injury to her own dignity. She would debase herself a hundred times a day if it would keep the king's lust directed at her and not at the children.

But with every day that passed, Nefertiti suspected that her attempts to distract the Pharaoh from his daughters grew more hopeless. Akhenaten knew, as all the court did, that Nefertiti could bear no more children. And above all else, he worshiped the force of creation. The potency of her astounding fertility was gone now, dried up like a droplet of water flung onto a hot stone. She could no longer offer what the king most prized, and soon, she knew, he would seek it elsewhere.

I ought to be thankful for Baketaten, then, she told herself as she watched the new King's Wife caress the Pharaoh's back with a gentle hand, smiling at him with every appearance of sincerity. *He will turn his lusts to her, the poor child, and spare my daughters.*

But for how long? Sooner or later, Baketaten would be cast off, too, just as Mutbenret was flicked aside—as Nefertiti soon would be. And when she was no longer the High Priestess of the Sun, would there be anything Nefertiti could do to protect her children? To spare her daughters seemed as impossible now as keeping Ay at arm's length. All the strength Nefertiti had wrought was crumbling, wearing away, fading under the glare of the sun.

Please, gods. Please, Mother Mut, Lady Iset, you protectors of mothers and of women. There must be a way. She prayed with all the desperation in her heart, but no thrill of warmth answered her.

Of course there is no answer, she scolded herself, turning away from the sight of Akhenaten with his fond, chattering children. *The gods no longer dwell here in the City of the Sun. Why should they remain? They were so cruelly banished, their priests stripped of their incomes and all their attending power. And all to glorify an uncaring ball of fire. All to glorify the Pharaoh— my own husband.*

A flicker in the flower beds caught her eye, white and slim, moving with a rough jerk of determined force. Nefertiti gasped and stared.

"What is it?" Akhenaten asked, breaking from his conversation with Meritaten, who still perched happily on his knee. "Nefertiti, you're so pale."

She forced a smile. "I thought I saw something, that's all. There, behind the pink roses. But it was only a shadow."

A shadow, indeed. She was *certain* the white figure had been Sitamun, rounding on the Pharaoh with fury, raising one thin arm, one tight-clenched fist, to strike him down. But of course, Sitamun was long dead. If she'd seen anything at all, Nefertiti chided herself, it was only a memory, an echo of days and sorrows past.

The girls went on frolicking around their father, and Baketaten laughed musically at something one of them said. Nefertiti turned slowly, regarding the new King's Wife with misted eyes. *Nebetah*, she thought, and all her suspicion of the girl, all her envy and mistrust, faded into pained regret.

Sitamun had vowed that her daughter would never enter the harem—would never be subjected to Akhenaten's lust. Kiya had told Nefertiti all about the fearful pledge Sitamun had made on the night of her death. And yet here Nebetah was, despite her mother's determination to keep her well beyond Akhenaten's reach. True, she now wore the guise of a new name and the mark of Tiy was everywhere upon her, but she was the same child whom Sitamun had loved—the same girl Sitamun had died defending. And she had landed in the king's bed after all.

Could I do the same for my daughters? Nefertiti wondered. *Could I strike against the king to spare them this pain?* Desperately, fervently, Nefertiti wanted to believe that she could die for her girls, and gladly, too—but what good had death done Sitamun or her child?

Perhaps the white shadow among the roses was no memory. Perhaps, Nefertiti thought, Sitamun had risen up from her tomb and sent her *ka* out to see what had become of her beloved child. Perhaps Sitamun knew now that all her love, all her sacrifice—her painful death—had been in vain. How the knowledge of that terrible futility must gall her. How it must tear at Sitamun's heart like the teeth of Ammit.

And I? Nefertiti thought dully. She watched Akhenaten kiss and stroke Meritaten's soft cheek. *What will I do when I am dead? Will I come back to walk the palace grounds, seeing everything, but forever barred from altering my children's fate? Will I haunt the City of the Sun, as useless and broken-hearted as Sitamun's ghost?*

Baketaten

*Year 13 of Akhenaten,
Beautiful Are the Manifestations,
Exalting the Name,
Beloved of the Sun*

"STAY A MOMENT, won't you?" the Pharaoh said quietly in Baketaten's ear.

The ceremony to welcome the Aten's morning rays had just concluded, and although the day was still quite young, already the interior of the Great Aten Temple was warming to an uncomfortable degree. Sweat collected under Baketaten's wig, trapped against her skin by the snug band of gold at her brow, and more trickled down her sides to dampen the linen of her white robe. But she smiled at the king, and nodded in acquiescence to his wishes.

Meritaten cast a sulky glance in Baketaten's direction as she herded her sisters—each as naked as she was—toward the temple's soaring gate. Meritaten's dark glances had increased in frequency and severity since Baketaten claimed her title as King's Wife. No doubt, the girl was jealous of the affection the Pharaoh showered on his new bride. Baketaten gave a soft sigh, an acceptance of the inevitable foolishness of children. Meritaten may be a King's Daughter, but she was still quite young. More to the point, Meritaten hadn't the benefit of Tiy's guidance. Tiy had turned Baketaten into a careful thinker, a keen observer—and she felt certain that Meritaten saw nothing more of the world around her than whatever was on its thin, inconsequential surface. She looked no deeper than her own petty envy, and resented the endearments and sweets, the casual affections the Pharaoh gave liberally to Baketaten. The king's time was limited, and whatever attention he paid to Baketaten meant neglect of his eldest daughter's vanity and pride. *Those* regrettable traits were already full-flowered in Meritaten's *ka*.

Baketaten shrugged, and Meritaten rolled her eyes and turned away, striding forcefully through the sand, dragging the reluctant Ankhesenpaaten by the hand. The other girls followed like goslings after a goose.

Baketaten nearly laughed aloud at the foolishness of it all. She had no thoughts to spare for the offended Meritaten. There were far heavier matters weighing on her heart, and a great duty to be done. Let every girl in the City of the Sun drown in her own petty whims. Baketaten cared nothing for Meritaten's wounded pride, or for the tender feelings of any other girl. She had her work ahead—divine work, and no one but she could do it.

"Your worship of the Aten is magnificent," the Pharaoh said when they were alone with the silence and the heat.

Baketaten turned her face demurely down. Waves of the sun's fire reflected up from the temple floor, striking her cheeks and forehead. "You flatter me too much, my lord. I only do as my heart directs. How can one not give praises to the sun when it shines so brightly and fills all the world with its power?"

"Yes—yes!" Akhenaten gripped her by the shoulders and gazed tenderly into her face. "That is just as I've always said. But only you seem to truly understand, Baketaten. Only you seem to feel as I do."

She smiled up at him, squinting against the sun's glare. Its brilliant halo backlit the king's head and shoulders, distorting his image, exaggerating his features like those of the great statues that gazed down from their rows, precisely spaced along the temple walls.

"Indeed, my lord, I feel as you do. The Aten burns within me, and I am aglow with his power."

He kissed her then. Baketaten relaxed her body, warding away the usual shiver of disgust that welled within her whenever the king touched her. She had grown quite adept at that, now—telling him the lies he wished to hear, giving him the illusion of love and fellow-feeling that he craved. *I will do what I must*, she told herself as his tongue invaded her mouth. *For Tiy's sake. For my mother's sake—my mother, whose life this mad creature wasted.*

"You must come to me tonight," the Pharaoh whispered. "Again."

"As you wish, my king."

A shudder of expectation wracked his body. The lazy lids of his eyes slid half-closed, and his smile was blissful, eager.

Now is the time. The small voice whispering in Baketaten's heart sounded very much like Tiy's. *While he's in your thrall—while he's clay to shape in your hands. Before you give him what he wants, extract from him the thing you need.*

Baketaten knew the counsel of her heart was sound. The time to set her plans into motion had come at last— the moment she had watched and worked for. The more time Baketaten spent around the King's Daughters—the evidence of his crippled fertility—the more certain she grew that he would never sire a son. Not on Baketaten, nor on any other woman.

She had worked with great focus and care, befriending quiet, withdrawn Mutbenret and gently extracting from her all the secrets of the Pharaoh's bed chamber. Thanks to Mutbenret's advice, Baketaten knew how to stir the king's passions. An impassioned man, carried away by the delights of his favorite pastimes, ought to conceive a son.

But his seed could sprout only female children, when it took root at all. It was the curse the gods had laid on him—and the secret salvation they had given to Egypt.

He sires only females, but I will not allow that to stop my work. I will conceive a son—the true royal heir.

And her son *would* be royal; she was certain of that. Tiy had entrusted her with one great secret—the pawn in reserve; the hidden power Tiy kept veiled behind silence and the danger of a long-ago ruse. Since she had first realized that the Pharaoh would sire no boys, Baketaten knew that she could make use of Tiy's secret. And she knew, with a sudden, heart-thudding conviction, that the time to act had come.

She laid a hand on the Pharaoh's wrist as they set off toward the temple gate. "Pharaoh, I must confess to you—lately my heart has been plagued by a terrible yearning."

He glanced down at her. Concern—apparently quite genuine—lengthened his solemn features. "Is that so?"

"It is."

"But what do you long for? I shall procure anything you desire—anything! Nothing is out of reach for you, the best of all my wives. Let me send out into the city and fetch an artist to create whatever you want—a new mural for your apartments, or a bust of your image—"

"What I want cannot be had in Akhet-Aten."

"Whatever do you mean? Akhet-Aten holds everything any person could ever need. It is self-contained, an island of perfection in an imperfect world." He gestured up at the white walls of the temple, at the enormous statues of his own image that leered silently down.

"Akhet-Aten is the greatest city in the Two Lands—that is true," Baketaten said. "But it is not the oldest city. Annu was the original home of the Aten, long ago, before the false gods infected the Two Lands with their lies."

Akhenaten said nothing. His feet hissed though through the sand as he paced along beside her.

"I crave to see the ancient sights," Baketaten told him. "I yearn to visit the temples where the Aten first rose in the hearts of men, in the days before he was forgotten and cast aside—when his power throughout the land was undisputed and accepted by all. Won't you let me go on a journey, my lord? Let me travel to the north and worship the one true god in his original home."

The king chuckled indulgently. "Perhaps you will be High Priestess of the Sun one day, just like Nefer-Neferu-Aten."

Again Baketaten lowered her eyes. "Perhaps I will, one day. I would do it gladly, if it would please you—and the Aten."

"But my darling, it is dangerous to travel so far from home. I have enemies everywhere, you know." He glanced up at the temple walls where a troop of guards made their usual rounds, protecting the king from the shadows that haunted his own heart.

Baketaten caught the eye of the guard on the temple gate. The man was young and handsome, broad-shouldered and square of jaw. He stood waiting to one side of the towering gate with his usual air of readiness, which masked from most observers—but not from Baketaten—the keen attention he paid to her, the lingering glances at her face and body. She had noticed the guard often, and did not dislike the curious hunger that burned in his eyes when Baketaten passed his station.

She gave the guard a tiny smile as they approached, and he smiled back, his face lighting with wonder at her sudden attention. Then he recalled himself and gazed steadily down at the ground, blanking his expression with admirable efficiency.

"I know you have enemies, my lord," Baketaten said to

the king. "But I might bring back some lost knowledge of the Aten from that holy source—his first temple! I shall travel in disguise, if you like—no one will recognize me. I am new enough to Akhet-Aten that the court hardly knows me as yet. And before you raised me up, I was a woman of no consequence. No one outside the City of the Sun knows me at all, and surely would not connect me to the throne. Of all your closest friends and family, only I can travel anonymously. Isn't it worth that very small risk to bring back the Aten's first fire?"

"Your idea does intrigue me," the king admitted. He paused in the gateway's mouth, considering. "But I cannot risk you, Baketaten. You are too dear to me."

He leaned close and kissed her again. A flush of shame—or perhaps annoyance—heated her cheeks; she would rather not have suffered the king's attentions before the eyes of the handsome guardsman. But Tiy had trained her well. By the time the king pulled back, beaming softly down at her, Baketaten's face was cool and untroubled. In the momentary silence, she heard the guardsman swallow hard.

An idea sparked in her heart, mischievous and daring. "I shall take a bodyguard with me," she said. "Just one, for more would make me conspicuous. He can defend me against any of your enemies."

"An excellent idea. I shall send Mahu to protect you."

Baketaten shook her head abruptly. "No, my king! You need Mahu here, to protect your holy person. As you say, your foes are everywhere. No, a simple guardsman will do for me, and the simpler the better. He shall be part of my disguise."

She shrugged, as if it made no matter who accompanied her, then pointed to the guard on the gate. "Why not him? You will keep me safe, won't you, soldier?"

"Of... of course, King's Wife," the guard stammered. He

had a deep voice, and Baketaten did not know whether its gruff, hoarse quality was its natural sound or due to the suddenness of this strange appointment. "As you command."

The Pharaoh laughed and pulled Baketaten against his chest in a long embrace. "You are persistent, Baketaten! My tender little gazelle!"

"If I am untoward in my persistence, it's because of my love for the Aten. My desire to know the one true god is great. I wish to embrace the god as fully as any human can—as I embrace you," she added, casting a coquettish smile up at the king.

"Very well, then. Perhaps after all you might bring back some hidden knowledge from Annu, and allow me to honor the god still more fully than I do." Akhenaten sketched a curt gesture toward the gate-guard. "Talk with your new mistress, man, and see to all her needs for the journey."

The soldier bowed low.

"But do it tomorrow," Akhenaten added, his mouth curling again with indolent anticipation. "The King's Wife has business with me tonight."

The Pharaoh strode away, leaving Baketaten standing beside her new bodyguard. She cut one surreptitious glance at the man from the corner of her eye and saw him quiver lightly, as if the ripple of revulsion that threatened to overtake Baketaten had leapt through the hot air between them or crossed the Aten-scorched sand, settling into his skin instead of hers.

Horemheb

Year 13 of Akhenaten,
Beautiful Are the Manifestations,
Exalting the Name,
Beloved of the Sun

THE RIVER WAS A DAZZLE of light, winking in a thousand shades of blue and green, of sunny gold and silver-white and the deep indigo of the water's shadow. The Iteru's current rocked the boat with a gentle hand as the small private ship drifted steadily to the north. Horemheb, leaning his back against the boat's rail astern, breathed deep of the Iteru's fresh, sweet perfume. He closed his eyes, raising his face to the breeze of the boat's steady movement, and allowed the rich air of the river to invigorate his *ka*.

He did not turn back to gaze at Akhet-Aten as it dwindled behind the boat, but he could feel the city growing smaller, less significant—could feel the great weight of his duties as a soldier and a husband lifting from his shoulders. The journey north to Annu would take more than two weeks, and Mutnodjmet had wept when she'd learned of Horemheb's going. Before, the soldiering life had kept him from her side for many days at a time, but never before had he left Akhet-Aten entirely. She had pleaded with him to stay, to pass the duty off to another man. Her tears had wrenched at Horemheb's heart, filling his gut with a deep, cold guilt. His remorse was all the greater for knowing he would not miss Mutnodjmet the way she would miss him.

But even if there had been some way to shirk this duty

and set it on Djedi's shoulders, or even another man's, Horemheb wouldn't have given in to Mutnodjmet's weeping. The king's unexpected command to accompany Baketaten on her journey seemed a great, astounding gift from the gods—a miracle he had not hoped to find, a blessing he clung to with both hands.

If you think I'll try to hand this treasure to another man, you're beyond mad, he'd told Mutnodjmet silently as she wrapped her arms around his neck and cried bitterly against his chest.

But he said only, "It was a direct order from the Pharaoh himself, my sweet. There is nothing I can do, except obey."

The night before he was set to embark on this miraculous journey, Horemheb had lain awake beside Mutnodjmet, staring up at the blackness of his room's low ceiling, imagining every moment of the trek—Baketaten's low, soft voice; her graceful movements; the music of her laugh; the delicate way she would touch his wrist as she spoke to him, and the witty remarks with which he would entertain her. As he drifted in and out of shallow sleep, his dreams and fantasies of the King's Wife blended and blurred, stretching into one long, unbroken vision of Baketaten singing, Baketaten smiling, the sway of her slender hips as she walked, the turn of her face toward the sun. He had staggered from bed at the first blush of dawn, exhausted from the night's desperate longings. As he'd made his way through the still-sleeping districts of Akhet-Aten, Horemheb's heart beat calm and low in his chest, and he knew himself ready for this duty, eager for the hours he would spend in Baketaten's company.

But when he saw the King's Wife safely aboard her little sailing ship, Horemheb found that he was too choked by his own expectations, and too fearful of offending her with his coarse, uncourtly ways, to speak to his beautiful young mistress. The sailors cast off their lines and the boat drifted away from the Akhet-Aten quay. Horemheb huddled against the side of the amidship cabin with its canopy of blue linen flapping in the breeze. He watched Baketaten from afar as she conversed with the steward Huya, who had accompanied her on the journey as a sort of errand-man. He eyed her as she took a morning meal, eating with delicate grace and tossing her bread crumbs overboard for the birds that cried in the boat's wake to squabble over. Trembling with the poignant pain of love, he observed her as she lingered in the prow of the ship, laughing to herself over the dense, green beauty of the land and the rhythm of the river. That pure, childlike pleasure was so at odds with her usual air of confident self-control. Horemheb couldn't trust himself to draw too near. He felt instinctively that if he grew close to her—if she would deign to humor his aching heart at all—the gods would only spirit her away again. They would take back the unexpected blessing of her presence, like a child dangling a string before a kitten and then snatching it away again—just for the amusement of the act.

But the first night of their journey fell. The cool of the evening seemed to soothe some of the panicked disbelief from Horemheb's heart. As he sipped from a cup of wine, he edged nearer to Baketaten. Now and then when their eyes chanced to meet he smiled at her, and received a warm tilt of her head, a curve of those soft-looking lips, in return. The enchantment of starlight hung all about her, casting a sheen on her skin that was like the color of a dream—an indescribable shade, but vivid and compelling, inscribing its memory on the heart. Baketaten's smile widened as he stood gaping at her like a clubbed fish. Her dark eyes sparkled with amusement. She lifted one small hand, beckoning him to her side. Horemheb moved with all the grace of a fish on land, too, thumping across the boat's deck on feet gone numb with anxiety.

"Sit with me, guardsman," Baketaten said.

She indicated two low, folding stools in the prow,

evidently vacated by the sailors who had been coiling the lines that lay nearby. Nodding at her command, he sank down beside her, balancing his cup of wine upon one knee. They remained silent for a time, listening to the whirr of insects in the shoreline reeds and the soft, hollow groan of the boat tugging at its night-time anchor.

"I love the moon," she said, breaking the silence at last with words that were so soft they were nearly a sigh. She turned her face up to the great, pale face of the moon, bathed in its silvery light. "I have always adored it."

"I thought you loved the sun, my lady. You certainly seem to adore the Aten in the temples."

She made no reply at first, but only smiled at him with a gleam of comfortable conspiracy in her eyes. At last, she said, "You watch me often at the temples."

Horemheb was grateful for the dimness of the night, for in the glare of day there would have been no hiding his sudden flush. There was no denying her playful accusation, either. "You've noticed, then."

She shrugged. "I have little else to do during the long praises to the god, other than watching the watchmen. But you needn't worry. I am flattered, not offended."

Her voice was lilting, toying—and her tone said she was more than flattered. Horemheb's heart surged with joy before he recalled that he had a good and loyal wife—and that Baketaten had a husband, who was, as it happened, the king of Egypt. He cleared his throat and sipped from his wine, and thought it wisest to ignore her teasing.

"Tell my why you're traveling to Annu," he ventured. "Is it truly to visit the original sun temples?"

She smiled again, holding his gaze for a long time. Caught by her wide, enchanting eyes, Horemheb felt his pulse race—but she did not answer his question. Instead she asked, "What is your name, guardsman?"

"Horemheb."

"A good name. A strong name, for a strong and honest man."

Horemheb finished the last of his wine in one long swallow. Its sweetness turned bitter on his tongue. *Honest, indeed*, he thought mockingly, picturing Mutnodjmet's tragic face as she bade him good-bye that morning. But even as he berated himself for his disloyal longing, he could not wish himself parted from Baketaten. Her silent contentment as she sat beside him, bathing in the moon's gentle light, filled his heart more completely than Mutnodjmet—or any other woman—had before.

As they drifted north with the current, the Two Lands unfolded around them like a rich carpet, woven in intricate patterns of green and gold, shadow and light. Vast beds of papyrus swayed in the breeze, and unseen birds, sheltering within the pale, downy tassels of the plants, called sweetly to the boat as it passed. Rustic villages clustered on any small rise of land; women gathered at wells turned to gaze at the ship, and children playing in the warm shallows of irrigation canals shouted and waved or left their games to race the boat along the shore. Where the river slowed, great arcing coves of still water glimmered white and pink beneath the sun, the surface bursting with lotus flowers like fruits spilled from a basket. Horemheb's heart sank deep into the serenity of the voyage, and as the days passed, he grew ever more comfortable in Baketaten's presence. The beauty of the land soothed him, until it felt right—perfectly, purely *maat*—merely to stand at Baketaten's side.

On the fourth night of their voyage, after the anchor had been set and their simple supper of flat bread, cheese, and coal-roasted fish was finished, Horemheb settled into the contented silence to which he'd grown accustomed, perched on the low stool in the boat's prow with Baketaten beside him.

STORM IN THE SKY

"How did you come to be in Mahu's service, Horemheb?" she asked lightly, gazing up at the moon.

"What else was I to do? Soldiering is the only trade I have, and these days there is little work for men like me, except in Akhet-Aten."

"Do you enjoy serving my husband?"

The question sent a jolt of surprise through Horemheb's bones. In the bliss of their peaceful journey, he had all but forgotten that Baketaten was the Pharaoh's wife—that Mutnodjmet stood between them, too. It had been so easy to fall under her spell, to pretend as if nothing in the world existed but the two of them and this boat, and Huya the steward with his little crew of specially hired sailors. Now realization flooded back into his heart, thick and uncomfortable. He twitched his shoulders as if he felt the sudden, sharp stab of a fly's bite.

"Again," he answered after a moment's thought, "what choice do I have? I go where I am sent, and do my duty."

"But you do not love the Pharaoh?"

"My lady, you ask me to put my hand into a nest of cobras. The only truthful answer I can give is that I am loyal, and always do what I must."

She nodded as if that were quite satisfactory, and no more than what she had expected.

They lapsed into silence again. A terrible, pressing weight settled onto Horemheb's shoulders, then plummeted dark and cold into his heart. He opened his mouth to speak, then closed it again, and finally, after bracing himself deliberately like a man about to face an army of spears unarmored, he asked the question that was gnawing at him. Though it was foolish even to hope, still he needed to know. "And you, my lady? Do you love the Pharaoh?"

She turned to him, and in the moonlight her smile lost its usual playful air. Her great, dark eyes were veiled by sorrow. "I am loyal," she said softly, "and always do what I must."

"Do you... is there anyone you love?" His throat tightened, and he coughed, shaking his head. "Forgive me. It is not my place to ask. Please, forget I—"

To Horemheb's surprise—to his leaping, bird-fluttering joy—she took his hand.

"Duty compels me," she said. "Obligation. I owe a great debt to my grandmother, Tiy, who kept me safe when I was a child and educated me. And I owe something to my mother as well. If I do not see to that calling, I fear her *ka* will never rest."

He waited, sensing something more to come, and content just to feel the warmth of her hand in his own.

"But," Baketaten said at length, "I think if I were not so tightly bound by duty I could be free to follow my heart."

She gazed up at him, too buffeted by emotion—or too wily and cautious—to say more. But Horemheb needed no more words. Baketaten's meaning was clear enough, shining in her eyes, dancing in the light that reflected from her gathering tears.

A soft rustle and thump sounded across the ship's deck—the last sailor rolling out his bedding, settling in for a night's sleep. Huya had long since retreated to his little curtained cabin. Horemheb was alone with his mistress—as alone as they could be on a river voyage. The current thrummed gently along the wood of the ship; Horemheb felt that sweet tension vibrating deep in his own gut.

Baketaten, blinking back her tears, leaned toward him. Horemheb held quite still, afraid that if he moved or shifted or breathed she would take fright and bound away, a gazelle in a field, elegant and fleeting. He watched her lips draw ever closer, and then, as the drum of his heart beat to its crescendo, he watched her slow, and pause. Her mouth was just inches from his own.

Torn between desire and duty, Horemheb swallowed hard. He was afraid to deny Baketaten what she so clearly wanted—and to deny himself what he yearned for. But he also feared to trespass on the Pharaoh's house, his property—his wife. He did not know which fear was the greater, and so he held perfectly still, caught between two impossible choices. He felt her warm, myrrh-scented breath on his cheek, its light brush across his skin. It was a more intimate caress than any he had ever shared with Mutnodjmet.

Then, in a heartbeat, Baketaten turned away. She rose and went to the ship's rail, leaning out over the water, watching the night-darkened reeds along the shoreline with a soft, contented smile.

Is she angry with me? Horemheb wondered. *Have I disappointed her? Will she send me back to Akhet-Aten now, and call for another guardsman—one who is bolder than I?*

But she did not seem offended by his failure to kiss her. Baketaten never seemed upset, in truth. Still, Horemheb had spent enough time in her company—oh, those four glorious, gods-gifted days!—that he could read her emotions well enough. She was pleased—satisfied with his nearness, and with the gentle touch of the moonlight.

SEVERAL DAYS BEFORE Horemheb expected to reach Annu, the boat put in at a small, inconsequential village on the river's western shore. Horemheb eyed the village curiously. Mudbrick huts were interspersed with finer, but still rather small and simple, estates. Many of the walls surrounding the larger properties had great tumbles of bright-green vines spilling over their edges, and Horemheb could smell the first, sweet notes of early grapes on the air.

The steward Huya gathered a few of this belongings into a sack and slung it over one shoulder. He nodded curtly to the captain of the boat, then addressed the entire crew as they worked over their lines and stowed the boat's oars. "I have hand-selected each of you," he said, "so I know you can be trusted. But still, I must stress the importance of remaining silent about today's port of call. We were never here. We sailed past this place and continued toward Annu. Is that clear?"

The crew saluted and affirmed in one voice, and Huya turned away, apparently satisfied.

Baketaten, finishing a breakfast of bread and honey in the prow of the ship, rose from her seat, scattered her crumbs overboard for the birds to feast upon, and calmly made her way to her curtained cabin. She tucked one of the lengths of blue linen back, and Horemheb peered through as she sorted through her few belongings, folding articles of clothing neatly on her bedroll, then tucking them into her bag.

"Where are you going?" Horemheb asked her.

"Ashore."

"Has Huya put in here to gather more supplies? There's no need for you to go ashore, too, but if you wish to set your feet on land again, I'll—"

"No," she said. "You misunderstand. I've reached my destination."

Horemheb shook his head in bewilderment. He was no great traveler, but even he knew that the boat had stopped well south of Annu.

He shifted uneasily. "My lady, we still have several days to go before we reach your destination."

Her hands paused in the act of folding a silken robe. She looked up at him sadly, and the laughter froze on Horemheb's tongue.

Baketaten stood and cupped his cheek with one small, cool hand. "Dear Horemheb. I will tell you where we are and why we have come, because I know I can trust you." She gave a self-deprecating laugh, a small huff of bitter amusement. "And even so, although I know that you are the most loyal man alive, you must swear secrecy. For if anyone learns of my business here, my life will be forfeit. I know I can trust you with my secret, but swear to keep it all the same."

"I swear on the At—" he began.

Baketaten hushed him with an impatient shake of her head. "Swear on Amun or Mut or Horus. Swear on Set, for all I care. But do not swear on the Pharaoh's god."

He watched her in silence for a long time, anxiety coiling in his gut. Finally he said, "Very well. I swear on Amun. I will keep your secret as closely as if my own life depended on it."

A pair of sailors walked by, carrying several oars across their shoulders. Baketaten held her tongue until they had passed. Then she placed a hand low on her abdomen and gazed up at Horemheb with wide, earnest eyes.

"I have come here to conceive an heir for the king—a son."

Horemheb shook his head, uncomprehending. A mist of confusion seemed to swallow him up like Ammit's maw, obscuring his senses until the only clarity in all the world was Baketaten—her small, confident figure, her low voice, the scent of myrrh rising from her body.

"Conceive a son?" he said cautiously. "With whom?"

Her reply was a faint whisper. "With the last hope Egypt still holds: my mother's brother, Smenkhkare."

Her words wrenched the breath from Horemheb's lungs. A sudden, bitter knowledge assailed him: that she would be in another man's arms tonight, and every night until she could be sure her womb had quickened. His heart was leaden and dull, and his middle was as hollow as an empty gourd.

"I'm sorry," she said. There was real pain in her voice. "I would have it otherwise, if the choice were mine—if my duty did not compel me."

"I would have it otherwise, too." He remembered Mutnodjmet, her arms around his neck, her tears falling hot upon his chest—and felt like a traitor to more than just the throne.

"I have my obligations." Baketaten hefted her bag and secured its strap over one shoulder.

He placed one hand on the hilt of his blade and fell into step behind her as she made for the boat's ramp. "As do I," he said quietly, and schooled his face to stoic calm, as strong and proper as any guard should be.

Baketaten

*Year 13 of Akhenaten,
Beautiful Are the Manifestations,
Exalting the Name,
Beloved of the Sun*

THE VILLAGE OF KHEPESH was all bustle and dust. Children scampered across the broad road—the only real avenue in the town—giggling and shouting as they kicked a large, leather-wrapped ball to and fro. From one of the many narrow alleys that fed into the road, a skinny, blue-eyed dog eyed Baketaten as she passed, barked once, and retreated. Where the avenue widened around a covered well, a handful of local merchants hawked their wares from donkey carts and rickety tables—poor stuff, compared to the goods available in the wealthy City of the Sun, yet Baketaten found herself charmed by the colorful baskets, clay pots, and beaded jewelry the merchants held up for her inspection as she breezed past. The rustic pleasures of this small town were nearly enough to lift the weight of Horemheb's disappointment—and her own—from Baketaten's heart.

Huya led the way through Khepesh as expertly as if he'd spent his entire life there. Baketaten felt Horemheb striding at her back, close enough to protect her if any danger should arise, but just far enough to balm the wound of her revelation. *I should have told him my secret sooner*, she thought, *before he could grow close to me—or I to him*. It was a misstep Tiy never would have made. *She* would have been canny enough to detect the guardsman's growing affection and cut off any hope for love, long before emotion could interfere with duty.

Baketaten clenched her fists as she followed Huya, firming her resolve. *I must be more like Tiy in all things. Too much depends on keeping a level heart. I mustn't allow foolish feelings to rule me again.*

Within minutes, the small, busy market district of Khepesh fell away behind them. Huya turned down a long, dusty cart track that wended out into a grove of fruit trees, where the shade was dappled and kind. Beyond, the track ran straight along the top of a causeway; the fields to either side were lush with the soft-green stalks of early barley. On a small rise at the track's end, a little walled estate stood, well back from the river and surrounded by olive trees.

Huya nodded toward the house. "There is our final destination."

Baketaten paused and stared at the tiny estate, at its stillness and seclusion. Through a clinging veil of grape vines she could make out mudbrick walls, brown, sun-dried, and unadorned by plaster or bright-painted murals. The villa would never be considered fashionable or fine in Akhet-Aten, yet there the secret hope of the throne had spent the past thirteen years, growing from a boy to a man. *Please, gods,* Baketaten prayed, *let him be capable and strong. Let him be good and wise. Let him not be mad like the men who came before him.*

"Very well," she said to Huya. "Let us do what we've come to do." She settled her bag's straps more comfortably on her shoulder and refused to glance in Horemheb's direction as she continued down the cart track toward Smenkhkare's home.

When they passed through the villa's low gate, undecorated except by the twining limbs of the grape vines, an elderly servant dressed in a plain white kilt came to greet them.

"Tell your master Huya has come," the steward said to

the old man. "He will recognize my name."

"And..." The servant eyed Baketaten and Horemheb with a question in his raised, grizzled brow.

But Huya said only, "My name will be enough to satisfy Master Nebre."

The servant bowed and beckoned them to follow, then settled them in a small waiting room. By comparison to the halls of Akhet-Aten, the room was very dark and plain, with a distressingly low ceiling. But Baketaten thanked the servant for his hospitality and settled onto the hard, narrow couch as easily as if it were the finest, down-stuffed silk in the City of the Sun.

"Master Nebre?" she said to Huya when they were alone.

Huya turned a sharp, considering gaze to Horemheb and made no reply.

"Horemheb is loyal to me," she assured him. "I trust him with my life." A little sardonic laugh escaped her throat. "And that *is* the truth. I've told him my mission already, Huya, and he knows who we've come seeking. He knows, too, that it's my death—and his—if anyone learns our secret."

Huya's eyes flicked to Horemheb again. He gave the guardsman a flat-eyed frown. No doubt, Baketaten thought, Huya considered Horemheb expendable anyway. A young soldier without any fellows to protect him could be gotten rid of quite easily, should the need arise. After a moment, apparently satisfied with Horemheb's inclusion in the conspiracy, Huya shrugged and turned back to Baketaten.

"It has been necessary, of course, to maintain the anonymity of—er—*our man*. Nebre is the name he uses here in Khepesh. It's the identity he took on when I first brought him here, thirteen years ago. The whole village knows him as Nebre, including his servants. We must go on addressing him as such."

"Wise," Baketaten agreed.

As they waited in silence, she examined the little house. Though it was simply made—at least by the standards she was used to—it was tidy and appointed just well enough to be functional. A small writing desk stood below a narrow window; the stools on which Huya and Horemheb sat were of old, pitted wood, but looked sturdy and well made. A faded carpet covered the floor, woven in a pattern of gazelles and flying geese. It was worn in some places, but clean, and Baketaten could see brighter threads here and there, where thin patches had been expertly repaired.

A narrow doorway led out to a flourishing garden. The arch of light darkened with the silhouette of a man, tall and broad-shouldered, his unseen face framed by a blunt-cut wig. Baketaten blinked as the light streamed in brightly all around him, casting him in a halo of fire, robbing him of every detail except shape. She held up one hand to shield her eyes from the brightness, to try to discern his features.

He stepped over the threshold, dusting his hands together, and as he came into the room Baketaten could see that black earth clung to his fingers and palms. Above his plain, soil-stained kilt, his abdomen and chest were flat and strong-looking, though not heavily muscled. His skin was very brown from many hours spent working in the sun. Baketaten examined him, searching for any sign of familiarity—and found it at once in his pointed chin and narrow face, his thin nose and heavy-lidded eyes. She inhaled sharply at sight of those eyes, so very like Akhenaten's. But when Smenkhkare met her gaze, she could see at once that his *ba* was whole and sound. His eyes, despite their superficial resemblance to Akhenaten's, were free from the slow fire and distant glaze of madness. Baketaten sighed in deep relief.

Smenkhkare's face went still and thoughtful as he took in the sight of Baketaten, sitting on his humble couch as poised as a heron in the reeds. He turned to Huya with his brows raised. "It has been long since I saw you last, Master Huya. I am always pleased to share my home with you." Smenkhkare's voice was as rich and smooth as well-polished wood. "But who have you brought with you?"

Huya rose from his stool. "Nebre—you look well. As for this woman's identity, I will respectfully withdraw, and allow her to tell you what she will." He gave a commanding nod to Horemheb, who, with one pained glance at Baketaten, followed Huya out into the garden.

Smenkhkare turned to Baketaten with a baffled smile. "Was your journey long, my lady? Let me bring you something to refresh yourself. Some cold beer, or—" He started toward a dim corner of the room, where Baketaten supposed he must have a pantry. But then he caught sight of his own hands, swinging near the sash of his kilt, and he paused, laughing softly at his thoughtlessness. "A moment. I was working in the garden, you see..."

Smenkhkare took a thick clay pitcher, fired in a bright-blue glaze, from a stand beside the garden door. He stepped just outside, back into the halo of bright light, and poured water over one hand, then the other, rinsing the last traces of soil away. Baketaten watched him with no small amount of wonder as he bent to this simple task of washing. He looked so very like the Pharaoh, long and lean, solemn-faced even as a backlit silhouette. In his familiar features, Baketaten saw the image of what Akhenaten might have been if the madness had passed him by. *What Egypt might have had*, she thought sadly. *A Pharaoh who is kind and good, thoughtful and sincere.*

He returned to the room and sat a little awkwardly on one of the stools the other men had vacated. He clasped his hands in his lap and looked at Baketaten with a tight-lipped, anxious smile.

"Your home is charming," she said. "And your garden—I can see from here how lush it is."

"I enjoy working out there, among the grape vines and the olive trees. I've lived in this house for many years, since I was just a boy. I was alone in the world from a young age, and so I was taken in by Sary, the High Priest of Ptah. He was an old man, but very kind and wise. He taught me well, and saw that I had everything I needed. When he died a few years ago, he left his house to me, for he had no children of his own. Sometimes I think I can still feel Sary's presence out there in the garden, when I tend the vines he planted or harvest the olives he so loved."

"Olives are difficult to grow in the Two Lands."

He laughed—a sudden, joyous sound, boyish and charming. "Difficult, indeed! I work very hard in service to Sary's olive trees. Sometimes they keep me occupied from sunrise to sunset. But I wouldn't have it any other way. I loved Sary dearly, you see—just as if he'd been my true father. The olive trees keep his memory alive."

"Do you remember your true father?" Baketaten said. "Your true family?"

Smenkhkare inhaled, and his eyes narrowed warily. "Yes," he admitted with obvious reluctance. "Sary was always straightforward with me—well, from an age when I could be trusted not to say anything foolish, and doom myself by my own innocence. You know how children can be. I know who I am—what I am."

"Do you know why I have come?"

Slowly, he shook his head. "I do not even know your name. You are a mystery to me, I'm afraid—although I can't help but feel that I've seen you before... somewhere, long ago. Impossible, of course; you are so young."

She decided it was best to hold nothing back—to go straight to the point of her visit. *I must trust that the gods will be merciful and carry me through this duty.* "I know that you are not truly Nebre. Your name is Smenkhkare, son of

Amunhotep and Tiy, brother of Akhenaten, the Pharaoh."

Pale and sober-faced, he nodded.

"My name is Baketaten," she said. "Though once I was called Nebetah. My mother was—"

"Sitamun," Smenkhkare interjected. He sat back abruptly. "Forgive my rudeness, but yes—I see it now. I know now why you seem so familiar. I recall that she gave birth to a daughter named Nebetah shortly after I left the West Bank. Mother told me all about it in a letter."

Baketaten hesitated. "Did Tiy also tell you that Sitamun is dead?"

He nodded once, with hard acceptance. "I heard. I confess that I wept when the news reached me. Sitamun was always a good sister to me, gentle and kind. I loved her. I would have spared her such a violent, painful death if I could have done it."

A deep sense of satisfaction, of calm reassurance, warmed Baketaten's chest. There was no hint of madness in Smenkhkare—none of the wild craving for divine power that had so blighted his brother and his father. He was pure—good. He could be relied upon to do as the gods directed and to keep silent when the act was finished. Baketaten was sure of it. She trusted to the deep, cool sense of certainty that Tiy had trained into her. If Tiy had been present to challenge Baketaten's assessment, to question how she knew that Smenkhkare was whole of heart, Baketaten never could have said. She simply knew that this man's *ba* was unfractured, his *ka* strong and clean. Perhaps it was the clarity of his speech, or the way his eyes grew liquid with sympathy for poor, lost Sitamun. Perhaps it was the glimpse he gave of an Egypt that might have been. Baketaten felt a stab of sorrow as she watched him marshal his emotions. He seemed to her a stark image of lost potential—a clear view of what Akhenaten might have become, if the gods had not bent the Pharaoh to their inscrutable whims and tainted him with madness.

When Smenkhkare seemed in control of his feelings once more, Baketaten spoke on. "Tiy raised me after Sitamun's death, you know. I don't suppose she told you that in her letters."

"No. Over the years I have heard very little from my mother. It has been Huya, for the most part, who has kept me informed of my family's affairs. I didn't think to inquire after the fate of Sitamun's daughter. I suppose—" He gave a small, embarrassed shrug. "I suppose I thought you'd gone into the harem, to be raised among the other royal children."

"Tiy saw great value in me—potential that would be wasted in the harem. As a daughter of Sitamun, I carry the royal blood. Nefertiti and Kiya—and their children—do not."

He said nothing, but tilted his head as he watched her, waiting for her to reveal more.

"Smenkhkare, the throne needs your aid. All of Egypt needs you. And Egypt needs me, too." Speaking quickly, half-afraid that he would cut her off and refuse the dangerous scheme she proposed, Baketaten explained her plan. She spoke of Akhenaten's inability to conceive a son, and went on at passionate length, describing what a royal son would mean to the Two Lands—the leverage it might provide over Akhenaten's zeal, his ever-increasing recklessness. A son might even, she told Smenkhkare, provide an immediate, clear heir to the throne—in the event that something sudden and tragic should befall the king. Something utterly unforeseen, of course.

But he did not stop her from speaking. Nor did he leap to his feet, or even shake his head in fearful denial. He listened to her talk of treason with a thoughtful air and said nothing. At length he rose and paced to the garden door. There he hesitated with the sunlight streaming all around him, emphasizing his youth and strength, his wholeness of body and heart. Then he walked outside without a word, without a backward glance.

A stifling silence descended on the room. Baketaten chewed her lip. Then she forced herself to stop, imagining a sharp admonition from Tiy. *Don't give away your plans; don't wear your thoughts on your face like a mask for anyone to see.*

When her face was once more unreadable, Baketaten rose from the hard couch and drifted to the garden door. She paused on the threshold, gazing out into the garden, searching for some sign of Smenkhkare. A slow blur of color caught her attention, the deep brown of his skin and the paleness of his dust-covered kilt drifting between the trunks of the olive trees, pacing in silent thought. Even as he vanished once more from her sight, disappearing slowly amid the violet shade beneath the rattle of the wind-stirred leaves, Baketaten could see how this duty hung heavy from his shoulders.

It was not necessary to like Smenkhkare in order to do the task the gods had set before her. But she did like him, she realized—and respected him, too. And that made the prospect more pleasant.

He re-emerged from among the olives, trailing a slim, broken branch absently in his hand. Staring through his garden wall into a vast distance, he shook his head with emphatic force, and Baketaten's heart sank. *He will reject the plan. He will send me away, and I must find another—a man who is not of the true, royal blood.* Or, worse, Egypt's final hope would die.

But then Smenkhkare looked up, and the mist of that daunting distance cleared from his eyes. He saw Baketaten waiting in the arch of the narrow garden door. Silent and grim-faced, he came toward her.

Before he had crossed half the distance that separated them, Smenkhkare reached out a hand. Baketaten's legs shook with a violent, throbbing relief. But she made herself walk steadily to Smenkhkare's side with her head raised high. Holding his gaze soberly, she placed her hand into his own.

BAKETATEN REMAINED at Smenkhkare's villa for twenty days, walking in the whispering shade of the olives, reading story-scrolls in the tangled peace of his small vineyard—and going to his bed, every night, like a broodmare led to a stallion. She took no pleasure in the work, and as she lay back on his humble bed to do her divine task, all her thoughts were for Egypt. But Smenkhkare was gentle, and Baketaten was grateful for his kindness. In the cool of the evening, as they took their supper together, or when they strolled arm in arm in the privacy of Smenkhkare's small but well-kept garden, Baketaten found that she could joke and laugh with him, and even shared with Smenkhkare some of her most precious thoughts and dreams.

But although she appreciated his kindness, Smenkhkare's attentions had the feel of simple courtesy. There was no passion blooming between them, as with Horemheb on the voyage north. It was not Smenkhkare's face Baketaten pictured when she slipped beneath her blankets each night, her body still aching from the effort of her sacred duty. She was glad for the distance between herself and Smenkhkare. It allowed her to remain focused on her obligations, her goal—and allowed Horemheb to remain in the special place she had made for him, deep within her heart. She had built a gilded throne there, and she would have been displeased had she found anyone other than Horemheb sitting upon it.

When the moon turned and her courses did not come, Baketaten slipped out into the starlit garden and crouched down among the grape vines, pressing her hands to her face, shaking with the force of her relief. Her perilous plan—the first part of it, at least—had succeeded. Only the gods could say whether the child that took root inside her was male. But there amid the peace of the twining vines, brushed by the soft blessing of the stars, she felt certain that a son of the royal line was coming. Control over the unpredictable Pharaoh, surety in the face of his downfall, and safety for the Two Lands seemed to rest at last in her hands.

After an hour of grateful prayer in the vineyard, Baketaten rose, brushed the soil from her sleep-shift, and picked her way quietly back through the garden toward Smenkhkare's darkened house. Something long and low moved heavily beneath an olive tree; Baketaten paused, staring into the night-dark shadows. After a moment, she relaxed with a pained little sigh. It was only Horemheb, tossing on his bedroll, gripped by some restless dream.

Horemheb had struck the only sour note during the otherwise pleasant weeks spent in Smenkhkare's company. The guardsman remained ever close to Baketaten, yet somehow still distant—silent, cool, cloaked in professional courtesy. Most nights he slept in the garden, preferring his rough bedroll to Smenkhkare's humble hospitality, and sometimes, when her night's work was through, Baketaten would steal from Smenkhkare's bed and peer from his narrow window, watching Horemheb as he slept. More often than not, the guardsman rolled and muttered in his sleep. Baketaten would watch his face in the starlight, its features distorted by the pain of some haunting dream. The agony she saw in Horemheb, sleeping and waking, stabbed into Baketaten's own heart and left her aching with its bitter reflection.

On that last night, when she knew her work was half finished, Horemheb woke from his fitful slumber and raised himself on one elbow. He gazed directly at Baketaten, as if a voice had whispered in his ear, directing him toward her pale shape in the garden. He stared at her, and even though shadows veiled his face, Baketaten could feel the hurt and the accusation in his eyes.

"I would have it otherwise," she whispered, though she was too far off for him to hear. "If only the gods would allow it."

When the dawn came, she informed Smenkhkare that his part of their secret task was finished, and she must return to the City of the Sun.

He paused in the act of cracking his boiled duck's egg, staring at her with faint remorse. "I am sorry to hear it," he said. "I have grown quite fond of you."

This confession startled Baketaten. In all her many calculations, her careful assessments, she had not factored in this risk—that Smenkhkare might come to love her. Her face heated. She stared down at her breakfast, unable to return his simple affection.

"I am grateful for all you've done," she finally said, and as she continued to stare blindly at her bread and cheese, she heard the shell of the egg crack again, the whisper of its separation from the white meat within.

Smenkhkare accompanied the little party down the cart track, back to the wide avenue of the village of Khepesh. He walked in silence at Baketaten's side, all the way down to the riverfront. She allowed him to bid her a tender good-bye, with a lingering kiss on the cheek and a warm hand on the small of her back—and all the while she could feel Horemheb's grief pouring over her like a strong, cold current.

Baketaten didn't know whether to feel relief of loss when the boat cast off and ran up its single, red sail for the return voyage southward. Her duty was halfway done, but she had found peace at Smenkhkare's small estate, a quiet security unlike any she had known before. From this day on, Akhet-Aten would hold her more firmly than ever before. She would be forever wrapped in the tangle of its thick, constricting vines.

She hoped that at least she might enjoy some of the warmth she'd shared with Horemheb on the journey north. But he was distant and wounded, wearing his obedient efficiency like armor. Baketaten took to the seclusion of her canopied cabin, resolved to allow Horemheb the time he needed to sort through his emotions. The gods knew she needed to order her thoughts as well.

On the fourth night of their journey, with Akhet-Aten looming ever nearer, Horemheb strode to her across the deck, cutting through the starlight like an ax through soft cheese. The boat's crew had long since gone to sleep, and Baketaten was alone in the prow with the new, pale sliver of the moon hanging high above her. She looked up, startled, as Horemheb approached. Before she could speak, he reached for her hand and raised it, turned it. His lips found the inside of her wrist, and his chin, in want of a shave, scratched the sensitive skin of her forearm. Baketaten's blood turned to fire in an instant, as it never had with Smenkhkare—and certainly never with the Pharaoh.

"Give me just one night," Horemheb whispered, close beside her ear. "One night to hold you—to love you."

She wanted to throw her arms around his neck, to press herself against his firm, strong body and tell him, *Yes—yes! And more than one night. Every night, for as long as I live!* But the weight of duty pressed down upon her until her back ached from it, until her shoulders sagged.

"The child I carry is divine," she said. "And more than that, he is the final hope of the Two Lands. I cannot risk this pregnancy, Horemheb. You know that passion could upset the child within me, or turn him female. For Egypt's sake, I must remain untouched. I will tell the Pharaoh when I return that I conceived the baby before I left Akhet-Aten—and then I will deny even the king's affection. I must remain chaste until I am delivered."

"You would deny yourself—" Horemheb began, his voice rough with anger.

"Yes," Baketaten said. "For Egypt's sake. Even if it destroys my own heart."

She reached up and caressed Horemheb's face, running her palm over the stubble of his jaw, begging silently for his forgiveness. And then, because her chest was bursting with need for him, she gave in to one small passion—only one—and kissed him. It was a long and lingering kiss. She savored it, although its taste was bitter, for she knew it was likely the only kiss they would ever share.

"I love you," she told him. "My time with Smenkhkare made me sure of that, at least."

He answered sadly, "Swear it."

"I swear it by Amun and Mut and Hathor. I swear it by Horus and Iset. By all the gods, save one. By all the gods that are true."

Horemheb nodded, his face paled by tragedy and starlight. Then he turned and walked away.

Tiy

Year 13 of Akhenaten,
Beautiful Are the Manifestations,
Exalting the Name,
Beloved of the Sun

SHEMU AND THE INUNDATION came and went, and Peret, the season of fertility, opened. Short, soft carpets of sprouted seeds covered the fields of the western bank. At every sunrise, the sky over Tiy's garden rang with the cries of birds, underscored by the high-pitched calls of their pink, featherless young in the nests. The omens of growth and renewal were good. She waited patiently for word to cross the Iteru that Baketaten's labor was begun.

The baby Baketaten carried had grown quite large, and the midwives exclaimed that any day now the child would arrive. Tiy had been readmitted to the court and restored to nominal favor, by dint of the fact that she had gifted Baketaten to the king. But she preferred to dwell on the western shore, where it seemed she could watch the Pharaoh and his family from a wider view, a superior angle. Even though she visited the palace only for feasts and ceremonies, still Tiy had noted the subtle shifting of the sands, the slide of power from one hand to another. She had watched with satisfaction as Baketaten, buoyed by her great, round belly, rose within the court like the first star of the evening—had watched as Nefertiti's lovely face firmed into a mask of helpless disbelief, and Kiya shrank quietly, gratefully, into the mercy of anonymity.

But as Baketaten's labor drew ever closer, Tiy feared for

the girl and the babe she carried. The plague that came to Akhet-Aten with the Tribute Festival remained long after the foreigners had departed. The illness had settled into the young bones of a city that was far more beautiful than it was functional. Waste from Akhet-Aten's homes flowed in sluggish trenches toward the river, stinking and rotting beneath the hot sun, and there the illness flourished, with outbreaks of the strange, often deadly fever rising every few months, spreading outward from the poorest districts that stood closest to the waste-filled ditches. And each time the sickness rose in Akhet-Aten, it held on a little longer and claimed a few more lives.

The plague seemed to strike infants hardest of all, carrying their tiny *kas* away within hours of the first symptoms. Mothers who had recently given birth were almost as susceptible. The thought of Baketaten, whom Tiy had nurtured so carefully, succumbing to that vile illness was more than she could bear. Three times a day, in the most secluded corner of her garden, Tiy burned offerings to Heka, god of healing spells, pleading with him to have mercy on Baketaten and her child.

The prayers and offerings seemed a small and ineffectual gesture, yet it was the best Tiy could do, the only protection she could offer. She would have removed Baketaten from the city if the king had permitted it—sent her back to Khepesh where she would be safe from the foul air and demons that carried the blight across Akhet-Aten. But no one—no humble craftsman, no courtier, and certainly not a King's Wife—was permitted to pass beyond the stone monuments that marked the boundaries of Akhet-Aten.

Many had tried, Tiy knew. Even in the western farms, the lanes and courtyards rustled with whispers—stories of the men and women who had tried to flee the plague that only grew deadlier with each successive recurrence. Mahu and his men were as thick in the rugged hills as fleas on a dog, and all those who had attempted to escape the City of the Sun had been apprehended and made to face the king's justice.

The king's justice was nothing Tiy would wish to confront. Akhenaten grew more incensed with each attempt at defection. At first, the culprits had been thrown into the little jail cells that Mahu had constructed on the southern edge of the city. The plague quickly overwhelmed the cells, and all who entered died in agony within days. The Pharaoh soon moved on to death by beheading, but when the attempts to escape were not quelled, he staked men out on the floor of the Great Aten Temple at dawn. By noon, their piteous screams filled the air, but by sunset they were silent, their lives snuffed out by the terrible heat hammering from above and from the temple walls. Mahu spread these tales to the people he captured in the hills and offered them a choice: go into the Great Aten Temple and lie exposed to the god's judgment—or leap from the cliff tops. There was no escape.

If ever we needed an heir, Tiy prayed—to which gods, she could not say— *if ever the land cried out for a new Pharaoh, a righteous and true man—or at least a child I can rear properly...* Surely the time had long since come to pull this mad king from his throne and restore *maat* to the land.

Tiy's prayers went on for only a few days longer. At last, in the full heat of midday, she looked out from her rooftop canopy to see a small vessel gliding swiftly across the river, its many oars working at a furious pace. She knew, with her usual observant certainty, that Baketaten's time had come.

Tiy raced down the steps into the garden, moving with a speed she thought impossible in her twilight years. She pushed through the tangled vines that shrouded her outer gate and was waiting at the end of her little stone quay before the boat reached its mooring.

Huya reached out from its prow, clinging to the quay to

hold the boat still. "I've only just heard. Baketaten entered the birth bower not two hours ago," he said.

Tiy scrambled down into the boat and sat hunched with anxiety as it sped back across the river. She expected the labor would be long; first births typically lasted for hours. But by the time the boat landed at the palace quay, cymbals were ringing from the walls and roofs; shouts of glad tidings filled the air.

Tiy hiked the hem of her robe high and rushed across the garden, following the cheers of servants and the exclamations of the harem women who sat on the lake's retaining wall, sharing the tender spears of new lettuce leaves, a symbol of masculinity. She rounded a bend in the path, and there before her, flanked by two great, red rose bushes in fragrant bloom, was the tall, narrow birthing bower. Its linen curtains stirred in the breeze.

Tiy paused, listening through the shouts in the garden and the clangor from the rooftops, hoping for some hint of the birth's outcome before she entered the bower. Were those sobs she heard? If the midwives were weeping, then the child was lost, and all Baketaten's careful work had been in vain.

But then, gusty and sharp, a baby's cry split the air. A midwife with blood to her elbows ducked though the bower's curtained door. "A son!" the woman cried. "The king has a son!"

Tiy staggered backward. Huya's arm slid quickly around her shoulders. She sagged against him for a moment, and whispered to all the gods—to any god who might be listening, "Thank you."

Tiy was the first well-wisher to enter the birthing pavilion. Baketaten reclined easily on a bed of cushions, her forehead sweat-dampened but her expression serene.

"A boy," she said to Tiy, and there was more triumph in her voice than exhaustion.

One of the midwives bustled over, bearing cool wine for Baketaten to sip. "I've never seen such a young woman make the passage through birth so quickly, nor so well. Our King's Wife hardly even cried out. She has the heart of a lioness!"

Tiy bent and pressed her lips against Baketaten's forehead. The salt of her sweat was sharp on Tiy's tongue.

"Well done," Tiy said, and Baketaten smiled up at her with eyes as cool and self-satisfied as those of a desert fox.

Tiy remained in the shade of the bower for a few minutes, holding Baketaten's hand as the first of her well-wishers filed in. The women cooed over the baby boy, red and squalling in a midwife's arms, and praised Baketaten for her quick, easy delivery. When Tiy was satisfied that the girl and the baby were in no imminent danger, she slipped away, making straight for Akhenaten's private chambers, determined to be the first to bear the news to the king.

She found Akhenaten in his private garden, kneeling on the grass, murmuring prayers up toward the glowing disc of the sun. Tiy cleared her throat, disliking the need to interrupt the Pharaoh in his religious ecstasy. He could be unpredictable at such times. But the gods were kind to Tiy. Though Akhenaten had heard the bells and cymbals ringing, he had not yet received news of the child, or of Baketaten's health. He rounded on her, scowling at the interruption, but when he saw that it was his mother who stood beside him, Akhenaten's expression softened into worry. He clambered to his feet.

"News?" he said anxiously. "Is there news?"

"Indeed there is, my lord," Tiy said, smiling broadly. "Baketaten is well. And you have a healthy, lively son."

"A son!" He breathed the word, awed by its sound, its import. Then he cut a caper in the grass, dancing with the sheer joy of the tidings.

Akhenaten raised wordless shouts to mingle with the ringing bells. Tiy watched the Pharaoh's unbridled pleasure with wry satisfaction. *Baketaten has done well, indeed.* The girl had more than lived up to the slyness and resolve Tiy had trained into her *ba*. Baketaten had taken a terrible risk to secure the heir Egypt so desperately needed. And her gamble had paid off handsomely. Now that the work was done, Tiy prayed, the gods would be good, and remove this jigging fool from the throne. The Two Lands would return to security.

"My king!"

Tiy and Akhenaten both turned suddenly at the interruption. Nefertiti had joined them in the garden, resplendent in the white robe of the Aten temple, wearing the blue, flat-topped crown that she favored. Meritaten lingered just behind, toeing the grass with a sulky air.

Nefertiti's smile was warm, but Tiy noted the strain around her eyes, the way her lips twitched with the effort. "So you have heard the good news already, I see." She flicked one sharp glance of resentment toward Tiy, but her smile never faltered.

"I have reached my pinnacle, just as you once promised, Nefer-Neferu-Aten—my great beauty, my High Priestess of the Sun! How wonderful is your power, how far-seeing your eye!"

Nefertiti nodded in acceptance of his praise.

"The height of my power has at last arrived." Akhenaten's face went slack with rapture, his eyes distant and wide.

Nefertiti broke smoothly into the king's reverie. "Baketaten has chosen a name for your son."

"Ah," Tiy said. "What is it? I'm sure we are all eager to hear."

"She calls him Tutankhaten."

"The Living Image of the Aten," the king repeated,

beaming. "Yes—that is good. Very good, indeed! When can I see him? I want to look upon this glorious child at once! I want to behold this wonder I have created."

Tiy eyed the Pharaoh's face, his stiff neck and trembling shoulders. Zeal burned in him like a fierce, hungry fire. *Baketaten chose the name wisely.* No doubt the girl had carefully selected just the right name to harness the king's passions and bend his madness to her whims. *The smallest of her actions is carefully planned, marvelously wise*, Tiy reflected. She turned her face away so neither the king nor Nefertiti could see her wry little smile. *This wonder I have created, indeed.*

The king's fervent enthusiasm for his son was already wild and fierce, and he hadn't yet laid eyes on the boy. Perhaps this new bundle of dawning potential, this Tutankhaten, would be the strong rein Egypt so desperately needed, after all. It all looked so favorable, certain to turn out well, that Tiy nearly allowed herself to hope.

Nefertiti

*Year 14 of Akhenaten,
Beautiful Are the Manifestations,
Exalting the Name,
Beloved of the Sun*

THE CHARIOT LURCHED, and Nefertiti braced herself with a tight grip on its gilded rail. Crowds usually thronged the Royal Road in the morning, waiting for a glimpse of the royal family on their progress to the Great Aten Temple. But today the crowd was denser than ever before, and seemed to boil with a dark, edgy passion that made her stomach clench with anxiety. The horses slowed to a trot and the chariot swerved to avoid a small knot of men that surged out from the crowd lining the right-hand side of the avenue. They reached toward the chariot with hands like a lion's claws, and Nefertiti drew back, bumping Akhenaten with her shoulder and hip. Mahu's men dodged in, a flurry of striped kilts and raised clubs, restoring order with shouts and the threats of blows.

Nefertiti had never been fool enough to believe the crowds along the Royal Road indicated any real enthusiasm for the Pharaoh and his family. There were few pastimes in Akhet-Aten, and the ritual drive to and from the temple was simply an excuse for courtiers to leave their homes, to behold a sight other than their rooftop lounges and the vast, sparkling monotony of the Iteru cutting through the land. The crowds had always been lazy, disengaged, cheering day after day with a rote duty that comforted

Nefertiti with its sameness.

But little by little, as the plague took a firmer hold on Akhet-Aten and Mahu tightened his fist around the city's borders, the daily throng of citizens shed their habitual laziness, and a palpable anger took its place. Where before Mahu's men had been only a ceremonial presence, now the soldiers were required to look sharp and act quickly to keep the crowd in check.

The chariot lurched again as several men broke past the restraint of Mahu's guards. They ran into the road and locked arms, forming a wall to block the Pharaoh's progress.

The men raised hoarse shouts, challenges to the king. "Plague! A divine curse! If you are chosen of divinity, then lift this curse from your city!"

The watching throng cheered their agreement, and the high, shining walls of estates and villas echoed back that fierce roar.

The horses balked at the noise and the sight of the men who barred their way. The chariot rolled backward; Nefertiti gripped the rail tighter.

"Fools!" Akhenaten hissed under his breath. He juggled the reins, pulling hard at the horses' mouths to keep them from wheeling and fleeing back to the palace.

"Make way for the king," one of Mahu's men shouted.

A man from the barricade lifted his fist in defiance. "Not until the king turns his heart to the suffering of his people, instead of to the worship of his god!"

The roar of the crowd surged. That boil of anger was louder than before. The horses tossed their heads, screaming in fear, and Nefertiti gasped as her heart seemed to leap into her throat. Behind the chariot she heard the pounding of many running feet and sent up a frantic prayer for protection. She was certain the crowd had rallied, and was rising up at last to attack the Pharaoh with fists and feet. She braced for the impact and the pain of hundreds of hands tearing at her, beating her, pulling her down from the height of power. But a heartbeat later, in a blue-and-red blur, a troop of Mahu's soldiers rushed past the royal chariot, brandishing clubs over the wall of their shields.

The line of protestors broke at once. The men scattered in all directions; the crowds along the road opened around them and closed again on the instant, absorbing them into the vast throng, hiding them from sight. Mahu's men landed a few blows on the nearest onlookers all the same, but the offending men had vanished, and the troop soon subsided, scowling and cursing.

"Aten save me," Nefertiti whispered, mindful, even through her terror, of the Pharaoh's nearness. He snaked an arm around her shoulders—a gesture that was no doubt meant to be protective, but only served to make Nefertiti feel more exposed and helpless before the hard glares and angry shouts of Akhet-Aten's citizens.

The chariot drove on. Nefertiti cut wary glances into the crowd as she passed, and wished she could call out to them—reassure them that she agreed with them entirely—that she was doing all she could, whatever she could, to set Egypt to rights. The plague worried her as much as it did them. Its specter drove off sleep nearly every night and left her tossing on her bed, dampened by the sweat of helpless fear. She had done all she could think of to bring the outbreak under control—had listened to several stewards and physicians propose various means of countering the illness, or of eradicating it entirely. She had approved most of the plans, willing to try anything—everything—if it might bring the terrible illness to heel.

She, Nefertiti, had done this—and no one else. Akhenaten remained completely uninterested in the plague that, month after month, ate away at the population of his great city like a nest of mice in a grain sack. The Pharaoh cared for nothing anymore save for his sun-worship, his daily appearances before cheering crowds, and the affections of his children.

And his enthusiasm for the children worried Nefertiti at least as much as the plague. But while she could take the counsel of learned men, and burn herbs against the illness or cast spells over the palace to protect it from disease-bearing demons, there was nothing she could do to divert the Pharaoh's eye from his daughters.

At last, when Nefertiti's heart had grown so heavy with her troubles that she feared she would weep before the crowd, the chariot reached the temple gates. Gratefully, she stepped down, ringed by the guards who held the hard-eyed citizens back. She gathered up her skirt in trembling hands and edged toward the temple, but a call from the crowd brought her up short.

"King's Wife, may I beg a word with you?"

The man leaned over one guard's shoulder to gain her attention. The guard made as if to bat him away, but Nefertiti stayed him with a gesture. She recognized the man who called out to her, and flushed with guilt. It was Senedj, the ambassador to Kadesh. He had been tasked with negotiating complacency with the Kadeshis, who were feeling the crush of their enemies all around them, yet received no assistance from Egypt, no matter how they pleaded with Akhenaten. In truth, the Kadeshis begged *Nefertiti*—as did the Hurrians, the Phoenicians, the Canaanites, and the Palmyrenes. It was Nefertiti who fielded all missives to the throne, ruling from the shadows as Tiy had done before her.

But where Tiy had been prepared—canny and well-trained for her secret role—Nefertiti had been raised and trained for motherhood, for the value of her womb and blood. *And*, she reminded herself bitterly, *to be an instrument in Ay's hand.* Now that she had put Ay off, deflecting his schemes and ambitions, she didn't even have *him* to turn to. There was no one to help her sort out the mess of the northern cities—no one but a few stewards, who understood this complex tangle of statecraft little better than she. Nefertiti was doing the best she could for Egypt, but each day she grew more painfully aware that her best effort simply wasn't enough. Not by a very long way.

"Senedj," she said, "I am so sorry. I missed our appointment this morning—we were meant to discuss Kadesh. Another matter kept me. Please accept my apologies."

That other matter was the plague, of course—a more immediate threat, since it was so close to the palace walls. Yet Nefertiti could not interest the Pharaoh in even that imminent and deadly threat.

Senedj bowed graciously over the soldier's arm. "Please don't fret, High Priestess. I know that many grave matters occupy you, these days. I shall send my steward to yours to schedule another audience."

"Yes, that would be best. And this time," she added with a sheepish smile, "I shall be true to my word."

"I have no doubt of that." He leaned a little closer and spoke low across the guard's shoulder. "It is difficult work, running the Two Lands by one's self. I shall be patient."

Senedj's words lingered in Nefertiti's heart all through the long rites of praise to the Aten. The ambassador's confidence in her abilities soothed much of the doubt from her heart. As the sun passed its high point and the rites dragged on, his quiet show of belief in her ability even seemed to cool the fiery heat of the temple, and Nefertiti found herself smiling as her misgivings fled one by one.

Indeed, she realized, *I am the only force holding this city together.* Aside from Mahu's increasing violence, of course, which only kept the citizens of Akhet-Aten penned like sheep between the high, red cliffs. If there was still any integrity to the City of the Sun, it was solely due to Nefertiti's efforts—because she had stepped in to rule, silently—and, she hoped, *invisibly* to all but the ambassadors and stewards.

As the final hymn to the Aten rose into the sweltering sky, Nefertiti realized with a chill of not-unpleasant surprise that she was effectively the Pharaoh. The fate of the Two Lands lay in her hands alone—but so too did its power. If only *she* had the divine blessing of the gods, instead of Akhenaten—then she could move with audacity, discarding her caution, free to make the changes this broken regime so badly needed. If she had the gods' blessing, she could command Mahu herself, and back him away from the people of the city—pull in his fury like a hound on a leash. *And*, she thought with cold calculation, *I could do to Ay whatever my heart desires.*

Is this how Hatshepsut felt? she wondered as she climbed back into the chariot beside her crowned and beaming husband. *Is this how the female Pharaoh's rise to the throne began—slowly, subtly, cloaked in delicate shadows? And when Hatshepsut realized her own strength and import, did she feel, as I do, that it was* maat?

As they returned down the long, broad avenue of the Royal Road, still clamoring with the angry shouts of Akhet-Aten's citizens, all Nefertiti could see before her was her father's face. Even in her imagining, Ay looked arrogant and smug, but Nefertiti smiled serenely at the vision. Ay did not yet realize who was *truly* in control of the throne, and his ignorance gave Nefertiti a distinct advantage.

Suddenly the desire to have her vengeance, to pay back her father for all the pain he had wrought in her life and Mutbenret's—and the pain his greed and ambition had forced Nefertiti to inflict upon her sister—reared up in her heart like a horse breaking free of its handler. She would use her new power to give Ay his due—to pay him back in kind. Oh, yes, she would guide Egypt as it needed guiding and be conscientious, a good ruler-from-the-shadows. But most of all, and before any other consideration, she would bring Ay's harvest in from the field. Now that the power was undeniably hers, nothing would stand in her way. She would pay back the grim debt Ay had incurred.

THAT EVENING, alone in the privacy of her chamber, Nefertiti sipped at a cup of warm wine, hoping the lulling sweetness might overtake her worries and coax sleep to her side. The hour was late, and most of her maids had retired to their small chambers down the hall, so the light tap at her outer door surprised her.

For a moment she wondered whether it was Akhenaten out there in the corridor, seeking the crude use of her body. Only yesterday, that notion would have flooded her with relief—for if the king was coming to Nefertiti's bed, then he hadn't yet aimed his bow for Meritaten. But now Nefertiti felt a surge of annoyance, a rapid welling of exasperation so strong it made her queasy. It was she who controlled Egypt now, not that skulking creature Akhenaten. And there was no good reason why Nefertiti should suffer the Pharaoh's despicable touch any longer.

Her night maid came bowing into her bed chamber, and the faintly amused lift of the woman's brows told Nefertiti that it was not the Pharaoh who'd come tapping at her door.

"Who is it?" Nefertiti asked.

"Nann, my lady."

Nefertiti pursed her lips in thought. The name was vaguely familiar, but she could not place it.

"The maid of King's Wife Kiya," the night maid added.

"Ah." She recalled the pert Hurrian servant with the missing front tooth. *What does Kiya want with me?* Her irritation was replaced in a heartbeat by suspicion.

Nann bowed low when Nefertiti swept into the receiving room. When the woman straightened, she leaned rather presumptuously toward Nefertiti, and her whispered words lisped through the gap in her teeth. "Great Wife, my mistress begs an audience with you."

"What, now?" Nefertiti scoffed.

"It must be now," Nann murmured. "The king cannot know."

Nefertiti blinked at the woman in dull confusion. "Where, then? This had best be truly urgent, Nann, or I'll be very displeased with you *and* Lady Kiya."

"Believe me, Great Wife, it's of the utmost importance. Kiya waits in the central garden, near the little house where Sitamun lived."

Nefertiti pulled on a violet over-robe to cover her sleeping shift, then paused in her doorway while Nann slipped away into the dark of the corridor. When a long enough interval had elapsed that no observer could think the two walked together, Nefertiti set off after Nann. Even her soft-soled slippers raised faint echoes from the tile floors, and every step clicked and repeated among the shadows that roofed the pillars of the corridor. Long before she passed beneath the garden portico, striding out into the wash of moonlight that paled the blue-dim garden, the fine hairs on Nefertiti's arms stood on end. She moved quickly along the path toward Sitamun's old chambers, her spine prickling as if the eyes of a predator tracked her between the flower beds.

When she reached the small, round pond outside Sitamun's apartments, Kiya stepped out from behind a cluster of date palms. The Hurrian's hands were clasped in a posture of unease, but she smiled in welcome as Nefertiti approached.

Nefertiti realized with some startlement that she hadn't spoken to Kiya privately for a long time—since the days before Baketaten arrived at court. The Pharaoh had quickly grown distracted by his newest wife, and Kiya seemed all too happy to vanish from his thoughts, hiding in her beautiful, private palace at the northern end of the valley, a timid mouse in a gilded hole.

Now that Baketaten has done the impossible and birthed a son, the king may give her the palace instead, Nefertiti thought. She eyed Kiya critically, taking in the woman's meek posture, her downcast eyes, robbed of their vivid green color by the veil of moonlight. *She hasn't changed, in all the long months since I spoke with her last. Always humble, always sweet.* No doubt that humble nature meant that Kiya would raise no protest if—*when*—the Pharaoh gifted the northern palace to his new pet wife. Perhaps she would even be grateful to fall from Akhenaten's favor. *I believe it's seclusion our little mouse values, and not the fine adornments of her lair.*

"You have some important business with me?" Nefertiti prompted.

Kiya turned to Nann and spoke a few low words of dismissal. The maid drifted back down the path, far enough to offer privacy, but near enough to give the alarm if anyone approached.

"You are well?" Kiya asked.

Nefertiti lifted a brow. "Quite."

The Hurrian also affirmed her health, then launched into an unnecessary, if rather amusing, tale about one of her servants. At first Nefertiti felt annoyed, impatient to return to her bedchamber. But Kiya's story was rather entertaining, and despite her irritation, Nefertiti gave a low chuckle. It occurred to her that Kiya was lonely, and only wished to share her little stories, her thoughts and feelings, with a friend. Soon Nefertiti's annoyance evaporated completely, and she was surprised to find pleasure in the other woman's company. *Perhaps I am lonely, too—or at least in need of a distraction from my worries.*

As Kiya laughed softly over one of her anecdotes, the corners of her eyes creased, and the tracks of fine lines spread across her pale, freckled cheeks. They were the same lines, the same creases, Nefertiti had noted in her own reflection.

We will soon be old women, Nefertiti thought sadly. *Or past our middle years, at least. How strange it is, that Kiya and I have spent our adult lives in virtually the same manner—married to the same man, shouldering the same burdens, subject to the same expectations. We even share the lines on our faces.*

They should have been friends, Nefertiti knew. They should have grown as close as sisters. They had suffered identical pains, endured similar woes. They could have understood one another, if they'd tried, and given each other comfort. But they had lived all these years as distant as the bitterest enemies.

Kiya's amusing tale of servants' follies soon took a darker turn. "It's well that it was only spoiled milk causing all this evil," Kiya said. "As soon as my maid Iah started vomiting, I was sure the plague had reached the northern palace, and we were all just sitting at death's door."

Nefertiti chewed her lip. *Plague. It always comes back to the plague.* Sooner or later, every conversation in Akhet-Aten veered toward that persistent illness. It lurked behind every story and hung like a curse between the notes of every song.

Kiya's chatter finally ceased. She fell into an awkward silence, obviously aware that Nefertiti's mood had shifted.

"I've been doing everything I can to eradicate the plague," Nefertiti said rather defensively. "Or to find some way to counter its worst effects, if any way exists. But no matter what the stewards and guards suggest, no matter what charms the magicians prescribe, it keeps coming back again." The damnable illness was as regular as the river's flood, and was proving to be just as permanent.

"You have been working very hard to stop the disease," Kiya said carefully. "I have noticed."

"Well, someone must do the work. It's certain the Pharaoh will do nothing."

Kiya hesitated, peering off into the garden's dim shadows almost shyly. Then she said, "Don't you wish to lay down that burden, Nefertiti? Wouldn't you like to return to a gentler life?"

Nefertiti laughed. She wished for her wine cup, just so that she might raise a salute to Kiya's foolish innocence. "What choice do I have but to carry the burden? I do what I must, because *somebody* must."

And a week ago, or only that very morning, her words would have been the entirety of the truth. But now a sly, compelling current ran through Nefertiti's heart, and she thought, *No, Kiya, I don't want to return to a gentler life—a life of waiting on Akhenaten's whim, or my father's. Ay raised me to rule, taught me the skills any king needs, though even he didn't see it, for all he prides himself on his keen observation. The throne should be mine. This is no burden to me.* Maat *is never a burden to the righteous. And even if it were, I would not surrender it for anything. Not now—now that I see what I may do with this power.*

Kiya fidgeted, glancing about the garden as if she suspected demons among the flower beds. Nefertiti opened her mouth to ask whether Kiya was keeping back some secret, but the Hurrian spoke first.

"I know something, Nefertiti—something I've kept concealed from you, and everybody else, for many years. But I tell you now because I believe it might be of use to you—and to the whole city, stricken as we are by this plague and hemmed in by Mahu's soldiers. Perhaps there is a way to break the Pharaoh's grip on us all."

Now it was Nefertiti who peered about the garden, eyeing the path and the dark, empty windows of Sitamun's old quarters to be sure there were no servants lurking, no soldiers listening. Finally she gestured for Kiya to speak.

"You remember, of course, how all the land mourned when Thutmose was killed—and mourned doubly when the King's Son Smenkhkare followed him in death."

"Of course," Nefertiti replied, stifling her impatience.

"What would you say if I told you Smenkhkare didn't die? It was all a ruse—an arrangement meant to protect him, and hold him in reserve in case a new Pharaoh was needed."

Nefertiti stared at her flatly. Finally she overcame her shock enough to speak. "But we saw Smenkhkare buried. I personally was there; I saw his body wrapped in its death-shroud and sealed in his coffins."

Kiya shook her head. "It was the body of a child similar to Smenkhkare in age and size. Tiy spirited Smenkhkare away to the north, and there he has remained, waiting for the call to return to the capital city and take his place as the heir to the throne."

Fury engulfed Nefertiti, hot and fierce. Such an elaborate scheme—and one so successful—*would* come from Tiy's heart. She said abruptly, "But the throne has its heir now. Tutankhaten—"

"Tutankhaten is only a baby," Kiya said. "He provides some security, I will grant you. But he will not be old enough to rule yet for many years. Smenkhkare, on the other hand, is twenty-five years old, and surely Tiy has not neglected to see to his education—proper training for an heir and ruler."

Nefertiti struggled to keep from her face the stark emotions that assailed her: horror, shock, envy. But it was more than she could do. She felt her cool mask crumble, replaced by a cringe of insecurity, for which she instantly cursed herself.

Kiya was humble and retiring, but she was not dull-witted. She caught the look of fear and rage on Nefertiti's face, and her eyes widened. Kiya swallowed hard and gave Nefertiti a trembling smile.

She sees that it was a mistake to share her secret with me.

With a breathy little laugh that did not hide her desperation, Kiya attempted to undo the damage. "Well, after all, we don't know this Smenkhkare—the man he has become. He may be as mad as his brother. Or worse! It's a gamble, to recall an unknown man to the throne. And what would we do with him once he was here? Akhenaten wouldn't like it, and—"

"Who else knows about this?"

Kiya shook her head, quick and emphatic. "No one. Only Sitamun knew, and she is no threat to anybody now."

Obviously Tiy knows. But even in Tiy's fallen state, Nefertiti did not care to match wits with her aunt. Could she act on this knowledge without approaching Tiy? A complicated equation tumbled through her thoughts, and she felt dizzy, disoriented, as if the stars reeled above her. *At least Tiy is still of no consequence. Without the support of Akhet-Aten's nobles—virtually all of them—she cannot recall Smenkhkare and put him on the throne. My throne.* No doubt, that was why Smenkhkare had remained in hiding for so many years. Tiy was as clever as she ever was, and Nefertiti was certain that her aunt still hungered after power, but Tiy was a political nobody. She was nothing now but a *stela* in the sands, a marker to commemorate a failed battle—a warning sign to any who had eyes to see.

I will not give my throne to Smenkhkare, Nefertiti decided with violent conviction, *nor to any other man. I am already more powerful than Akhenaten, though he doesn't know it yet. I can control him. Even if he rescinds my title and makes Baketaten the King's Great Wife, I have time, and now, knowing Smenkhkare is alive, I have leverage over the throne.*

But as I am, aging and barren, I would be cast off entirely by a new king. No—the throne is mine now, and mine it shall remain. At least until I've dealt with Ay.

After that, Tiy can do to Egypt whatever she pleases.

Kiya shifted, and peered over her shoulder at Sitamun's old quarters. A shiver ran through Nefertiti's blood. She recalled the pale image of Sitamun walking among the roses, reaching in anger toward the Pharaoh, vanishing again before *maat* could be done.

"Sitamun was the lucky one," Nefertiti muttered darkly. "Gone to the Underworld before this mess could reveal itself. The poor woman—all she wanted was for her daughter to be free of the Pharaoh, and look what's become of Baketaten. Look what's become of us all. Sitamun was the luckiest, and yet I pity her."

Kiya folded her arms tight beneath her breasts and raised one eyebrow. "Sitamun is not to be pitied, Nefertiti—believe me."

"Of course she is. Her daughter—"

"Sitamun was a cold-hearted killer."

Nefertiti stared at Kiya for a long while, squinting in disbelief. Then she gave a short, sharp burst of laughter. It echoed from the garden wall, and Nefertiti stifled herself with a hand over her mouth.

But Kiya did not laugh. "It was Sitamun who murdered Amunhotep."

Nefertiti drew back from Kiya, numb with shock. She waited for the sensation to abate, but the chill in her gut only intensified. Something in Kiya's demeanor—her wide, earnest eyes—spoke clearly of knowledge and truth.

If Sitamun killed Amunhotep, then she murdered Thutmose, too.

Sickening awareness dawned over Nefertiti. *It was Sitamun who killed my love, the brother of my heart. To think that I pitied her, and tried to live with her as a sister!*

But why would Sitamun do such a thing? Why take Thutmose's life? Nefertiti shook her head, staring blankly at the empty quarters—the smooth, unadorned mudbrick walls, the windows like the eye sockets of a skull. Had Sitamun simply been evil—a bad seed? If so, then the blight of her blood lived on in Baketaten, and in Baketaten's squalling boy.

They cannot be trusted, Nefertiti realized, her mouth going dry and her heart racing. *Neither Baketaten nor her child. They are both tainted by Sitamun's vileness, with the foul blood of a kin-killer.*

A bleak resolve grew like a stone monument in Nefertiti's heart. She must not allow the throne of the King's Great Wife to pass to Baketaten. And more importantly, her son, Tutankhaten, must never inherit the throne. The Two Lands had suffered all they could stand of tainted blood. The Horus Throne must be protected from the touch of a kin-slayer if Egypt were to have any hope of recovering from the chaos Akhenaten had wrought. Any wickedness was preferable to allowing inborn evil to rule for another generation.

And Kiya—she could not be trusted, either. Nefertiti saw that plainly. She knew too much, and the mouse was capable of much more than Nefertiti had ever suspected—involving herself in dark schemes, and keeping her silence for so many years. Now that the plague had made Kiya desperate enough to spill her long-tended secrets, she might dole out the same tale again—to anyone who might help her bring Smenkhkare to the City of the Sun.

And Nefertiti knew that there was only one man remaining who might offer Kiya the help she required: Ay.

He will not have this knowledge. Nefertiti, cool and composed again, watched Kiya's pretty face—a face that could have been as welcome and dear to her as a sister's. *I will see to it. I will do whatever I must to protect my kingdom from disaster. And Ay must never know that Smenkhkare still lives.*

"I TAKE MY ORDERS from the king." Mahu set his heavy bowl of beer on the table between them and gazed at Nefertiti with wry expectation.

It had taken several days to track down the chief of Akhenaten's soldiers. Soldiering had become quite popular in Akhet-Aten; it was the only job in the city that still afforded men any power, and so each day the young sons of the city's nobles competed to carve out a place in the Pharaoh's personal army. Mahu, naturally, remained quite busy, overseeing this force that grew vaster all the time—and more difficult for escaping citizens to evade. Nefertiti had been obliged to send her most trusted maids out into the city several times, seeking Mahu with an urgent message. With all those forays into streets and alleys, Nefertiti was more fearful than ever before that the plague might find its way into the palace. But her maids had done their duty well, and now Mahu sat before her, lazily toying with his beer in Nefertiti's receiving room, waiting on the negotiations to begin.

Nefertiti had always been disgusted by the huge, unfeeling man, with his hands that were apt to ball into fists at the slightest provocation and his face like a hunk of raw meat—square, red, tough and cold.

But he will be no more unpleasant to negotiate with than any ambassador or steward, she told herself firmly. *All men are the same inside their hearts. They all want something, and once one knows their desires, one may bring them to heel.*

"I understand that the king gives the orders," she said, "but Kiya poses a great threat to the Pharaoh himself. She must be removed before she can spread her treasonous influence to others and start an uprising against Akhenaten."

"I won't do it," he said. "Kiya is the king's favorite."

"Not anymore," Nefertiti countered. "The king has turned his heart toward Baketaten. And why not? Baketaten has given him a son—his only son—whereas Kiya has birthed but one daughter, and borne no other children for many years. She is nothing to him now."

"Still," Mahu insisted, "I take my orders from the king."

Curse you, she spat inside her heart, watching Mahu's slow, confident smile. *I am the true king now. Akhenaten is an ineffectual, corrupted freak who spends his days writhing in a beam of sunlight. Who do you think runs Egypt? Not he!*

But she bit her tongue and schooled her face to a placid mask. After all, Mahu was dangerous—his handling of those who tried to escape the plague proved just how cold and terrible he could be. He might decide to act on his own, independent of any order from the king, despite his assertions to the contrary. He might remove Nefertiti instead of Kiya, if she didn't place her pawns with care.

"I can pay you well," she said.

Mahu leaned back on his stool, eyeing her with speculation.

"Ten weights of gold," she said.

Mahu only laughed, a hoarse, deep rasp like a mason planing stone.

No matter, Nefertiti thought coolly. She had expected him to laugh. She had negotiated with cannier men than Mahu, and she knew that to open with her highest offer would only make her seem desperate and put her opponent at an advantage.

She feigned reluctant consideration, then said slowly, "Twenty. And I will give you that mirror on the wall—that one, there. Its frame is cedar—very expensive."

"Mmmm." He cupped his chin with one slab of a hand, gazed at her silently for a moment, then shook his head. "You speak of removing a King's Wife. Dangerous work. Surely a hazard so great is worth real compensation."

"Very well," Nefertiti said, "I will also give you a certain estate on the West Bank."

"The West Bank?" Mahu snorted. "What need have I of the West Bank? The throne is here in Akhet-Aten, and so I will remain here."

"Even a man as loyal as you might enjoy a holiday from his service now and then," Nefertiti said. "After all, your army has grown so large, with so many lieutenants and captains. Surely you can spare yourself some time now and then. Ay's estate was the finest in the West Bank—it still is, I have no doubt. And if you do this one small task for me, his great house will be yours."

"Ay's house?" Mahu tilted his head and hummed deep in his throat, as if he considered rejecting the deal. But Nefertiti, her eye sharpened by so many negotiations with much brighter, subtler men, noted the spark of greed in Mahu's lazy half-smile. She knew that Kiya was as good as dead already.

When Mahu left her, bowing and chuckling, she remained at the table, staring in silence at Mahu's empty beer bowl. A dull weight of shock settled in her gut. She could have been the closest friend to Kiya—*should* have been, in truth. But the salvation of Egypt was more important than any friendship, any woman or man. Nefertiti would not allow the throne to be wrested from her grip by any hands—not even hands she might have loved.

Meritaten

Year 14 of Akhenaten
Beautiful Are the Manifestations,
Exalting the Name,
Beloved of the Sun

A PAIR OF JUGGLERS MOVED with easy grace down the central aisle, their gold-powdered bodies slipping between the feast tables, passing brightly colored balls between them in an intricate, rapid blur. Reed flutes piped an energetic tune, and the drums clattered like water spilled from a fountain, a raucous, rolling cascade. It was the Feast of the Longest Day, a celebration of the extended blessings the Aten conferred upon the world when his holy light outlasted the night's dark. A joyous occasion, and Meritaten should have been free to immerse herself in the pleasures of the festival. Instead she had been relegated to the children's table, as if she were still a useless girl, just like all her sisters.

She scowled at her cup of watered wine, wishing the pipes would play even louder and drown out Meketaten's ceaseless, silly chatter about her pet cat.

"And then, can you guess what Miu-Miu did?" Meketaten said, heedless of Meritaten's obvious disinterest. "He jumped right on my lap and knocked my embroidery frame into the dust! Oh, he's terribly naughty, but I love him all the same."

Meritaten rolled her eyes and reached for a handful of dates. *If only Meketaten would stuff her mouth with dates*, she thought sourly, *and spare me all these pointless, dull cat stories!*

She sighed and peered over her shoulder at the royal dais. Her mother, as King's Great Wife, sat beside the Pharaoh. That was to be expected, of course. But Baketaten, as the king's favorite, also enjoyed the relative peace of an elevated seat, to say nothing of the honor and attention she received, so high above the heads of the noble guests, glittering like a star in the sky.

It's not fair. I'm a woman now, not a child. I am due more honor than this. True, her womanhood was only recently arrived—her first blood had come five days before. *But still, I am a lady of the court now, and no longer a child.*

Meritaten drank deeply from her thinned wine, imagining it was stronger stuff, wishing it would make her drunk and blot out Meketaten's inane ramblings and the squeals of the littlest girls as they squirmed and fussed beside their nurses.

At least Ankhesenpaaten was quiet, as usual. The girl had not quite reached her tenth year, but *she* understood the dignity a King's Daughter must assume, if none of Meritaten's other sisters did. Ankhesenpaaten nibbled at her food, watching the jugglers and acrobats perform with polite interest, only speaking when she was spoken to—and even then, her replies were pleasant enough, but brief.

If only Kayet would take her cue from Ankhesenpaaten! Kiya's daughter was sulky and morose, alternating between glaring at the other girls and bursting into tears as she clung to her nurse's arms or neck. It was embarrassing—behavior not becoming of a King's Daughter.

Of course, Meritaten couldn't truly blame Kayet for being so unstable. Her mother, Kiya, had vanished more than a week ago—simply disappeared from her northern palace one day when the Pharaoh sent a messenger to inform her that he would be paying a visit that night. No one could say where Kiya had gone, or so the rumors told—not even

MERITATEN

her Hurrian servant, who had been distraught, clinging to the other women and wailing, making a fool of herself until she was finally led away.

The back of Meritaten's neck tingled under the locks of her new, grown-woman's wig. She brushed at her skin, but he prickling sensation only grew more persistent. Slowly, she turned again and stared up at the dais. It looked eerily empty, with only two King's Wives beside the Pharaoh. Kiya should have been there, as she always had been before. Meritaten chewed her lip, wondering what truly had become of Kiya. If she'd fallen victim to the plague, the court would have heard the news before the illness claimed her. Or at least, her household servants would have known, and told the Pharaoh's messenger. But it seemed that Kiya had gone without any trace, and the mystery of it both titillated and worried Meritaten.

Tasherit began making a donkey of herself, packing bread into her cheeks until they puffed out like an inflated sheep's bladder. The twins squealed and clapped, and Tasherit's nurse scolded her, all the while fighting to keep the grin from her face. Meritaten sighed at the spectacle.

I'd give anything to be up on that dais with the King's Wives. She pictured herself there—how elegant and mature she would look to all the courtiers gathered below! How they would exclaim over her beauty, her grace, her fine taste, reflected in her gown and jewels! And how she would gaze back at the guests with cool detachment, as high above them as the sun at midday.

Baketaten gets to sit up there, gazing down at me with cool detachment. She probably gloats over her position every night. She's probably laughing silently at me, right now. I remember when she was just Nebetah, the unwanted child, hidden away in the corner of the garden. But look at her now, and look at me!

Everything was better for King's Wives. It simply wasn't fair.

I could be a King's Wife, too, if only the Aten would favor me. Baketaten was not much older than Meritaten herself. In fact, Baketaten was named King's Wife at age thirteen—the same age Meritaten was now. Thirteen—and with free access to everything Meritaten desired: jewels and silks and fine linens, a private apartment in the palace, and most of all, the affection of the Pharaoh. The king had once played games with Meritaten in the garden. He had kissed Meritaten's cheek, and patted her head and praised her, and brought her sweets and presents. Now, though, he seldom paid her heed at all, unless she happened to cross his path. Meritaten was forever cast from the Pharaoh's heart. He had no room in his thoughts for anything anymore, save for the Aten, Baketaten, and her baby boy.

The jugglers finished their act, and the feast hall broke into applause. Kitchen servants made their way through the aisles, clearing away empty dishes and presenting the final course—an array of candied fruits, arranged on each platter in the shape of the sun-disc encircled by rings of colorful sweets. Meritaten refused the sweets and turned her face away from the table as Meketaten began another boring tale of Miu-Miu.

She caught sight of Nefertiti on the dais. The Great Wife also turned away the candied fruits with an elegant shake of her head, and as she did so, she caught Meritaten's eye. Nefertiti watched her thoughtfully for a moment, then nodded surreptitiously toward the portico and the garden beyond.

Meritaten glanced around, certain Nefertiti had invited someone else to stroll with her in the garden. But there was no one nearby of any consequence, and when she looked up at the dais again, Nefertiti smiled lightly at her, an amused confirmation.

Meritaten pushed back her stool and rose quickly.

"Where are you going?" Meketaten said. "I'm coming,

too!"

The younger girl made as if to rise, but Meritaten pushed her back down with a hand on top of her head. "I'm only going to the privy. Don't be such a goose; I'll be back before you know it. Stay here with Ankhesenpaaten. She can't wait to hear more stories about Miu-Miu."

Ankhesenpaaten looked up from the platter of fruits with goggling eyes, but Meritaten spun away from the table. The guests had begun to leave their tables, too. Men in their long, formal kilts mingled with women in vibrant linens and silks; laughter and half-drunken song rang loud among the pillars. Meritaten dodged and wove into the crowd, then pushed beyond to the open air of the garden. A group of servants moved about the portico, lighting dozens of bright-glazed lamps. The lamps and their flames shimmered in the darkness of the portico like the night's earliest stars.

A late twilight had fallen at last over the garden, just beginning to touch the paths and ponds with the dim, soothing violet of night. Nefertiti was unmistakable, moving with her characteristic grace through the veils of evening. Meritaten glided to her mother's side, keeping her hands clasped at her waist in a manner she hoped was elegant and dignified.

"A lovely night," Nefertiti said. They moved down the path together, and Meritaten finally felt like the woman she was—poised and admirable, worthy of quiet conversation with the King's Great Wife.

"Did you enjoy the feast?"

Nefertiti dismissed the question with a wave of her hand. "It was a feast like all the hundreds of feasts that came before it. Did you enjoy it?"

Meritaten shrugged. "I would have liked it more if I weren't seated with the children." She watched her mother carefully from the corner of her eye, hopeful that

Nefertiti would pick up on her hint.

"Where would you prefer to sit, if not with your royal sisters?"

"The dais would be lovely. I'm a King's Daughter, so I'm nearly as important as a King's Wife."

"At the next feast, I shall see that you're placed beside Baketaten."

Meritaten wrinkled her nose. "I would rather sit beside you."

"You don't like Baketaten, do you?" Nefertiti observed.

"How can I like her? She's so cool and unapproachable, as if she thinks she's made of gold! And she has everything—a fine apartment, and all the jewels and wealth she could hope for, while I am stuck living like a child. But I'm not a child! I am a woman now."

"Do you long for Baketaten's life?"

"Yes," Meritaten admitted. "She lives in ease and beauty, *and* she has the affection of the king."

Nefertiti drifted from the garden path toward a small, round pool. The water's surface was as dark as indigo dye; it shone like a well-polished mirror. The stars of early evening reflected in its surface, and as Meritaten gazed at the simple beauty, carp rose from the pond's depth, dimpling the surface of the pool with their mouths, shattering the sky's reflection.

At last, Nefertiti broke her pensive silence. "You can have all the things Baketaten has, too." Her words carried a clear note of confidence, but a shadow passed across her face. Meritaten could see that ripple of doubt clearly, even in the dimness of the evening.

"All the things Baketaten has? What do you mean, exactly?"

Nefertiti did not answer for a long time. She watched

the fish rising in the pond, and her lovely face was still and sad. But finally she looked up and smiled lightly at Meritaten. "I have a great duty for you—a task. Now that Kiya is gone, the Pharaoh needs another King's Wife. Why should it not be you?"

Meritaten's eyes widened. Her heart leaped with disbelief, and her spine tingled with a sudden, wild thrill.

"Would you like that?" Nefertiti said.

Meritaten could hardly manage to answer. Her throat was tight with anticipation and possibility. "To be a King's Wife—oh, it would be so grand! But I am a King's Daughter. I can't take on the role... can I?"

"You can." Nefertiti's mouth tightened, and again Meritaten had the impression that her mother was not entirely pleased. But she went on. "I will see to it that the king accepts you as his wife, but under this very important condition: you must remain close to me. We shall work together, you and I, to keep the king's favor."

To keep his favor, and shepherd him, like a pair of rekhet *girls driving a gander down the road*. That was Nefertiti's meaning—her purpose. Meritaten couldn't say what it was in her mother's voice or stance that said those words so clearly, but she heard Nefertiti's true meaning, as loud as if the Great Wife had shouted in her ear. Briefly, Meritaten wondered how it could even be possible, for two women to control a king. *But if it means having the life of a King's Wife—the private apartment and all the fine, luxurious things...* She was willing to try, willing to make herself her mother's ally. She would do anything, if it meant she could rise to the very pinnacle of the court.

"I'll do it," Meritaten said.

"Don't be so quick to agree. You must do... *certain things* as a King's Wife. If the idea is disagreeable to you, say so now, while you can still decline. For after you're wedded to Akhenaten, there will be no denying him."

"Tell me."

Meritaten sat on the pond's wall and Nefertiti sank down slowly, reluctantly, beside her. As the twilight deepened, then finally yielded its soft, violet glow to the deepness of true night, Nefertiti explained the duties of a King's Wife, speaking in halting, almost bashful terms. Meritaten listened in silence. Somehow it had never occurred to her before, in all her daydreaming about King's Wives and the enviable lives they led, precisely what it meant for a woman to serve the king.

As Nefertiti's explanations continued, Meritaten felt a moment of blinding revulsion—a hard, fast roiling in her gut—over the thought of lying with her father. But then she thought of the daily processions to the temple—the citizens shouting their acclaim as the royal family drove their chariot down the broad avenue. She recalled how the nobles gathered below the Window of Appearances, begging the favor of the king—and of the King's Wives.

They worship Akhenaten, she realized with a quivering thrill. *As he worships the god, so the people worship him—and my mother, though perhaps she does not see it. Or perhaps she wishes to ignore it.*

If I am a King's Wife, they will worship me, too. I will be like a goddess on the earth.

"I'll do it," she said. "I'll work with you. I will do whatever I must to become a King's Wife." *To become as divine and untouchable as the sun itself.*

"Good," Nefertiti said. But her smile was sad, and had something of self-loathing in it.

Meritaten gazed up at her mother gratefully and took her hand. She couldn't understand why Nefertiti should look so despondent. Wasn't it the very finest thing, to be a goddess on the earth?

THE REALITIES OF BEING a King's Wife far outstripped Meritaten's expectations—and even her most wistful hopes. Nefertiti's wedding gift to Meritaten was the little northern palace that had belonged to Kiya. Meritaten gleefully moved in, and began ordering her household—her *own* household!—as she saw fit. She sent to the best markets in Akhet-Aten, buying new furnishings and fine ornaments for all the rooms. She filled the menagerie stalls with her own pets, and hired as many servants as she pleased to tend the beasts and her little, sweet-smelling, entirely private garden. The palace was hers—all of it—and best of all, her noisy, clamoring, meddling sisters were nowhere to be seen. In the seclusion of the palace, alone on her high walls with only the cliffs and the temple in her view, Meritaten could pretend that she was the only woman in the world—or at least, the only King's Wife in Akhet-Aten.

Her duties as a wife began at once, of course, only hours after the wedding. But Nefertiti had told her what to expect, and Meritaten was well prepared. She wore a face of hard bronze, showing so little emotion that she soon found that she felt no emotion, either. Indeed, there were still moments when Meritaten's skin crawled or her stomach turned, but most often she found herself able to shut her eyes and ignore her unappealing task, which after all was not physically trying, and was usually finished with merciful speed. The filthy residue she sometimes felt settling onto her skin was worth the reward of the palace, the riches that filled her chests and wardrobes, and certainly worth the acclaim of the court.

Meritaten had grown up a King's Daughter, and so she had been praised for many things—beauty, perseverance, and charm—but never for keen intelligence. Still, even she was bright enough to grasp what specific role Nefertiti wished her to play, her true purpose in the machinations of the Great Wife. Meritaten was intended to replace Kiya.

Nefertiti meant her as a sop to the Pharaoh's emotions, a distraction from Kiya's strange and tragic loss. Because she was determined to do her work well—to be worthy of her new place in the world—Meritaten did her best to emulate Kiya in all things. She adopted the Hurrian's downcast, shy looks; her reserve; her appealing mildness, even though such affectations ran counter to Meritaten's nature.

Most days, she felt she did a passable job of wearing Kiya's mask, and the Pharaoh certainly seemed charmed by her efforts. The guise became so familiar to her that she donned it without thinking, and sometimes even displayed Kiya's habits and spoke with her soft, self-deprecating tones in the privacy of her palace.

But she could not maintain that Kiya-like distance and calm all the time. And one day, a month after her wedding, as the family concluded worship at the Great Aten Temple, Kiya's mask fell away entirely, and the old, true Meritaten reared up in her place.

The line of girls had just begun to file out of the sanctuary, all of them naked as usual, save for Meketaten, who had just experienced her first blood. Kayet's sorrow over her mother's disappearance had never abated. If anything, the girl had only grown more withdrawn, and Meritaten could see Kayet's distraction as she went blindly through the motions of the ceremony. As the girls passed, Kayet staggered in the deep sand, blundering hard into Meritaten's shoulder.

Meritaten was thrown off balance; she was obliged to catch herself against one of her father's great statues to keep from falling face-first into the hot sand. Her crown flew from her head, landing in a puff of dust on the sanctuary floor, and the stone of the statue scraped her palms.

Meritaten righted herself and jerked her white priestess's

robe straight. The king and Nefertiti were sequestered with the Ben-ben stone, and so it fell to Meritaten to handle Kayet's insubordination on her own. She retrieved her crown from the sand, shook it clean, and rounded on Kayet, scowling.

"What was that for, you clumsy cow?"

"It was only an accident," Kayet muttered.

"An accident—ha! That was no mistake. You shoved me, you envious flea!"

Kayet's eyes narrowed, and she braced her fists on narrow hips. "Why ever should I envy *you?*"

"Because I'm a King's Wife, and you are nothing!"

"King's Wife, indeed! You aren't half the King's Wife my mother was."

"Your mother ran away and abandoned you, so what do you care for her, anyway?"

Baketaten glided over smoothly from the direction of the Ben-ben stone, and stepped between Kayet and Meritaten. "Don't fight," she said with a note of confident command.

To Meritaten's annoyance, she found herself obeying that assertive tone without hesitation.

"My mother didn't run away," Kayet cried. "She would never have left me here! She is dead—*dead!* And *you* had her killed, Meritaten!"

Meritaten was so shocked that she forgot the dignity of a King's Wife and gasped aloud. The younger girls stopped fidgeting in their line and stared, open-mouthed.

"That's ridiculous," Meritaten said. "Don't dare to insult me with your vile accusations!"

"You *did* do it!" Kayet was screeching now, leaning across the restraint of Baketaten's arm. "You killed her—why else would you have her palace now?"

"Because the Pharaoh favors me," Meritaten said calmly. She cast a sideways glance at Baketaten. "I had no need to kill anybody, least of all your mother, who was useless years ago and already half-forgotten."

"I don't believe you!"

Kayet dodged around Baketaten, swift as a darting fish, and swung her fist through the hot air. She was not a strong girl, and the one blow she landed on Meritaten's cheek barely hurt at all. Baketaten caught Kayet around the shoulders and pulled her back. She warned the girl to stillness with a foreboding glare.

Meritaten pressed her hand against her cheek, but she was more shocked than injured. She gaped at Kayet for a moment, astounded, robbed of speech. Soon enough, though, the words came hurtling back into her heart and spilled from her tongue like a serpent's venom. "You beast! You filthy creature! How dare you strike a King's Wife?"

"I'm not afraid of you," Kayet growled.

"You ought to be. I have more power than you can imagine!"

Baketaten, still restraining Kayet, gave a delicate snort of amusement.

Meritaten rounded on the other King's Wife, burning with rage. "So you think I have no power, Baketaten? And you, Kayet? Then consider this: *I banish you, Kayet. You must leave Akhet-Aten at once!*"

Kayet gasped, and her eyes filled with tears. "Banish me? You can't!"

"I can. Allow me to remind you that I am King's Wife, since you have clearly forgotten." Again she touched her stinging cheek. "You'll go off to Annu, far in the north, to become a priestess of Aten in some old, crumbling temple. Just *see* if I can't make it happen. I'll tell the Pharaoh, and he'll think it a splendid idea to send you off for priestess training, and you'll be gone by sunset. You'd best start packing your little bags when you return to your chamber. The journey is a very long one."

The tears spilled over Kayet's cheeks.

The girl must see now, Meritaten thought with satisfaction, *that what I say is true.* And her threat had been no bluster. If she put the idea into Akhenaten's heart, he would think it utterly brilliant to send Kayet away to learn the arts of the priestess in Aten's ancient town.

"I don't want to go to Annu," Kayet sobbed.

Surely not. Akhet-Aten was the only home Kayet had known since her earliest days. Certainly the prospect was terrifying—being thrown out into the wide, cruel, unknown world without her mother or even a friend to guide her. But Meritaten did not relent or withdraw her terrible threat.

Baketaten's grip on the girl's shoulders loosened. She slid one arm around Kayet, pulling her into a comforting embrace. "Don't weep," Baketaten said. "If you are sent away, you'll be one of the lucky ones."

"Lucky?" Kayet sniffed miserably.

"Yes. Once you're outside the boundaries of Akhet-Aten, beyond where Mahu's guards can get you, look for an opportunity to escape. Simply run away—you *can* do that much, once you're past Mahu's reach. The Pharaoh will not try to catch you. His attention is here, at the temple. You can slip away and make a new life for yourself in some other town. You'll be free of this madness for good."

"Madness?" Meritaten scowled at her fellow King's Wife. "Be careful I don't send *you* off, too."

Baketaten threw back her head and laughed. The sound of it rebounded from the temple walls, mocking and sharp. "Just try to root me out of the palace, you ignorant fool. It's my own domain. I belong there far more than you do. It's mine, perhaps even more than it is Nefertiti's—or Akhenaten's."

"You think you're so grand," Meritaten hissed, "just because you've had a son. Well, he is only the *first* son to be born to the Pharaoh. I'll give the king more sons—better sons, and stronger. Then you won't ride so high on your horse."

"Oh, will you?" Baketaten smiled coldly. "Meritaten thinks to give the Pharaoh a son—I wonder if it will come to pass. I wonder if you can."

"I will," Meritaten vowed, "and when I do, you had best watch your back."

"Come, girls," Baketaten said to the assembled children. "Worship is done for the day. Kayet, dry your eyes." The girls resumed their line and turned for the temple gate, with Baketaten taking up the rear. But she hung back, and when the children had moved well ahead she turned back to Meritaten with a grim smile. "It's not I who should watch my back," she said softly.

And the confidence in her voice—the crackling, black fire in her eyes—made Meritaten shiver.

Nefertiti

*Year 14 of Akhenaten
Beautiful Are the Manifestations,
Exalting the Name,
Beloved of the Sun*

THE YEAR DREW to a welcome close. The Feast of the Year's End—the last before the New Year celebrations would begin—bubbled over with real joy, with honest laughter and ready warmth. The plague that had gripped Akhet-Aten tightly for so many months hadn't re-emerged from its filthy trenches in several weeks—a longer respite than the city had yet seen, and every man and woman in the City of the Sun felt justified in celebrating.

Nefertiti wasn't fool enough to believe the plague had finally gone. Disease had a way of resurfacing just when it was thought eradicated, and she was braced for another outbreak. But the interval since the last eruption of illness had been a long one, and she dared to feel some small measure of hope. Perhaps when the plague returned, it would not be as harsh. Perhaps it would take fewer lives— or none at all. She had no way of knowing what to expect when it came again, but the present lull was encouraging, and Nefertiti allowed the festive air in the great hall to buoy her heart.

Meritaten lounged comfortably on a great, gilded chair to Nefertiti's left hand. She laughed with appreciation as a troupe of tumblers entered the hall, springing hand over foot, trailing the wisps of silk that served as their costumes through the myrrh-scented air. Nefertiti smiled at her daughter, and passed her a dish of figs. Meritaten was quite suitable as a King's Wife. The girl had embraced the work so completely that Nefertiti often chided herself for the way she had once fretted over her safety. True, this marriage of father to daughter was strange, and still struck her now and again with a faint sensation of distaste. But Meritaten seemed no worse for the arrangement. In fact she had embraced it, and appeared to thrive in the self-contained realm of her little northern palace.

Is it Akhenaten's blood in her veins that causes her to enjoy such filthy activities? Is his madness her birthright, and has it gripped her already? She thought it better not to question the arrangement. So long as Meritaten remained in the king's favor, then Nefertiti's purposes were served.

Meritaten had taken to her role so readily that no one spoke of the little northern palace as Kiya's any longer. Indeed, with Kayet sent off to Annu to learn the ancient ways of the sun cult, no one in Akhet-Aten mentioned Kiya at all. The Hurrian had spent her final years studiously vanishing. Now it seemed that she had done her job too well. Kiya had made herself so invisible that in the end she was not missed—not truly. If the Pharaoh hadn't had Baketaten to distract him, he might have grieved more for Kiya's unexplained disappearance, but his devotion to the sun god and to the watchful, enigmatic new King's Wife kept Akhenaten well occupied. The pale, half-seen ghost of Kiya's memory faded more each day. Nefertiti was nearly able to forget, most days—in the light of day, at least—that the woman's disappearance had been her own doing.

Meritaten's rise to the throne had combined with the recession of the plague to produce an unexpectedly grand result. The newest King's Wife was obviously Nefertiti's close ally—naturally, of course—and the easing of the plague's crisis shifted the subtle balance of power more firmly in Nefertiti's favor. Without the need to desperately face down the ravaging disease, Nefertiti was more stable on her shadowy throne than ever before. Ay evidently sensed this, and kept his distance, retreating from all but the most necessary of court functions. Apparently, Nefertiti realized with smug satisfaction, Ay felt no more need to ingratiate himself with the king, no need to insert himself into the throne room so that he might apply himself more readily toward future meddling.

The simple absence of Ay made Nefertiti's *ka* soar freer than it had since the days of her youth. She was secure in her strength. The spirit of *maat* sat with her upon the dais, guiding her hand where it rested on the Pharaoh's shoulder. In the weeks prior to the Feast of the Year's End she had almost begun to enjoy life in Akhet-Aten—and would have enjoyed it in truth, if not for the continued complaints of the northern territories, the tangle of which still needed unraveling.

Ah, well, she told herself, watching contentedly as the acrobats cavorted among the guests' tables, *time enough to put the north in order after the New Year.* She was certain the puzzle of the north could be solved, its broken pieces mended. And she felt every confidence, deep and reassuring, in her own ability. She had done better as the shadow-Pharaoh than Akhenaten had done in the light— the glaring, hot, unfeeling light of his beloved sun.

The acrobats finished their routine, bowed to the throne, and filed from the hall. Nefertiti lifted her hand to gesture for more entertainment, but Akhenaten rose to his feet, holding up his hands for silence.

Nefertiti turned to him, irritated that he would presume to intrude upon the festivities she had arranged—until she recalled that he was the Pharaoh, in name if not in truth. She smoothed the scowl from her face and smiled at her husband with mild curiosity.

"I have news," Akhenaten said. His voice carried down

the great length of the feast hall, echoing faintly from its rear wall. "Wonderful, joyous news."

The crowd quieted, waiting on the king's announcement, and as the court's last murmurs died away a chill of foreboding crept up Nefertiti's back.

Akhenaten beamed out at the court, soft-eyed, his smile wide and dreamy. "I wish to tell you all that my newest King's Wife, my own beautiful daughter, is with child."

Nefertiti turned to Meritaten, her brows raised in surprise. Meritaten had been as good as her word, and had met regularly with Nefertiti, disclosing whatever information she had learned of the king's plans, his ambitions and dreams. But as closely as they'd worked together, Nefertiti had heard nothing of this news. Nor had she seen any sign of pregnancy about Meritaten's body—no swelling of the breasts, no change in her skin or hair.

Meritaten stared back at her, brow furrowed in confusion. Then she shook her head at her mother, and mouthed, *No.*

"It's only his madness." Nefertiti breathed the words so softly in Meritaten's ear that not even the servants at the foot of the dais could hear. *A delusion—a fantasy brought about by his wild zeal.*

She felt the court's collective gaze shift from Akhenaten to Meritaten, to Nefertiti beside her, and she withered inside with embarrassment. *What a curse, that the king's mad fantasy should play out before the entire court! The gods have saddled me with a fool for a husband, and left Egypt with a madman on the throne.*

But a heartbeat later, that wilting embarrassment turned to hot, panicked disbelief—and mortification, too. The flame of rage leapt in Nefertiti's gut. For Akhenaten gestured to the side of the dais, and from behind the heavy winter draperies that flowed down the soaring pillars, little Meketaten emerged. Her face, still round with the softness of childhood, hung shyly downcast. She climbed the steps of the dais in utter silence; not a breath, not even a gasp of shock, came from the assembled crowd.

Nefertiti's face heated in horror; tears of helpless fury sprang to her eyes.

I gave you Meritaten, she hissed silently at the king, within the confines of her pounding heart. *I sacrificed one daughter to you. Wasn't she enough?*

Certainly Nefertiti had not consented to Akhenaten taking Meketaten as a King's Wife, and never would have allowed the girl into his bed. *She is not yet twelve!* The girl was far too soft and fragile-hearted to withstand any form of abuse, unlike her more ambitious and self-driven sister.

Nefertiti's stomach roiled on the rich foods of the feast. The dais seemed to close around her, a trap snapping shut about a wild creature. It pinned her, weak and helpless, before the eyes of the court. For the damage done to Meketaten was terrible enough, but the Pharaoh had just confessed, before hundreds of witnesses, to treating young girls—his own daughters, barely entered into womanhood!—like harem ornaments, plucked and used for his pleasure. Her heart plunged into her gut; guilt flooded her limbs.

She fought back the urge to leap to her feet and scream defenses, accusations—excuses—at the court. *Ours is the divine blood*, she might have cried. *We do as the gods do, for we are gods on earth!*

But gods wed brother to sister, not father to daughter.

And Meketaten was far too young.

The girl came obediently to Akhenaten's side and stood, flushed with a pink tint of shame. She met no one's eye while the king stroked her bare shoulder and kissed the top of her head.

The silence in the hall was absolute, as present and towering as the colossal statues inside the Great Aten

Temple. The sharp, judging stares of every nobleman and every lady bore into Nefertiti's flesh, burrowing toward her heart, and although she was raised high above them on the dais, she felt as if she crouched in the temple's hot sand with the glare of a thousand condemnations beating down from above.

She snapped her fingers at the gaping musicians. "Play," she commanded, her voice an inelegant croak in the silence.

The musicians struck up a cheery tune, its notes swaying drunkenly, faltering amid the shocked whispers and wide-eyed stares of the court. Desperately, Nefertiti urged them to play louder. But even as the notes of the harp and lute clamored up toward the high ceiling, drowning out the murmurs of the guests, Nefertiti's heart pounded louder in her ears. Nothing could quiet its hard, terrible beat.

THE FEAST CAME to a merciful close in a clamor of forced cheer, and Nefertiti swept from the dais and out of the hall at her first opportunity. The Pharaoh, too, had gone, smiling softly to himself as he walked through the feast hall. A way had cleared before him as the court drew back from his presence in fear and disgust, but he did not notice his subjects' disapproval.

Nefertiti took a circuitous route toward his chambers, but fury drove her stride, and she reached the colonnade outside his apartments just as the king did. She caught Akhenaten by his arm. Her fingers with their sharp nails locked into the flesh of his inner elbow so tightly that he cried out in alarm, and Nefertiti gave a great wrench, whirling him about. The flash of fear in his eyes—the bald panic—gratified her, but when he realized it was only Nefertiti who confronted him, and not the shadowy assassins he feared, all his fear evaporated. A slow, mocking smile spread across his womanish lips.

"What in the name of the sun are you *doing?*" Nefertiti shouted. "Meketaten? I gave you *Meritaten* for a wife! And yet you have dared to touch another of my daughters!"

"Your daughter—and my wife," he said calmly.

"Meketaten is not your wife."

"She is," Akhenaten replied coolly.

"By what authority? I witnessed no wedding!"

"By my own authority," he said, amused. "I am the Pharaoh, Nefertiti. It is within my power to wed as I will—you recall how I took Kiya and Sitamun into my household that day at the Circuit of the Sun."

"You had no right," she cried, "Pharaoh or not! No right to touch her!"

He scowled at her a moment, then opened his door and ushered her inside his chamber, where at least their quarrel would not be exposed to the eyes of the palace servants. The interior was already lit, lamps glowing against the winter's darkness with a cheer that mocked Nefertiti's helpless rage.

When the door was safely shut again, Nefertiti rounded on him. "No right," she repeated. "You are a hideous, predatory monster!"

He took her outburst calmly. "I am a king. And I am much more than any king who has come before me. You told me yourself, Nefertiti, that your numerous daughters were a sign of fertility—of the might of creation. Each and every one of them is like goddess to me, a bringer of yet more fecundity, a vessel through which I shall express my greatest power."

No, she thought in panic. Her golden necklaces suddenly felt much too tight around her throat, and she clawed at them like a feral dog struggling to free itself from a collar.

The king went on, "Through my daughters, I will conceive

a new, godly line. The children I sire upon them will bear elements of the Aten within their flesh and blood. They will be gods in truth—new gods for Egypt."

"You're mad. As mad as your father ever was—*worse!*"

"Meketaten is part of my ascendancy," he said, as if she hadn't flung the accusation of madness at his feet. "As the first to bear my divine issue, she is the most blessed. But her sisters will join her in that holy work, when the time is right for each—when the Aten decrees it."

Frantically, Nefertiti shook her head. "No. *Never*. It shall never happen. I'll send to the city for an herb-woman; Meketaten will be freed from this, and she'll go off to a temple, just as your sisters did, where she can be safe from you. You'll never see her again! Nor will you see the others. I'll send them all away—Meritaten, too!"

"An herb-woman?" Akhenaten's eyes lost their dreamy distance, sharpening on Nefertiti's face with sudden hatred. "Try to find one in the City of the Sun. They've all been driven out—filthy, murderous whores."

"Driven out?"

"Mahu saw to it long ago, at my command. I'll suffer no one in my city who goes against the will of the god—who casts children from the womb!"

"Then I'll send to Waset," she said. Her heart counseled her to silence—for she knew that if she concealed her plan from Akhenaten, then perhaps it stood some small chance of success. But her tongue disregarded that wise advice and ran on without her, goaded by the terror that flooded her. "There are herb-women by the hundreds in Waset! I'll bring them all here—every last one!"

"By the god, you will not." His voice was low, dangerous, and his eyes glittered with grim promise.

But a far greater danger drove Nefertiti on. "It will kill Meketaten to give birth! She is too small, too young!"

"She is protected by the Aten. Don't be such a fool; you're hysterical."

"She is protected by *me* now," Nefertiti said fiercely. "And she shall have the herbs that cleanse her womb. You'll get no god-child from her, nor from any of my daughters!"

"You, my own wife, my High Priestess of the Sun, would go against the god's will, and destroy the very best of the Aten's creations? Such a thing is abhorrent to the god, and to me!"

Before she could note the movement of his hand, or detect any shift in his weight, the king's fist crashed against Nefertiti's face. She staggered sideways, stumbling into a small table, and the lamp that lay upon it shattered on the floor. A puddle of oil spread. Flames leaped up from the tile floor in a dance of wild panic.

Nefertiti stared mutely at the flames. She had never been struck by anyone before, not even by her father, and the shock of the act itself stunned her for one frantic heartbeat. Then the pain of the blow arrived. She cried out, clutching her face, and her breath came short and harsh.

Calmly, Akhenaten crushed the flames beneath his foot, snuffing their life with the sole of his sandal. Then he turned and advanced on Nefertiti, raising his fist to strike again.

She dodged backward. Her legs connected with another piece of furniture, too heavy to upset—his writing desk. She groped blindly behind her and seized the first object that her hand touched. It was the little statue of Kiya, the one Akhenaten had doted over in the days of the West Bank. She heaved the thing at him, smiling grimly as its solid mass flew from her hand. But Akhenaten stepped easily aside. The statue crashed onto the floor, the seated figure snapping from its small stone plinth.

"You will not do it," the king said softly. "You will summon no herb woman. You will not destroy what the

Aten has created."

"I will!" There were no more missiles within her reach. She forced herself to face his rage, unprotected, alone. *Stand strong like the Pharaoh you are*, she told herself. *You are the true might—the strength of Egypt.*

But when his fist punched hard into her stomach, she doubled over despite her will, breathless and pained. All pretense of power left her in an instant. Another blow fell across her back; she sprawled to the hard ground, and the greasy, dark scent of singed lamp oil filled her nostrils and mouth. Nefertiti spat blood on the Pharaoh's floor, not knowing where it had come from, why it filled her mouth so suddenly.

Is this how Sitamun died? The thought was distant and light, absurdly gentle.

She gasped for air. When she could speak again, she climbed to her feet, slipping in the oil and wheezing.

"Birth will kill Meketaten," she gasped. "Perhaps... perhaps even just carrying the child to term will destroy her. If you are truly the earthly aspect of a benevolent god, then you will show mercy, and spare your daughter's life."

Nefertiti forced herself to straighten, though the pain in her middle was terrible, like a long, hot dagger stabbing into her stomach—her heart. She breathed deep. Her lungs expanded into her bruised gut with a wrench of agony, and she resisting the urge to cry out. With the tip of her tongue she explored the gash in her lip—she had bitten it when she fell. She was battered, but she faced the Pharaoh tall and straight, ready to fight for her children—to die for them, if the gods willed it.

"The Aten will protect my little wife," Akhenaten said. Then he shrugged, a gesture of heedless dismissal. "And even if the god in his wisdom decides to call her home, what does it matter? He has blessed me with five more fertility goddesses to bear my divine seed. I shall not weep if one is lost."

Ankhesenpaaten

Year 15 of Akhenaten
Beautiful Are the Manifestations,
Exalting the Name,
Beloved of the Sun

THE NIGHT WAS COOL and quiet, and the stars seemed weak, far away in the moonless sky. Ankhesenpaaten walked slowly along the western edge of the palace's high outer wall. She trailed her hand over the top of its waist-high barrier, feeling its dryness, the faint crumbling of the plaster beneath her fingertips, and the coarse mudbrick exposed underneath. The Iteru, an expanse like a great sheet of dark glass, reached outward from the palace's foot. The stars cast a sheen on the river's surface. The Iteru's rippling current winked with light, the sickly green shade of tarnished copper.

Ankhesenpaaten watched the river, eyeing its strong, silent, deep-cutting flow, feeling its cool lack of regard as it slid past Akhet-Aten. She watched the Iteru as she watched everything: calm, quiet, always assessing.

She had watched for months as Meketaten's child grew, distending her sister's belly into a grotesque swell. The roundness and largeness of it as it hung from Meketaten's small frame seemed a cruel joke, a mockery of the very concept of fertility.

She had watched as Nefertiti tried to cast the child out, using herbs and spells and desperate prayers to gods Ankhesenpaaten did not know. But each attempt availed nothing, and Ankhesenpaaten had watched, too, as bruises appeared on her mother's arms and face, like dreadful blossoms opening inside a sorrowful garden.

Ankhesenpaaten watched her sister grow paler and quieter with each passing week, and soon she realized what Meketaten's fading color and gaunt, staring face meant. Long before Meketaten entered the birthing bower, Ankhesenpaaten knew that she would not come out again.

Meketaten had struggled in the bower, down in the garden below, for a day and most of a night. Ankhesenpaaten had spent that time in prayer, leaving the relative seclusion of the wall only when she must, begging the Aten unceasingly for his mercy, pleading with the god to be kind and take Meketaten quickly up into the sky. But all her efforts proved futile. The Aten only drew out Meketaten's misery, sustaining the fragile girl's suffering with cruel relish.

Now and then one of Meketaten's weak cries had reached up to the wall where Ankhesenpaaten huddled. The cries were no more than whispers at such a great distance, yet still they stabbed at her heart and wrenched quiet sobs from her chest.

When night fell and the Aten faded from the sky, leaving Meketaten alone to face her agony, Ankhesenpaaten whispered a new prayer to the darkness. "Anupu, Dark Jackal, guardian of the dead," she muttered, "come for my sister now, and ease her suffering."

She did not know who Anupu the Dark Jackal was. She had only heard her mother mutter a prayer to that forbidden god—for all gods save the Aten were forbidden—but Nefertiti had begged Anupu to pass Meketaten by, to spare her life and leave the family in peace.

"Come for her now." She chanted the words beneath her breath as she paced along the western wall, her eyes on the river. "Anupu, Dark Jackal, come for my sister now, and end her suffering."

She did not know how long she had walked and prayed.

It was difficult to judge the passage of time on a night without a moon. But when the first wail pierced the night—a woman's scream of loss, not a child's cry of pain—Ankhesenpaaten sighed in relief. The Dark Jackal had come. Meketaten was freed at last from her torment.

One wail turned to many. The garden filled with the terrible, discordant song of grief, and it poured up into the night sky until the sound seemed to fill the whole valley—the whole world.

Trembling, not knowing what she must do now, Ankhesenpaaten gazed around the wall's narrow terrace in a stupor. A large, blocky figure paced slowly toward her, walking the wall's perimeter. As the man drew closer, she could see the blue-and-red striped kilt swaying around his knees. *One of the guards.*

She stood in his path and waited for him to approach. He slowed as he neared, eyeing her with frank curiosity, but his gaze was tinged with sadness.

The guard halted, staring down at Ankhesenpaaten. He watched her for a long, silent moment, and she watched him in return, noting how grief sat comfortably on his face and his broad shoulders, as if sadness had found long residence in his *ka*. This soldier's grief was not for Meketaten—or, not *only* for her. Some old pain haunted him, although he seemed a young man.

He finally spoke in a quiet, not unkindly voice. "You should go down into the garden, King's Daughter. I fear your sister is dead."

Ankhesenpaaten turned on her heel and made briskly for the long, narrow staircase that led to the garden. The cries of mourning seemed to reach for her with cold hands, seizing her by her tunic, dragging her onward and down.

The birth bower was across the grounds, a pale, eerie temple standing out in stark definition against the dark shapes of flower beds and the low walls of fish ponds.

Ankhesenpaaten paused, staring across that distance to the small pavilion where Meketaten labored and died. Was Anupu the Dark Jackal still present? Would he take Ankhesenpaaten away, too, if she came too near?

As she hesitated, a servant woman stumbled past, tearing at her hair, weeping up toward the cold, uncaring stars. "Dead! The King's Daughter is dead! And her son—stillborn! Oh, gods, it is an evil night!"

The Pharaoh's son, born without breath. A chill ran down Ankhesenpaaten's arms. *A terrible omen for the king.*

She turned away from the garden, ducked into the darkness beneath the nearest portico. At first she did not know where she was going—only that she didn't wish to be anywhere near Meketaten's birthing bower. She moved easily through the black halls, guiding herself with one hand brushing the wall when there was no distant flicker of lamplight to dimly show the way.

Before long her hands found a smooth, recessed door. She ran her fingers along its surface, feeling the great, embossed image of the Aten. She recognized the door to Nefertiti's quarters, even in the dark.

Mother will not be there, she told herself. *Mother will be at Meketaten's side, weeping and tearing at her dress. But I can wait here for her return. Here I will be safe from the Dark Jackal.*

Ankhesenpaaten pushed the door open and slipped inside the large apartment. She expected darkness within, as complete and dense as the darkness that shrouded the hallways. But a lamp flickered in Nefertiti's bed chamber, and slowly, with dragging steps, Ankhesenpaaten went toward it. As she crossed the receiving chamber her scalp tingled. The room held a profound sense of emptiness, although she could see, in the weak gleam of the lamp, that all of Nefertiti's belongings were still present, still in their accustomed places. Yet the room—the whole of the quarters—was so very *vacant*. The sense of desolation had a certain finality that swelled her heart and made her throat constrict with a poignant sense of loss.

But she found that the apartments were not entirely empty. Not yet. Somehow Ankhesenpaaten knew—perhaps she had heard her ragged breath or smelled her perfume—that Nefertiti was there. She found her mother in her dressing room, seated before the great, oval mirror. One lamp burned on the table beside her, its small flame glittering over all the finery of the King's Great Wife. The cries from the garden made their way faintly into the chamber like sighs from a tomb, and Ankhesenpaaten knew that she had no need to impart the news to Nefertiti.

Nefertiti's gaze, unfocused in the mirror, suddenly sharpened, and her reflected image held Ankhesenpaaten's eye. The Great Wife said nothing, keeping her silence as assiduously as Ankhesenpaaten did. But the anguish in Nefertiti's face, in the set of her neck and shoulders, was voluble.

Nefertiti reached up and unhooked the clasp of her wide, bright-banded collar. She laid it on the table with a heavy clatter. She removed her turquoise earrings, one by one, then slipped the dozens of bracelets from her wrists, dropping them atop the collar. A pile of gold and electrum, of turquoise and malachite shone on the table before her. She rose from her bench and loosed the knots of her fine robe, shook the linen out, and folded it carefully across the bench. The cobra crown of the Great Wife went next, joining the rest of the ornaments she had discarded on the table.

Nefertiti slipped her wig from her head. Her hand fell to her side, and the heavy wig slid to the floor with a soft thump. She stared at herself in the mirror, naked and exposed, and Ankhesenpaaten stared, too. She saw a body once young, once lush and beautiful, distorted now by motherhood. Yet through the sagging and rounded flesh, Ankhesenpaaten still noted hints of refinement, of proud carriage and natural grace.

There were bruises on her mother's body, crossing her back, darkening her stomach, marring the skin of her legs. Some were faded, hazy marks of faint purple and sickly yellow. But others were blue-black and painfully new.

Nefertiti pulled a simple sleeping shift from a basket near her feet. She donned the garment, then loosed the pins from her hair and picked up a small, ivory brush. With long, methodical strokes, she combed out her black hair until it hung like a smooth cape across her shoulders. Then she turned away from her mirror without another glance at her reflection.

She walked past Ankhesenpaaten, silent and serene—and on, out into her garden, toward the small gate that led from her private sanctuary past the palace walls to the road that ran to the lesser Aten Temple and the eastern cliffs beyond.

Ankhesenpaaten followed her mother out into the cool of the night. "Where are you going?"

Nefertiti paused, gazing down at her daughter with a broken sigh. "I have failed you," she said. "All of you—all my precious girls. I don't deserve to go on as I have done... *ruling.*" She said the word as if it were a curse. "I am going away, Ankhesenpaaten. You will not see me again. But you must be brave and good."

"Don't go." Ankhesenpaaten tried to keep the pleading tone from her voice, but it worked its way out all the same. She shivered against the cold, against the sound of her own desperation.

Nefertiti shook her head mutely. She gazed up at the stars for a moment, then managed, "Stay close to your aunt Baketaten. And to Tiy."

"I thought you didn't like Baketaten. Or Tiy."

"Who ever told you that?"

Ankhesenpaaten shrugged. No one had told her; she had seen it.

"Stay close to them," Nefertiti repeated. "And be sure your sisters stay close, too. If anyone in this city can protect you—anyone in this gods-blasted family—it's Tiy, or Baketaten. They have the strength. And, I pray, the wisdom. I have neither."

Nefertiti bent and kissed her forehead lightly, then moved on toward the little, vine-wrapped gate. Ankhesenpaaten watched her pass through it, struck immobile by disbelief and fear. Then, when Nefertiti vanished through the tangle of vines, the spell broke. Ankhesenpaaten turned and ran.

She ran back through the great central garden, through the crowds of servants and harem girls that staggered and wailed in their grief. She dodged between their bodies, evaded their clasping hands, and she was quite breathless before she found the long stairway to the wall's upper terrace. But she willed her legs to keep moving, and pelted up the stairs as fast as she could go, despite the burning in her lungs.

Ankhesenpaaten ran to the wall's edge and leaned out over the low, mudbrick barrier. She shook violently, panting and weak from her flight.

Far below, on the temple road, she found the small, distant form of Nefertiti drifting through the streets of Akhet-Aten. The simple shift she wore was as pale as a ghost in the starlight.

Footsteps scraped along the terrace, drawing near to Ankhesenpaaten. She did not need to look around to know that the guard had joined her—the one who had spoken to her earlier that night. He stood at a respectful distance, but still he came near enough that Ankhesenpaaten didn't feel so terribly alone. She stared silently after Nefertiti for a while longer, tracking her progress through the city. Finally she looked up at the guard.

"What are you looking at, King's Daughter?"

She did not reply.

"My name is Horemheb," he offered. "It is a sad night. I am sorry for your loss."

Still she made no response, but her brow furrowed in careful thought as she gazed up at him. She read pity on his face—pity and rage, barely suppressed. His lips thinned as he considered her in his turn, and it seemed to Ankhesenpaaten that she could all but hear his thoughts: *How old is this child? Eleven? Twelve, at the most? How long before she, too, finds herself trapped in the agony of the birth bower?*

Ankhesenpaaten turned away from Horemheb's pitying stare. She searched the streets below for the white ghost of her mother. "I think we will have a new Great Wife now."

Horemheb drew back as if she had spat a curse at him. "Who?" he said, and his voice was demanding, almost fearful. "Will it be Baketaten?"

This man wouldn't like that, Ankhesenpaaten realized. *He wouldn't like to see Baketaten tied more tightly to the Pharaoh.*

But she couldn't answer with any truth or surety, so she only shrugged. She scanned the streets of Akhet-Aten fruitlessly, desperate for one last sight of her mother.

In the garden below the wails of mourning went on, unceasing.

Meritaten

*Year 15 of Akhenaten
Beautiful Are the Manifestations,
Exalting the Name,
Beloved of the Sun*

MERITATEN HADN'T YET WASHED the dust of the funeral procession from her body when the knock sounded on her chamber door.

"Come," she called.

Two servants entered, bearing a large, lidded basket between them. The basket shifted and rocked in their arms, and a peeved, spiteful hiss came from within.

"Here he is, my lady." The women eased their burden to the ground, and one toed the basket gently with a fond smile. Then she removed the basket's cover and a pale streak sprang forth. The cat danced a few steps toward Meritaten, back arched and tail puffed like a bundle of papyrus tassels. It spat, exposing a pink tongue, and its eyes—one green, one blue—narrowed in mistrust.

"You mustn't mind him, my lady," the other servant said. "He was indignant at being put into the basket, and the journey from the Pharaoh's palace to your own was long. But he will soon calm. He's a sweet cat, once you get to know him. We fed and brushed him often for your sister, may the Aten keep her."

"Thank you." Meritaten dismissed the women, then stood gazing down at Miu-Miu with hands on hips.

What am I going to do with a cat?

The mad impulse to take Miu-Miu into her household had seized Meritaten on the walk back from her sister's funeral rites. They had laid the girl and her stillborn son in one small, accessory chamber of the Pharaoh's own tomb. There had been no time to build for Meketaten a proper tomb of her own, for who ever expects a girl of twelve, well cared for and fit as a young horse, to die? As they returned from the Meketaten's makeshift eternity, a great, suffocating anger had risen up inside Meritaten's heart, and she didn't know just what had caused it. Was it only the fact that Meketaten had no tomb of her own?

And she deserves one! Meritaten drove a fist into her palm. The sound interrupted Miu-Miu, who, with his indignation duly expressed, had turned to the work of grooming his fur with ponderous dignity. The cat flicked his ears and glared at Meritaten again.

"She deserved better than an anonymous afterlife," Meritaten told him. "She deserved to live on, in this world and the next."

It was true that she had often found herself annoyed by her younger sister—by all of her sisters—but Meketaten especially, whose clingy ways and habit of copying everything Meritaten did grated on her nerves.

But she had never wished for Meketaten to die.

She bent and offered her hand to the cat. Miu-Miu ignored her while he raked his tongue over the long fur of his tail. Then, in his own good time, he rose and ambled to Meritaten. Then he sniffed her with an air of perfect arrogance. Gently, she stroked his head. His fur was as white as bleached linen, soft as a goose's breast.

"You're my cat now," she told Miu-Miu with finality. "You won't wander off to eat bird chicks and lizards in the garden. I'll feed you on the choicest meat from the kitchen, and keep your fur brushed and tidy. Meketaten would like that. I knew, after we sealed up her tomb—or, the chamber that must serve as her tomb—I knew she would want me to care for you, and see that you have the best of everything. For her sake, I will."

Miu-Miu, unimpressed with that revelation, turned and strolled away.

The next morning, when the praises to the Aten were finished, Meritaten did not return to her private dwelling, but wandered the halls and gardens of the great palace by the river. She felt instinctively that the quiet she had treasured in the northern palace would seem too vast and isolating now. She strolled aimlessly from the feasting hall to the throne room, then crossed the grounds to the large lake and stood staring blindly at its carpet of lotus blooms. When the sweet scent of the flowers turned cloying in her nostrils, she turned and walked without direction once more, until she found herself, quite unexpectedly, outside Nefertiti's chambers.

Seventy days had passed since Meketaten went to the god—since Nefertiti vanished, disappearing as completely as Kiya had the year before. Akhenaten had wept and raged over the loss of his High Priestess of the Sun, showing far more grief over Nefertiti than he had over the death of his daughter-wife.

The Pharaoh insisted that Nefertiti's rooms should remain untouched, maintained exactly as she had left them, as if he expected her to re-appear one day, to wink back into existence within the palace walls and pick up her life from where she had dropped it.

What a fool he is, Meritaten thought as she stood contemplating Nefertiti's closed door. *She is never coming back. She left us—she is finished with the City of the Sun, and all who dwell within its borders. Even with me.*

In the first few days after Nefertiti's disappearance, Meritaten had often come to peer through her mother's open door, spying on the king as he wept over some discarded article of clothing or some cast-off bracelet he'd found dropped on the floor. Sometimes Meritaten listened as the Pharaoh muttered darkly about the Aten—how the god had spirited the pure, sacred Nefer-Neferu-Aten away into the sky, as a punishment to the king for all his sins. He had only grown stranger thereafter. Often he remained in the temple from dawn to dusk, groveling in the glare of the sun's fierce light, never seeking shelter until his skin turned as dark as an ancient *rekhet's* and the pale, dry flesh of his lips cracked and bled.

Meritaten slipped quietly into Nefertiti's dim room. She drifted across the cold tiles of the floor to her mother's dressing table. The gown Nefertiti had discarded still lay folded over the bench. Meritaten lifted it, letting its soft, flowing linen slide across her hand like cool water. Then she sat on the bench and touched each piece of jewelry one by one, examining the ornaments, watching the distorted reflection of her own face in the ripple of hammered gold and the sheen of polished carnelian.

I don't know what to do with myself, what is expected of me, any more than the Pharaoh knows what he must do. Nefertiti's absence has left us all bereft and confused. The only thing she knew, with a terrible, deep certainty that churned like an illness in her stomach, was that she, Meritaten, would be required to step into the void Nefertiti had left behind. She frowned over a pair of her mother's earrings, rolling the turquoise drops in her palm. *How can I ever do it? And what will happen to Egypt—to me—if I fail?*

The image of Baketaten flashed into her mind, haughty and self-possessed. Meritaten blinked and tossed the earrings back onto the heap of golden things, shaking her head to clear away the unwelcome vision. Baketaten's intrusion into her thoughts was the last thing she wished for now, gripped by sorrow as she was.

Then Meritaten paused, considering the other King's Wife more deliberately. Would it be possible, she wondered, to forge some kind of alliance with Baketaten? Perhaps together, working hand in hand, they might discover how to act more effectively as King's Wives—to handle Egypt wisely and well, like Nefertiti before them, while Akhenaten sank ever deeper into his isolation and despondency.

For a moment the possibility warmed in Meritaten's heart, rising over her consciousness like the sun at dawn. But then she pushed herself away from the dressing table and pushed the foolish thought from her heart, too. She had never forgiven Baketaten for her arrogant words in the Great Temple, when she had implied that the palace was hers. Baketaten was self-important, haughty, and mean-spirited. Meritaten's stomach turned bitter, churning over the thought of cooperating with that smug, sneering creature.

I'll handle Egypt's reins on my own, she thought. *My mother was the Great Wife, and I shall be, too. I don't need Baketaten's help. I need no one's help, for the god is with me.*

She heard a soft sound, like the whisper of a mouse's feet on tiles. She turned quickly toward the bed-chamber door, fear racing fast and hot down her veins. Just *what* she was afraid of, Meritaten could not have said, but there was no mistaking the harsh, metallic tang in her throat, nor the shiver that ran up her spine.

But it was only Ankhesenpaaten, careful and quiet as she leaned against the doorjamb of Mother's chamber. She stared at Meritaten with solemn, nearly apologetic eyes.

"What do you want?" Meritaten asked, more sharply than she'd intended. The taste of fear faded slowly from her tongue.

"I'm afraid," Ankhesenpaaten said.

"Of what? You have nothing to fear."

From beyond Nefertiti's apartments, deep in the palace's

halls, a sound like a wounded animal rose, then fell again abruptly. It was the king—weeping, or shouting in rage at the god; Meritaten could not say. Ankhesenpaaten turned toward the sound, her small, pale face standing out against the darkness of the room with ominous clarity. Then she returned her gaze to Meritaten. And said nothing.

"You shouldn't fear Father," Meritaten said. But Ankhesenpaaten *should* fear the king, and Meritaten knew it. Meketaten should have feared him. They all must fear him now.

Ankhesenpaaten shifted on her small, slippered feet. "Mother warned me before she left to get away from our family. She told me to seek a protector—somebody who could watch over me and our younger sisters."

"You spoke to Mother before she left?"

Ankhesenpaaten did not respond to the sharp, desperate query. She only blinked at Meritaten from across the room.

"Where did she go?" Meritaten prompted. "What else did she say to you?"

Still Ankhesenpaaten said nothing. She sucked at her lower lip.

Meritaten tossed her head in irritation. "You needn't worry. I'll become King's Great Wife, and I will protect you and the little girls."

The smallest frown creased the girl's forehead. Her doubt was plain enough to read in that skeptical gaze, her shrinking posture as she leaned half in and half of the chamber.

Her sister's doubt sent rage flaring up in Meritaten's heart. "Get out!" she shouted.

Ankhesenpaaten made no move to depart, so Meritaten scooped up one of Nefertiti's cast-off slippers and hurled it at her sister. The younger girl ducked as the slipper flew past her. Then Ankhesenpaaten turned and vanished into the depths of the apartment.

The darkness of the chamber seemed to reach for Meritaten, offering a cold embrace with no comfort in it. *Don't go*, she almost called after her sister. *Please come back.*

But whether Ankhesenpaaten stayed or went, Meritaten would still be alone, struggling in isolation with the weight of a duty she knew already was too great for her shoulders to bear.

THE BURDEN OF the throne taxed Meritaten straight away. As the weeks passed, the pain of Meketaten's death dulled—or perhaps it was merely overshadowed by the towering monolith of Meritaten's duties. Matters of the court always required her attention, for Akhenaten, still mired in despair over Nefertiti's abandonment, spent nearly all his time in the temples, and showed less interest in the fate of Egypt than ever before. Most of her hours were passed in the throne room, seated on the dais beside Baketaten, where the two young King's Wives heard petitions and correspondence together.

On rare days, Meritaten could return to her northern palace for some short respite from the throne. During those hours—too few for her liking—she often wasted what should have been leisure time in the grip of a wild fury. Baketaten's presence, her easy superiority, haunted Meritaten. She seemed to glide through each day with an inborn strength, a thoughtless capability that made Meritaten burn with envy. The other King's Wife handled the requests of stewards and nobles, and even Akhenaten's moody behavior, with much more aplomb than Meritaten could muster, even on the days when she pushed her efforts to their limits.

"She's everything I wish to be," Meritaten told the white cat sadly one evening as she sat stroking his fur in the last, rosy-orange shaft of sunset's light. "Everything I *must* be, for what will Egypt become without *someone* minding the throne?"

Of course, Baketaten might have minded the throne herself. The haughty creature was capable enough, Meritaten bitterly conceded. But just the possibility of giving up her small measure of power—and the position and riches Nefertiti had secured for her—made Meritaten feel cold and sick.

"I must press on," she said to Miu-Miu. "I must become the King's Wife my mother was. I have no other choice."

The cat lashed his tail in agreement.

The following day, when Meritaten returned to the king's palace, she entered the throne with an efficient, direct stride, head held high and eyes sparking with purpose. But her air of confidence melted when she looked up at the dais. Ankhesenpaaten was seated on its highest step, thin, brown arms clasped around her knees. Directly behind the girl, Baketaten settled comfortably onto her throne.

Meritaten paused, narrowing her eyes at the scene. Of late Ankhesenpaaten had taken great pains to attach herself to Baketaten, and the King's Wife seemed perfectly happy to allow the girl to follow her about, clinging to her, watching her with wide, hopeful, awe-struck eyes. But never before had Baketaten allowed the girl to invade the throne room.

Meritaten lifted her skirt in both fists and hurried on. She stormed up the steps of the dais, then nudged Ankhesenpaaten with the toe of her sandal.

"What is she doing here?"

"Observing," Baketaten replied.

"There is nothing here for her to observe. Send her off to the harem garden with the other children."

"There is much here for the girl to see." Baketaten sipped nonchalantly from a cup of beer. "She will stay."

Meritaten scoffed. "What can she possibly see here? Throne business is nothing but a lot of court chatter and letter-reading; a lot of bowing and scraping and contorting for the king." *Or, as the case may be, the King's Wives.*

"Exactly. Ankhesenpaaten is intelligent; it's time she learned the ways of politics."

"She doesn't *need* to learn the ways of politics," Meritaten snapped.

"Every woman *should* learn." Baketaten cast a slow, significant glance at Meritaten on her throne.

Meritaten leaned back into her gilded seat, face throbbing with the heat of humiliation. The implication that Meritaten was ill-prepared for ruling stung all the more because she knew it was true. And as the day's business unfolded, she watched Ankhesenpaaten turn ever more toward her rival King's Wife for comfort and guidance—and Meritaten's resentment of Baketaten redoubled.

Does she think to outshine me even as a sister? Does she think to replace me in Ankhesenpaaten's heart—and in the little girls' hearts, too? It is well that Nefertiti has left us, or Baketaten would soon be working her way into my mother's best favor, too!

The morning hearings concluded—not a moment too soon, in Meritaten's estimation—and the hour came for the progress to the temple. Meritaten's anger and deep, quivering sense of helplessness blinded her as the chariots made their way down the Royal Road, and she saw nothing of the crowds that thronged the avenue, save for a great, colorless blur. It was not until she stepped down from her chariot outside the temple gate that her senses came back into focus—and her sudden awareness sent a sharp, chilling impact shuddering through her *ka*.

A woman surged out of the crowd, reaching for Meritaten with thin, claw-like hands. In a flash, Meritaten took in the woman's pale, sweating face; the dark rings around her eyes; the sickly, greenish cast about her mouth.

"Please, Lady," the woman cried, "bless me! Save me!"

The plague!

Meritaten lurched backward, stumbling away from the trembling hands. Mahu's soldiers moved quickly, ushering the ill woman back into the crowd, but Meritaten couldn't stop her staggering feet. She tottered sideways and collided with Ankhesenpaaten, who was just stepping down from the children's chariot. The girl's foot landed on Meritaten's hem, and the white robe tore.

Meritaten pushed her sister away roughly. "Watch where you're going!"

Baketaten dodged past her to sweep the edge of her red sun-cape over Ankhesenpaaten's shoulder. She pulled the girl close. "Leave her be, Meritaten."

"You will not give orders to me."

"Why not?" Baketaten said languidly. "You aren't the Great Wife yet." *And*, her tone implied, *you never will be*.

Meritaten narrowed her eyes at her rival King's Wife.

"It's I who've given the Pharaoh a son." Baketaten ushered the girl away from Meritaten and the milling crowd, directing her toward the temple. "Best make your peace with that."

She thinks herself untouchable. She thinks me an ineffectual fool! But I'll show her who is a fool, and who is untouchable. I'll teach her to respect me.

Meritaten allowed the procession to move on without her. Even the littlest girls preceded her into the temple; she let them all pass her by. She took up with the guardsmen as they marched between the great, pale pylons of the temple gate, and worked her way toward Mahu until at last she caught his dark, glittering eye.

"I have a task for you," she told the man.

He peered down at her with curiosity, those eyes like

two beads set in a rough slab of stone. But he said nothing.

"I want you to send a message to Baketaten."

"A message, King's Wife? Best find a maid to carry your letter. I have more important work to do."

"Not a letter—not that kind of message. I want her frightened. I want her to know it's *I* who have the power to frighten her. Do you take my meaning?"

Mahu stroked his chin and continued to regard her with dark deliberation.

"I don't want her harmed, of course," Meritaten added hastily. "Only frightened. My message must be strong. She must know that I *do* have power in the king's palace. She must know to keep to her place."

"And my pay?"

Meritaten blinked up at him in surprise. She hadn't planned to compensate the man. Indeed, she hadn't planned at all. She had assumed that Mahu would do as she commanded simply because she was the King's Wife.

I shan't give him any of my *gold or jewels*, she decided firmly.

Then she recalled Nefertiti's riches, left untouched in her chamber. How easy it would be to scoop up a bracelet here, a necklace there, and never trouble the palace's treasury, nor sacrifice even one of her own ornaments.

"Two fine bracelets," she said. "Gold, and fit for the King's Great Wife."

Mahu nodded at once. "Done."

Horemheb

Year 15 of Akhenaten
Beautiful Are the Manifestations,
Exalting the Name,
Beloved of the Sun

HOREMHEB PAUSED on the eastern wall of the palace. The moon was falling into an early set, sinking behind the high, black line of the cliffs, casting a low slant of silver across the streets of Akhet-Aten. The city seemed peaceful enough. Its villas and garden walls were softly luminescent in the failing moonlight, and in this quiet moment, with its roads so neat and orderly, it even looked beautiful—something Horemheb could not often say for the City of the Sun.

The cliffs seemed innocent enough, a simple, night-black wall surrounding Akhet-Aten, featureless and unthreatening. Yet Horemheb felt a chill of terrible foreboding as he gazed to the east. Somewhere in those rocky heights, tucked into a cold, black tomb, were the bodies of a dead girl and her baby— born of iniquity and sorrow—and both of them taken from the world long before their time.

Two children dead. And only to suit the whims of a man we must call Pharaoh.

He continued his circuit, pacing slowly along the eastern wall, watching the moonlight flow, liquid and pale, across the terrace. Doubt sat heavily in his heart and seemed to coat his mouth, so that each breath he drew tasted bitter. Could the gods he revered—the ones he still worshiped in his heart, despite their banishment from Akhet-Aten—truly approve of such an abomination? *Surely*, Horemheb thought desparetely, *it is not the will of my gods that a king like Akhenaten should continue in his iniquitous rule.*

He stopped his pacing again, but not through any intent. His feet had simply rooted to the ground; his legs went numb with the shock of his own musings.

What am I thinking? Am I truly considering...?

Sweat rose on his brow; he shivered. There was no greater wickedness than to kill a king—or even to displace one. What the gods decreed in their infinite mystery, in their inscrutable wisdom, was not for men to meddle with.

Yet what could he do? Allow Egypt to fall into this deadly depravity? Sit idly by while the city was overrun by plague—it had already resumed its spread from the sewage trenches and waste heaps—or protect the Pharaoh's person even as he defiled the innocent?

You trap me, gods. Horemheb smiled sourly at the moon—at the stars that burned above like the eyes of all divinity—and offered up his bitter prayer. *You show me how to save the Two Lands, and yet if I do, you will curse me for it and feed my heart to Ammit.*

He forced one foot to move, then the other. The regularity of his stride slowly drove back the quaking fear that threatened to overtake him, and his thoughts grew gentler.

And all of those thougths were for Baketaten. He loved her—there was no denying it. Whenever he looked upon Mutnodjmet's face, her smile and her large, trusting eyes were an accusation. He had tried to banish the memories—of Baketaten's soft lips, her vow of love. It would have been simpler to stop his heart from beating. He ached for Baketaten's touch; he burned with the need to hear her voice, to see the delicate, controlled movement of her hand, the confident tilt of her chin. He loved her—

he *loved* her! How could he leave the woman he loved in Akhenaten's hands? How long would it be until she, too, was shut away in a cold tomb, another victim of the king's selfish desires?

Remembrance of those precious days he had spent with Baketaten on her journey north filled Horemheb with a crushing, poignant pain. And although the memories were more bitter than sweet, they nevertheless made him feel far more vivid, more true, more undeniably *alive* than he ever had before. *I cannot live without her*, he thought in despair. *To be without Baketaten is to be like a* ba *unseated from its body, flitting about, lost and unsettled*.

He stared into the glow of the moon and nodded once to himself. His heart was made up: he would tell Baketaten how he felt—confess the totality of his love. He would beg her to leave Akhet-Aten with him, to run away and built a new life together, living in anonymity in some secluded village where the king and Mahu's soldiers would never find them.

Horemheb gave one short, wry laugh and turned away from the moon. It was a mad scheme, and he knew it, just as surely as he knew that Baketaten would refuse. Her sense of duty was too great; her obedience to the gods' will was the very breath of life within her.

But still, Horemheb thought sadly, *I must try. Even though I know she will call me a fool and send me away—I must try.*

A high, sharp scream ripped through the night, driving out all thoughts of Baketaten. Horemheb paused, listening—and almost at once the scream came again, frantic and harsh, wild with panic. It was a woman.

He ran to the edge of the terrace and looked down into the courtyards below. The screaming continued, and in moments, more cries of terror joined with the first. Horemheb tilted his head, trying to pinpoint the location of the chaos. The high, keening wails of women rose into the night sky like birds taking wing, all black clamor and fear. And then, through a slow fog of disbelief, Horemheb realized where the screams were coming from: Baketaten's apartments.

He did not remember sprinting down the long, narrow stairway that carried him from the top of the wall to the courtyard below. But when he found himself on level ground, he raced through the garden paths and pillared corridors as if Ammit himself were after him, coming to devour his cold, fast-beating heart. Horemheb skidded on the balls of his feet as he rounded a sharp corner. Baketaten's chambers chambers were just around that bend, and as he came into view he saw women spilling out of the apartments, a flood of palace servants and maids flailing at each other, clawing at their faces, tearing their night-dresses in their haste to flee. Some of them had blood on their hands or smeared across their short, white shifts.

Only one small figure among them was not screaming. Horemheb approached her, reaching out to catch her by the shoulder, thinking to question her. It was the girl Ankhesenpaaten, whom he had found on the wall terrace the night the Pharaoh's daughter had died. The girl looked up at Horemheb, pale-faced and wide-eyed.

"What happened?" he asked her. "Where is Baketaten?"

She did not answer, nor did she weep. But her small, thin body trembled in his grip.

Horemheb released the girl and bowled past the maids who crowded blindly around the door.

"Move!" he shouted. "King's guard; make way!"

The lamps in Baketaten's chambers were burning, but the receiving room, with its fine couches and ebony tables, its harps and chests and wall-hangings, was empty. He glanced down at the floor, and clutched his stomach as queasy fear overtook him. A trail of many footprints fanned out from the bed-chamber door, glistening slick and red. It was as if the disbelieving servants had crowded into the bed chamber, then rushed away again, scattering in all directions, tracking behind them the thick, warm evidence of the horror they had seen.

With feet as heavy as bricks of bronze, Horemheb followed the spray of footprints toward the bed-chamber door. Inside, and at first glance, the room appeared peaceful. It was tidy, appointed with only a few essential furnishings—a bed, a dressing table, one simple cedar closet—yet each was beautifully carved and tastefully arranged. It seemed a room where nothing untoward had happened, or could ever happen; a sanctuary of quiet, feminine dignity.

But the trail of bloody prints curved beyond the bed, and Horemheb could see, between the bed's lion-paw legs, a large, dark pool spreading slowly across the floor. Sick and weak with fear, not wanting to see what he knew must be lying there, Horemheb followed the footprints one reluctant step at a time.

When he saw Baketaten lying in a vast lake of her own blood, her once-beautiful face a ruin of red flesh and splintered bone, Horemheb fell to his knees. A wordless cry of pain ripped from his throat, splitting his chest, his heart, his very *ka* in two. His screams of agony and rage carried up to the heavens, where the moon she had so loved sank uncaring from the night sky.

He lifted her body from the pool of blood, cradling her against his chest, rocking and weeping. He could not look at her face—at the place where the mouth he had once kissed was wrecked and gone, staved in by some furious blow. But he knew who had done this thing. There was only one man in the palace who had the strength, the coldness and brutality to attack such a beautiful creature as Baketaten: Mahu. And Mahu moved only at the order of the king.

Gods curse this Pharaoh, and his whole, depraved family, Horemheb prayed as he held Baketaten against him. *And gods curse me, because I wasn't here to protect her.*

The last, faint warmth of her body faded into coldness, but still Horemheb clung to her, his cries of pain muted now by the force of his agony. He only let her go when soldiers came to carry her away, to lay her out on some slab of limestone for the embalmers to touch with their cold, stinking hands—for the Pharaoh to look upon.

When Baketaten was gone, Horemheb staggered to his feet. He saw nothing of the world, nothing but a wash of red that seemed to cover every object, every surface—the floor, her bed, one of her small slippers lying in a corner of the room, his hands and his kilt, his chest where he had cradled her. He staggered away from the carnage, retching, supporting himself against the walls with weak arms and shaking hands. At last he found his way out into the courtyard, gray and dull in the starlight. He stood shuddering and heaving in the night air, and felt Baketaten's blood turn cold and hard on his skin. The wailing women had gone, chased off by the soldiers, but distant cries still filled the night, echoing among the pillars and courtyards.

There was a small, shy tug on the hem of his blood-stained kilt.

Horemheb looked down into the face of the King's Daughter, Ankhesenpaaten.

"Who will protect me now?" she asked in a small, frightened voice.

Horemheb stared at her dully for a moment. "I don't know," he finally said.

"Will you do it? Will you be my body guard, and keep my sisters and me safe from all harm?"

He watched her again in stunned silence. Then a gruff

laugh erupted from his chest. His throat tightened and burned. "Child, there is no one who can keep you safe. No one."

The girl's eyes widened. Horemheb could not look at her frightened, innocent face. He turned away. Staggering like a drunk, he found the main path through the gardens and moved along it slowly with numb, dragging steps. He walked on past the palace gate and down the Royal Road.

Where am I going? He asked himself with distant curiosity.

Keep walking, he answered. *Go back to your home. Wake Mutnodjmet, collect a few things in travel bags—and press on.*

His fellow soldiers were in the hills, the cliffs. *I don't care. I'll fight the damned lot of them.* He would fight his way past any number of Mahu's men, and walk and walk, and leave Akhet-Aten far behind. He would find some place of peace and safety, some place that could erase the shadow of this mad king from his heart forever. It made no difference to him, whether he must go back to Waset, or north to the Delta, or cross the wide, green sea. He would go beyond to the farthest, war-torn reaches of the empire, or out into the brutal Red Land itself to wither and die beneath the hateful sun.

Any place was better than Akhet-Aten. Horemheb was certain of that now. He would leave, and once he was beyond this gods-blasted valley, he would never return.

Tiy

*Year 15 of Akhenaten
Beautiful Are the Manifestations,
Exalting the Name,
Beloved of the Sun*

THE FIRST BIRDS of the morning had hardly begun to sing when Tiy heard Huya's shout from her little stone quay. She rose abruptly from her breakfast table and pulled her light, red sun-cloak over her shoulders. As she fussed with its knot, she glanced down at the honey cakes and stewed figs she had been eating contentedly only moments before. Now the sight sent a swell of nausea through her gut. If Huya had traveled across the Iteru at such an early hour, his business could not possibly be pleasant.

She instructed her servants to remain in the house and went alone through the little garden to meet Huya. The season of the Inundation had just begun, and the morning was crisp with dew, the damp air soothing and richly perfumed. Tiy breathed deep, savoring the warm-green scent, knowing that soon the sun would reach its height and burn all the goodness from the land.

And whatever news Huya brings will burn the goodness from my heart. If there is any goodness left in it.

The steward was waiting at the head of the quay. He, too, wore a cape against the morning's damp chill, and its white folds reminded Tiy of the wings of Mother Mut. But these wings did not stretch strong and wide, offering the goddess's protection to her children. They hung limp and defeated—weak.

Tiy nodded a brusque greeting. "What is it? Why have you come?"

"My lady, I have sad news. Your granddaughters, Nefer-Neferu-Re and Setepenre, are dead."

Tiy pulled her red cape tighter, taking in his words with numb accptance. *The twins. But they were so young and spirited.* "Followed little Meketaten into that dark, cliffside tomb," she muttered. "How did it happen?"

But she had no need to ask—not truly. Only a week ago the plague had finally grown strong enough to overcome the relative seclusion of the royal palace. Tiy had heard the news. Several servants had fallen ill, including two of the girls' nurses and young Mutbenret. Mutbenret survived, thank the gods, though she was still quite weak and pale. But both the nurses had died, and now, it seemed, their little charges had also succumbed to the fever.

"I hadn't even heard that the twins were sick," Tiy said, before Huya could explain their deaths.

"It often happens that way. The youngest victims of the illness fall so quickly. Perhaps that is part of the gods' mercy, to spare them greater suffering."

"Perhaps."

Tiy turned away, gazing back into the green, peaceful depths of her garden. The birds were singing sweetly now, busy with their little lives, untroubled in the treetops. She listened to their chorus in silence. The sound did not ease her grief nor lift her heart. In truth, she felt almost no grief at all—just a blunt, cold force of... what? Shame? Anger? She couldn't put a name to the dull, insistent pressure inside her. It seemed she could muster no emotion anymore, save for heavy self-loathing.

Somehow, she told herself with grim certainty, *this is my doing. The plague, its rampages through the city... the deaths of my grandchildren.*

And Baketaten. That terrible loss was certainly Tiy's fault. For had she not tried to change the world—had she not tried to put right what the gods never saw as wrong... If she had not taken Baketaten and honed her into that sharp and subtle tool, but had allowed the girl to live a natural life, free from the court, free from pain....

Huya had carried the news of Baketaten's death across the river weeks ago, just as he had done this morning. And ever since learning of Baketaten's violent end, a shadow had cloaked Tiy's heart, deadening her thoughts in its ink-black folds. The girl had shown more promise than even Tiy had in her youth. For Baketaten to suffer that sudden and violent death seemed a terrible omen, a clear warning from the gods, a grim foreshadowing of the precipitous fall—Tiy's, or the whole damnable court's—which was surely coming soon. If it had not come already.

Tiy turned back to Huya. "What of the other girls?"

"Ankhesenpaaten is well, and Meritaten has kept herself shut away in her private palace. She has not fallen ill. But Tasherit is quite sick. I'm afraid the physicians doubt that she will survive."

Tiy nodded gravely, accepting the ill tidings. What could she do, but accept divine judgment? What could she do, but bear the punishment for her sins?

"And Tutankhaten?" Tiy asked. "What has become of Baketaten's boy?"

"Still well," Huya said. "But now that plague has overrun the palace's walls and struck down the youngest girls, only the gods know how long the boy might hold out."

The court—her power, such as it was—everything Tiy had built over the long years of her life—all of it was crumbling before her eyes, beneath her hands, like old mudbrick tossed under a chariot's wheel. Dulled by the inescapable fact of her fate, she moved a few paces away from Huya, drifting heedlessly back toward her home.

"My lady? What are your wishes?"

Tiy stopped, staring down at her beaded slippers. Dew had darkened their silken embroidery and chilled the tips of her toes. The hem of her robe was damp, too.

What are my wishes? I wish I had been born into a different family. I wish my brother were not a viper, who used me for his own ends. I wish I had never laid eyes on Amunhotep the Pharaoh. Tears welled in her eyes, bitter and burning with salt. *I wish I had smothered Akhenaten in the cradle, and spared Egypt this horror.*

She wanted only to vanish now, to disappear from the court and the world, to be forgotten. She had wished for an end to the farce of her life ever since learning of Baketaten's death. She had loved that girl—had believed Baketaten would be Egypt's true salvation. And in her heart, Tiy still believed that in one thing, at least—in educating Baketaten, preparing her for a great and valiant work—she had done right.

Baketaten's son remains trapped in the city. Tutankhaten may have been bred like an Apis bull, crafted from the royal blood, created for the gods' use. But he was still a child—a baby, innocent and fragile, helpless in the path of danger.

If I don't remove him from Akhet-Aten, he will surely sicken and die.

It was the one kindness Tiy could do, the one apology she could make to Baketaten's shade.

For your sake, Baketaten—for the sake of the girl I loved—I will see Tutankhaten to safety.

And when that work was done, Tiy would rest. The gods knew it was past time.

WHEN TIY AND HUYA reached the royal palace, she could see in the pale faces and trembling lips of servants and stewards alike that fear ruled Akhet-Aten now. Many of the palace workers still bore traces of the illness that had struck them—skin dewed by sweat, a faint trace of green around the lips, the sallow skin and sunken cheeks of dehydration. Tiy perceived at once that it would not be long—a few days, perhaps—before the whole of the royal household was tight in the plague's grip.

The king's court session was just concluding. It would be an early dismissal, so that Akhenaten could make haste to the temple, to pray for the Aten's mercy. A steward bustled about outside the great audience hall's doors, but he waved Tiy away.

"Come back tomorrow." He stuffed scrolls into his bag. "The king is needed urgently at the palace. Plague has fallen inside our walls, and—"

"Don't you know who—" Tiy began, but Huya strode forward, knocked the man aside with a bussiness-like flick of his hand, and shoved the hall's door open. The steward gave a squawk of alarm, then another of indignation, but Huya payed no heed, storming into the throne room as if he were the Pharaoh himself. Tiy's lips twitched with a tight smile. She nodded her thanks to the steward as she swept past him.

Mahu's soldiers leaped to bar their entry from the throne room's interior; one even raised his club over Huya's head, poised to strike. But Akhenaten, his hands braced on the arms of his throne, caught in the act of rising, stared at the commotion at the hall's end, then shouted for the guards to stand down.

"Mother," the king said when the guards had backed away. "What is this all about? I thought you'd come to your senses, and decided to remain sequestered in your estate for good."

"It would be wiser to stay there, Grandmother. Illness has overrun the palace." Meritaten looked small and fragile on the throne of the King's Great Wife. She had ascended there by default—the only King's Wife left alive—and although she sat straight and watched Tiy with a calm, emotionless mask, she made for a very pale and insufficient echo of Nefertiti. Her necklace, a wide collar of lapis bars, was threaded all about with fresh, green herbs—charms to drive away the plague, Tiy suspected.

"I know the fever has come," Tiy said. "That is why I'm here. I've heard the news of Setepenre and Nefer-Neferu-Re. This illness is striking the youngest, one by one."

"Tasherit has caught it, too," Meritaten said, her voice dulled by exhaustion.

Tiy nodded. "My king, what of your son?"

"Tutankhaten? I hadn't thought—"

"Let me take him away from this place before the illness strikes him, too. He is the youngest of all your children. I fear he will not survive, if the fever strikes him."

Akhenaten's grip eased from the arms of his throne. He sat for a moment in silent consideration, but Meritaten shifted uncomfortably in her seat.

"You raised Baketaten," she said to Tiy rather sharply, "and turned her into a force all her own." She regarded Akhenaten with smooth confidence, and her face in profile suddenly reminded Tiy very much of Nefertiti. Regal, self-possessed, just a touch haughty, Meritaten said, "My king, do we truly want another child raised under Tiy's thrall? What will a *son* be like, if Tiy plants her own thoughts in his heart?"

Tiy cut in smoothly. "My lord, I taught Baketaten to revere the one true god. She knew and loved the glory of the Aten, as few others in your city do. I will do the same for your son. I will make him a devotee of the only god that lives."

The Pharaoh stroked his long chin. "That is true," he said slowly. "Baketaten was devout." A distant fire lit his eyes and a hot flush of excitement bloomed on his narrow face. And Tiy could see that even now, surrounded by death as he was, Akhenaten's first allegiance was always to his strange, unknowable god.

"We don't need another tool sharpened by Tiy," Meritaten said to the king. "It will only cut us and make us bleed. We will regret it in the end."

Tiy bowed her head. "Great Wife, may I speak with you alone?"

Meritaten clicked her tongue in exasperation and seemed about to refuse. But Akhenaten raised his hand.

"I have urgent business with the god," he said. "Hear her petition, Meritaten. I shall trust to your judgment."

Tiy waited in silence while the Pharaoh drifted from the throne room. Then she dared to give Meritaten a sympathetic smile. "He shall trust to your judgment, indeed."

"He certainly never trusts to his own." Meritaten stood, arching her back in a long stretch, and then stepped lightly down from the dais. Nefertiti's inborn grace was in the girl's limbs, nascent and faint, but present. Face to face with Tiy, she said, "Now tell me your real business, Grandmother. What do you want with Tutankhaten? What new scheme have you made?"

"It is no scheme, my lady. I think only of the child's well-being."

"Tiy, you never think *only* of any one thing. Your heart is a honeycomb, full of chambers and wiles. Tutankhaten will be just as safe here as anywhere else in Akhet-Aten."

"Which is to say—" Tiy flicked her eyes down to the protective herbs Meritaten wore—"not safe at all. Let me do better for the boy. I will remove him from Akhet-Aten entirely. *And* from the western farms. I will send him away from this place, to someplace far distant, where he will be forgotten."

Meritaten tilted her head, considering.

"Think, Meritaten: if the boy is out of the Pharaoh's sight, he will also be out of the Pharaoh's heart. You will be free to give the king sons of your own, and you will rise even higher in his esteem."

Meritaten frowned. She turned toward the hall's doors as if she might flee the throne room entirely. A faint cry sounded from the hall beyond, a high-pitched wail of grief. Meritaten glanced up at the dais where the two thrones stood. Finally she nodded.

"Very well. You may take the boy. It is probably safer for him elsewhere. But you must keep him well away from the court, and you must stay far away yourself. Akhet-Aten is mine now, and it will remain in my hands. Your meddling isn't welcome anymore."

Tiy dismissed herself with a bow, then waited in the garden while Huya, brandishing orders marked with Meritaten's seal ring, went to collect the boy. She drifted down the wide paths, scowling at the dry, brown flower beds, at the petals falling from their blooms. The palace lacked the staff it needed to water and tend the garden. If the plague kept on—and it showed no signs of abating—these gardens, this palace, the whole of Akhet-Aten would revert to the dry, hot sand that had once covered this ground.

Tiy found her way to Sitamun's old quarters. The building was already crumbling in its forgotten corner. She stood watching the little home, struck by its smallness, its isolation. A poignant ache of loss and regret wracked Tiy's body, throbbing in her joints and heating her skin. She whispered her daughter's name.

"Sitamun."

The house made no reply. But as she turned away, Tiy could feel the cool, dark squares of its windows, watching—accusing.

Huya called from the center of the garden, and Tiy hurried toward him. Tutankhaten rode on the steward's hip, his small arms wrapped about Huya's neck. Tutankhaten's brow furrowed as Tiy approached.

"You have him." She touched his cheek. It was soft and smooth, and felt like a promise beneath her fingers.

"Yes. His nurses gave him up without much fuss. Shall we take him back to your estate, then, my lady?"

"No," Tiy said. "Not there."

It was not she who would raise the Pharaoh's son. Tiy had already proven herself unworthy of such an important task. That work would fall to another. For Tiy's part, she had but one more duty to the gods, and then her toil in this world would be done.

"Wait with Tutankhaten at the boat. I am going into the city. I shan't be long; I only have a message to deliver."

She walked alone to Ay's estate, noting the hollow emptiness of Akhet-Aten's streets, the shuttered businesses, the quiet, furtive movement of watchers on the rooftops. Everywhere, over doors and windows, in shops and at the wells, bunches of herbs hung as protection against disease, and spells to ensure good health were painted on the walls of every home. Now and then, when she caught some stray whisper from the roofs, Tiy heard the Aten's name invoked. Prayers went up to Akhenaten, too—but more often than the Pharaoh would have liked, the names of the old gods were spoken, raised in fragile hope and futile entreaty. *Heka, god of medicine*, the voices whispered. *Hathor, who protects children. Mut the merciful;*

Amun the wise; Anupu, who guards the dead.

When she reached Ay's estate and pulled back the hood of her sun cloak, the door guard announced her at once. She found herself standing in Ay's library for the last time. He was bent over his scrolls, studying and plotting. It seemed impossible to Tiy that she had ever seen her brother busy at another work. He had never done anything in the world, through all the years of his life, but pore over scrolls, sift through secrets, plan and plot and climb.

"What is it you want?" Ay asked impatiently. "If you hadn't noticed, Akhet-Aten is in crisis, and *somebody* must do something about the plague."

"You?" Tiy was genuinely startled. "You care about the plague?"

"Our Pharaoh is a sunstruck fool and his Great Wife is a selfish child. Who is to save the city, if not me?"

Tiy tilted her head in acceptance. *I have changed—abandoned my old ambitions for more worthy work. Why should Ay not do the same?*

"I have an admission," Tiy said. "I may regret this later, but I wish for you to hear it."

Ay raised his brows. "This sounds very like a deathbed confession, Tiy. Have you found early signs of the fever upon you?"

Tiy did not respond to his insinuation. Nor did she lapse into her old ways, engaging in Ay's coy games of secrets. She outed with her information straight away. "Smenkhkare still lives."

Ay sat back, stunned. The scroll he'd been reading rolled up in his lap with a snap so sudden it was almost comical.

"I sent Smenkhkare into hiding when Thutmose died," Tiy said, "to keep him in reserve against emergency. And we certainly face grave danger now. But I lost all my power, Ay, and never could have raised the support necessary to bring Smenkhkare to the throne."

Ay tapped his chin with one finger. "I see."

"You have that power now. As you say, the Pharaoh is a fool, and Meritaten is only a child. I suggest you marshal whatever men will back you, and recall Smenkhkare from the north."

Ay gazed out his window for a long moment, mulling over her news, examining the possibilities. At last, he said, "Do you know, everyone is so fearful of the plague—I believe they will be more reluctant now than ever before to remove the Pharaoh from the throne." He gave a single, dry laugh, a harsh outrushing of breath through his nose. "Isn't that just like the gods, to toy with mankind so?"

"Then do not remove Akhenaten. Raise Smenkhkare to a co-regency with his brother. He is an intelligent young man, and if he has the madness that has plagued the get of Amunhotep, I have found no hint of it in all my years of correspondence. He may be level-hearted enough to give you the leverage you need over Akhenaten and his Great Wife—to bring them under your sway."

"You would willingly place the throne in my control, Tiy? After opposing my efforts for so long?"

"I would willingly do whatever I must to save the Two Lands—if they can be saved at all. This is a gift I give you, Brother. You had best be grateful for it, and use it wisely. Don't let your ambition cloud your judgment. Work to restore Egypt to its former glory. Shape it into the country it should have been for all these many years. But you must remember that restoring *maat* to the land is much more important than your lust for power—or my pride."

"A co-regency," Ay mused. "Yes, it could work quite well. But the heir, Tutankhaten—"

"He will not be anywhere near the palace. I have him now, in fact. I will see that he is raised well, far away from his father and the Aten—as far from corruption as I can take him."

"Where, exactly?"

Tiy took a small step backward and pressed her lips tight. "Tutankhaten is the pawn *I* hold, Ay—Egypt's bulwark against your ambition. If you use Smenkhkare well, then Egypt's reins will remain in your hands. But if you misuse this gift, I can take back the Two Lands in a heartbeat. Do not forget that."

Slowly, Ay nodded. "Very well. With Smenkhkare, I believe I can do away with the corruption that has infected Egypt—yes, it is just possible. I can even, with time, restore the good graces of the priests whom the Aten has displaced." He tapped his chin again, and watched Tiy with bright, calculating eyes. "I may even see a way to bring the northern states back to order, and to ward off the marauders who harry them. I will act as Smenkhkare's advisor, and you may keep your bulwark—your little Tutankhaten. Egypt will not need him. Nor will I."

"I hope Egypt shall not need him. But remember, Ay: I will keep the boy safe and ready. He will learn all my ways." *Better—he will learn all* your *ways, Brother*. "And if you misstep, the throne will pass to Tutankhaten. So move with care, and leave your lust for personal gain aside. Egypt can tolerate no more of our games."

Nefertiti

*Year 15 of Akhenaten
Beautiful Are the Manifestations,
Exalting the Name,
Beloved of the Sun*

"LADY KHENUT!"

At the sound of her maid's call, Nefertiti made her way to the window of her bed chamber and leaned over the rough stone sill. She scanned the rows of her vineyards carefully and gazed for a long moment out over the barley field, looking for any sign of danger—one of the royal family's golden chariots, perhaps, or a man in the red-and-blue striped kilt of Mahu's vicious troops. Such caution had become her habit, but as always, the fields were empty of everyone save the few *rekhet* who tilled the soil and tended the plants.

She cupped her hands around her mouth and shouted toward the dusty lane, "What is it, Peshu?"

Peshu, thin and sharp-faced and past her middle years, came scrambling around the stone gate of the small, secluded farm. "There is a woman here to see you, Lady Khenut. She says her name is Tiy."

Nefertiti's heart froze in her chest. She stared at Peshu in cold silence, then swallowed the lump in her throat. It prickled like a burr going down.

How did the old cat find me?

Despite her cautious spying on the landscape, Nefertiti had truly thought her seclusion was complete. Yet somehow Tiy had tracked her to this sanctuary. Nefertiti forced herself to draw slow, steady breaths and shook her head at her own flighty thoughts. *Of course Tiy found me.* It wasn't worth wondering how the old woman had done it. There was no scrap of knowledge in the Two Lands that Tiy could not obtain.

Did Tiy ask for me by my true name? Did she ruin my disguise? A moment of panic overwhelmed her at the thought; her vision filled with a shower of white sparks and her senses reeled. She braced her arms against the window sill and breathed deep again, trying to slow her pounding heart.

But no. Peshu would be startled—shocked *to hear the name of Nefertiti here, on this humble farm*. There was no saying where Tiy had unearthed the secret of Nefertiti's hiding-place, but the old woman evidently had enough respect to honor the disguise. She had asked for Lady Khenut at the gate, and so Nefertiti's comforting seclusion was still intact.

For a moment she considered ordering Peshu to send Tiy away. But Nefertiti knew the old woman better than that. Now that Tiy had found her, she would never let up until she had concluded whatever business had brought her here into the quiet hills far south of Akhet-Aten.

"Admit my visitor," Nefertiti called out to Peshu. "Bring us beer, bread and cheese. And then you may join the other women in the vineyard."

She hurried to her small dressing table, brushing the dust of the farm from her wig and her simple, bleached-linen dress. It was the work of a few moments to make herself presentable—a woman of middling consequence, as Lady Khenut was, required no jewels or elaborate face-paints.

Nefertiti received Tiy in her humble living quarters with an icy look and a suspicious glance at the child the old woman carried. Tutankhaten. Nefertiti recognized the boy, but she found no pleasure in the sight of the child.

His features were so like those of all the royal family—he wore all the faces of Nefertiti's daughters in one soft mask, and the stark reminder of her failures and sins only sickened her with self-loathing.

Tiy set the boy on the floor. Tutankhaten toddled about the room, exploring the rustic furniture and simple rugs with his eager little hands.

"What do you want?" Nefertiti asked sharply when Tiy had settled into a leather-seated chair.

"Only to call upon you, Lady Khenut—to inquire after your health."

Nefertiti gestured grandly at her own person, at her plain clothing and unassuming appearance. "I am well enough, as you can see."

"How do you get by here? Are you not known?"

"I'm far enough from Akhet-Aten that no one in this village recognizes me by sight. Almost none of them have been near the city, let alone gone to court. I've put it about that Lady Khenut is a relative of Nefertiti, in case anyone chanced to see me in the City of the Sun—in case anyone should note a resemblance. But people see what they are told to see. I am safe enough."

Tiy nodded, a simple gesture of honest acceptance. "How did you come to be here, of all places?"

For a long moment Nefertiti did not reply. Peshu had set a tray on the room's lone, low table, and Nefertiti went to it, lifted a bowl of beer, and took a long sip of the earthy, bitter drink. Her eyes were unfocused, her thoughts distant. At length Tiy cleared her throat, and Nefertiti sank back onto her stool, the beer balanced on her knee.

"On the night I left Akhet-Aten," she said, "I walked alone. I had no plans, no thoughts at all in my heart—other than grief, of course, for Meketaten. I simply walked—past the temples, through the streets, up into the hills.

And then I climbed higher, into the cliffs.

"I think by the time I reached the cliff trails I hoped I would find Mahu's guards—or be found by them. I believe I hoped they would try to stop me, and then I could resist and be speared for my recalcitrance, or given the choice Mahu gave so many others: face the sun's judgment in the temple or leap from the highest cliff. I would have chosen either fate, gladly. Death was all I wanted by then.

"But for reasons I will never understand, the gods denied me a confrontation with the soldiers. I didn't question it at the time. I simply walked—and walked. I never saw a guardsman, nor heard any of their voices, and by the time the sun rose, I realized I was far beyond the borders of Akhet-Aten."

"Did you make it all the way to the Red Land?" Tiy asked.

"Nearly." Nefertiti sipped her beer again, recalling the terrible thirst that had gripped her as the red sun rose, as she faced the long, rolling plains of sand that stretched eastward into a hot, dry oblivion. "Perhaps I did reach the desert, in truth. I don't know its exact borders, but I know it isn't far from Akhet-Aten. A woman might get there in a single night of walking."

Tiy waved a hand. "Go on."

"When the morning came, I nearly took my own life. Or, I should say, I nearly gave my life to the sun-god. Aten, Horus, Amun-Re—what does the name matter? It is the same terrible ball of fire no matter what you call it. I thought to walk out into the dunes—out into the great, red expanse that stretched out before me—and lie down for the sun to claim me. Akhenaten did that in the temples, you know. He stretched his own subjects out and tied them to pegs, to suffer and weep beneath the sun's eye."

Tiy frowned and said softly, "I know."

"I thought it a fitting end for my life of misrule and poor choices. I thought it just; *maat*. I sat for a time and looked at the dunes. And then I got up and turned south, and left the Red Land behind me. I still don't know what motivated me, or what decided me to move south. I don't know why I chose to live."

Tiy smiled faintly, but did not speak. Tutankhaten came to the old woman's knee and grasped her skirt, staring up at her with dark, solemn eyes.

"I found this small estate on the second day of my wandering. I was hungry, suffering from thirst. Peshu found me—not here; she was traveling on the farm's business—and took me into her wagon. She nursed me back to health, and brought me to this little estate. She saw that I am a learned woman, literate, with a good command of numbers. She asked me to manage the farm, to become the mistress of this holding, for the farm's old master went to Akhet-Aten to sell some of his wares but never returned."

"The plague, no doubt," Tiy said.

"Certainly."

A streak of deep, glittering green flashed across Nefertiti's vision. She flinched, and recovered quickly—but not fast enough to avoid Tiy's sharp eye.

Tiy raised her brows, silently enquiring.

Nefertiti sighed, pressing her fingers to her temples. "It's nothing, Tiy."

"Oh, it's something, I think. You *saw* something, Nefertiti—something I did not. It frightened you. What was it?"

She shook her head, laughing softly at herself. "Perhaps I'm as unstable as Akhenaten. Is madness catching? If so, the gods know I've lived close beside it long enough that I ought to have lost my wits long before now."

"What did you see, Nefertiti?"

She sighed in surrender. What did it matter, after all, if she kept this secret—or any other? "I've seen it ever since that morning—when I sat at the edge of the Red Land and looked my death in its face."

"Tell me."

"It is my *ba*," Nefertiti admitted. "It follows me—everywhere, every day."

Tiy leaned back in her chair, the lines of her perpetual frown deepening with suspicion.

"I see it—the body of a bird, small and fluttering, and the face of a woman. My face. It is my spirit, Tiy. It has loosed itself from my body, vacated my being in anticipation of my end. And the end must come soon. Without my *ba* inside me I am not truly here. I go through the motions of life, of running this farm. I eat and drink, I sleep. But I do not feel.

"That is, I feel nothing but fear, and that only when I see my *ba* flying. It seems it's always there, darting, watching—taunting me for all the evil I've brought upon the world—upon my children."

Tiy turned her face away. She watched the boy play in silence for a moment, and then, avoiding Nefertiti's eyes, she asked, "Have you heard of the deaths of your two youngest?"

The light, delicate wings beat close beside Nefertiti's ear. Tiy's words fell heavy into her heart, landing there with a hollow sound that flooded her limbs and her head with a fierce, trembling pain. But she sat unmoving—numb, resigned. Finally she drew a ragged breath and said, "I rejoice to hear it. They will be spared all the evils to come."

"And Tasherit," Tiy said, "and Ankhesenpaaten—"

"Don't give me news of them!" A desperate pleading cracked Nefertiti's voice—a force of emotion she thought had left her forever. "I don't want to know. They will soon be old enough... they will soon be considered women. And I don't want to know what they must do, or face, or become."

The *ba* darted past her face, hovered around the window, dancing in a shaft of sunlight. Its emerald feathers glowed, ethereal and taunting, and it seemed to beat its wings too slowly. Its face—Nefertiti's own—stared at her with calm expectation.

"I know why you didn't kill yourself," Tiy said.

Nefertiti laughed. "Do you?"

"The gods didn't allow it."

"And yet the gods have allowed so many other evils to transpire. Three of my daughters are dead, and one of them is already in Akhenaten's grasp—where I myself put her. What is one more evil in the world? What is one more death?"

"You may die soon enough, for all I can tell," Tiy said with dry practicality. "But not just yet. Your work in this world is not finished. The gods still have a task for you."

Nefertiti tossed the locks of her simple wig. "Take your tasks and obligations away from me, old woman. I want nothing to do with the throne. Someday soon, the bird that follows me will leave me alone. My *ka* will fly out to join it, and then I'll get around to the only task that matters: dying—ridding the world of another of its evils."

"I think not," Tiy said. "The gods have provided us both a way to make everything right."

The leather chair creaked as Tiy leaned forward, stretching out her hands, calling to Tutankhaten. The boy went to her quickly enough, toddling on his strong little legs.

"Tut," Tiy said gently, "you will live here now with your Aunt Khenut. Isn't that a fine idea? Won't you like to live in this place?"

"No," Nefertiti said.

"Oh, yes," Tiy rejoined. "Only you can do this work properly, Nefertiti. Raise this boy in the old religion. Teach him of the gods that lived before Akhenaten's reign. Teach him how to bring about the end of the Pharaoh who rules Egypt now, and show him how to remake the world."

"I cannot," Nefertiti said. Tears sprang into her eyes, stinging and sharp. "I don't know how."

"A woman raised by *Ay* doesn't know how to bring down a Pharaoh? What foolishness you speak!"

"I am not worthy of this work. I have done too much harm to the world—and hurt too many children. My *own* children, Tiy! And besides," she added after a reluctant pause, "how can I teach this boy to defeat his father when I never could defeat my own?"

Tiy gazed at her with great sympathy—an expression Nefertiti had seldom seen before on her aunt's face. Then the old woman leaned a little closer and said in a conspiratorial, almost happy whisper, "Akhenaten is not the boy's father."

Nefertiti shrank against the back of her chair, cautious and afraid. But despite her wariness of the king—of Akhenaten and all the vast schemes that surrounded him—a flicker of hope flared deep inside her breast.

Tiy rose, gently removing Tutankhaten's fists from her skirt. As if the deal were done, the old woman stepped toward the door.

"Wait," Nefertiti said. "I never agreed—"

Tiy silenced her with a wave of one hard, slender hand. "Be a better mother to this boy than you or I were to our own children."

Then, with a last, loving glance at Tutankhaten, she stepped through the door.

Nefertiti swept the baby up in her arms. He gave a little cry of startlement or protest, but Nefertiti hushed him with an unthinking, instinctive kiss on his cheek. She rushed after Tiy and called out to the old woman just as her wrinkled hand fell upon the gate.

"Will you come back for him one day? Will you send me word, at least?"

Tiy turned and smiled. Nefertiti blinked; the vibrant green bird hovered beside Tiy, and its small, brown face, so like Nefertiti's, smiled at her, too.

"No," Tiy said. "I'm afraid you won't hear from me again, Lady Khenut. Take good care of this treasure. May *maat* bless you both."

Tiy

*Year 15 of Akhenaten
Beautiful Are the Manifestations,
Exalting the Name,
Beloved of the Sun*

IN THE DIM, violet-gray half-light that preceded the dawn, Huya's face was drawn and cast in deep, mournful shadows. He said nothing on the long walk from the palace quay down the Royal Road, but kept to Tiy's pace and offered his arm when she grew weary. When they reached the mouth of the Great Aten Temple, he turned to her and watched her in silence for a long moment, his eyes eloquent with pain.

The sun would rise soon, climbing to its victorious height. When its fire burned the sky Akhenaten would arrive too, and here he would remain all day—deep within the temple, prostrating himself, pleading on his belly in the sand. He would beg for mercy from a god that did not feel. He would seek the blessing of a god that was not there. The Aten was not there—but Tiy would be.

"Are you ready?" Tiy asked her steward.

Huya did not reply. For the first time in his long and loyal service, he could not respond to his mistress. She took his hand as they walked toward the temple's gate and held it tightly. He squeezed her fingers, and lightly, Tiy smiled.

The temple was cool now, as it never was in the light of day. Deep-blue shadows softened its hard corners, cloaking each colossal statue of the king. The sand of the temple floor was soft, welcoming, tinted a pale violet hue. In the peace before dawn it was a calmer and more beautiful place than it ever was beneath the glare of the sun.

When they reached the inner sanctuary Tiy looked up. The sky was a long, bare stretch of blue-toned gray, hemmed on all sides by the temple walls, empty of everything save for the last fading echoes of the stars. Soon that soft, placid blue would turn to rose, then to flame-orange, and then to the searing, yellow-white of the sun in its full and frightening power.

Tiy extended her hand. Huya hesitated only a moment, but he was always loyal, always quick to obey. He reached into the pouch at his belt, then passed her the phial of poison.

She lay down in the sand. It was as cool as the river at night, and gentle as a rocking current. Tiy watched the final stars fade in the swath of sky above. She smiled. A vastness seemed to stretch all around her; she felt the sands of Akhet-Aten flowing outward from her body, rushing beyond the walls of the temple that surrounded her. She felt the very ground beneath her body—her *ka*, her consciousness—reach out to the fire of the Red Land, and sink into the deep mud of the Black Land, into its endless rhythm of river's flood and field's growth, of harvest and renewal—of life and death.

Huya's frowning face, seen half in silhouette, half in the pale, dusty light of the oncoming dawn, hung in the air above her. Something darted across the sky—something dark and small with swift, confident wings. As it passed behind Huya she glimpsed its face—young and beautiful, with a knowing smile. It was the face that had stared back from her mirror in years long past, long buried.

She pulled the stopper from the phial and drank the poison down. It was bitter on her tongue, but bitterness had never bothered Tiy. She had lived with its taste all her life.

Huya sank to his knees beside her. To Tiy's glad surprise, he pressed a long kiss against her brow, and she felt a hot tear fall upon her cheek.

"My good and loyal man," Tiy said, her chest and eyes welling with affection. "You have always served me well."

He took her hand again, and she was content to leave it in his warm grasp.

Tiy watched the sky as the first blush of dawn appeared. The last silver star vanished.

Let me die before the sun rises, she prayed. *Let the next sunrise I see be in the afterlife. And let it be an afterlife full and proper, with the true gods there to meet me.*

Even if those gods condemned her and cast her down to the Eater of Hearts—even if she were damned—she wished to look upon the rightful gods of Egypt, to know that they still lived, before the Duat claimed her.

Be waiting for me, she prayed to Amun, to Mut. *Wait for your chance to return to the world and restore* maat *to the land. For I have made the way for you. I have done what work I could. Not to save my own soul—I think there is no hope of that. I have done it for the sake of the Two Lands.*

The poison began to do its work. Her gut burned, and her breath came harsh and shallow. She closed her eyes; a pink glow lit her eyelids as the sun broke, triumphant, into the sky.

But as the bitter drink marched on through her body, ravaging her blood, the glow of sunrise faded. Blackness closed around her, and she was wrapped in a merciful cloak of dark, even as the sunlight warmed her body and filled the Great Aten Temple with its fire.

There was a beating like a bird's wings in her ears.

Satisfaction glowed in her belly, a feeling so soft and reassuring that it nearly deadened the pain of the poison.

She tried to laugh at the darkness—at the wall that shut out the sun's rays—but the ache in her chest was too great, and she kept herself sober and still.

But she thought, *I have slipped from your grasp, Aten, you lone and silent god. And soon—soon, I pray, all of Egypt will break from you, too.*

ABOUT THE AUTHOR

Libbie Hawker writes historical and literary fiction featuring complex characters and rich details of time and place. In her free time she enjoys hiking, sailing, road-tripping through the American West, and working on her podcast about Jem and the Holograms.

She lives in the San Juan Islands with her husband Paul. Between her two pen names, she is the author of more than twenty books.

Find more, including contact information and updates about future releases, on her web site: LibbieHawker.com

Printed in Great Britain
by Amazon